The Captain's Old Love

One Night in Blackhaven
Book 1

MARY LANCASTER

ARE YOU SIGNED UP FOR DRAGONBLADE'S BLOG?

You'll get the latest news and information on exclusive giveaways, exclusive excerpts, coming releases, sales, free books, cover reveals and more.

Check out our complete list of authors, too!

No spam, no junk. That's a promise!

Sign Up Here

www.dragonbladepublishing.com

Dearest Reader;

Thank you for your support of a small press. At Dragonblade Publishing, we strive to bring you the highest quality Historical Romance from some of the best authors in the business. Without your support, there is no 'us', so we sincerely hope you adore these stories and find some new favorite authors along the way.

Happy Reading!

CEO, Dragonblade Publishing

Additional Dragonblade books by Author Mary Lancaster

One Night in Blackhaven Series
The Captain's Old Love (Book 1)

The Duel Series
Entangled (Book 1)
Captured (Book 2)
Deserted (Book 3)
Beloved (Book 4)

Last Flame of Alba Series
Rebellion's Fire (Book 1)
A Constant Blaze (Book 2)
Burning Embers (Book 3)

Gentlemen of Pleasure Series
The Devil and the Viscount (Book 1)
Temptation and the Artist (Book 2)
Sin and the Soldier (Book 3)
Debauchery and the Earl (Book 4)
Blue Skies (Novella)

Pleasure Garden Series
Unmasking the Hero (Book 1)
Unmasking Deception (Book 2)
Unmasking Sin (Book 3)
Unmasking the Duke (Book 4)
Unmasking the Thief (Book 5)

Crime & Passion Series
Mysterious Lover (Book 1)
Letters to a Lover (Book 2)
Dangerous Lover (Book 3)
Lost Lover (Book 4)
Merry Lover (Novella)
Ghostly Lover (Novella)

The Husband Dilemma Series
How to Fool a Duke (Book 1)

Season of Scandal Series
Pursued by the Rake (Book 1)
Abandoned to the Prodigal (Book 2)
Married to the Rogue (Book 3)
Unmasked by her Lover (Book 4)
Her Star from the East (Novella)

Imperial Season Series
Vienna Waltz (Book 1)
Vienna Woods (Book 2)
Vienna Dawn (Book 3)

Blackhaven Brides Series
The Wicked Baron (Book 1)
The Wicked Lady (Book 2)
The Wicked Rebel (Book 3)
The Wicked Husband (Book 4)
The Wicked Marquis (Book 5)
The Wicked Governess (Book 6)
The Wicked Spy (Book 7)
The Wicked Gypsy (Book 8)
The Wicked Wife (Book 9)
Wicked Christmas (Book 10)
The Wicked Waif (Book 11)
The Wicked Heir (Book 12)

The Wicked Captain (Book 13)
The Wicked Sister (Book 14)

Unmarriageable Series
The Deserted Heart (Book 1)
The Sinister Heart (Book 2)
The Vulgar Heart (Book 3)
The Broken Heart (Book 4)
The Weary Heart (Book 5)
The Secret Heart (Book 6)
Christmas Heart (Novella)

The Lyon's Den Series
Fed to the Lyon

De Wolfe Pack: The Series
The Wicked Wolfe
Vienna Wolfe

Also from Mary Lancaster
Madeleine (Novella)
The Others of Ochil (Novella)

To Violetta Rand
Rest in peace

Prologue

"**N**OW THAT WE are all together under one roof, we need to have a family congress."

Everyone present in the drawing room of Black Hill House regarded Lawrence Vale with varying degrees of interest, tolerance, and amusement. Clearly, they knew he spoke for his twin sister and himself—they were always in agreement. But since they were the youngest of the Vale siblings, Lawrence suspected that even together, the twins carried much less weight than any one of the others.

"Sounds ominous," Felicia, their widowed sister, said lightly, though she looked a shade anxious. "Are you not happy here?"

"Oh yes, we like the house," Leona, Lawrence's twin, said. "And Black Hill. And we very much like Blackhaven, too, which is what we want to talk to you about."

"Talk quickly," Aubrey said, pouring himself a large glass of brandy and throwing himself into the chair next to the decanter.

"Wait," Roderick said, glancing around the room. "One of us is missing."

"The vital one," Cornelius pointed out, "since all of this belongs to Julius."

"Yes, but it is Julius we want to talk to you about," Lawrence said.

"*He* isn't happy," Leona added.

They looked at her with more than a hint of discomfort, but no one denied it.

"He brought us all back here to give us a home," Lawrence said. "To look after us. I know it was always the family property, but if we were ever here, we've forgotten it. Lucy doesn't remember it either. It's *Julius's* home, and he, more than any of us, should be content here."

"I think he will be," Lucy said. "He is merely adjusting to life on land after decades at sea. I know he likes Blackhaven, and he wants us all to grow into the community."

"*Us* all," Lawrence said. "He has plans for the land, which Cornelius is managing, and the house and gardens which we are all helping with. But does it not seem to you that he has *retired*?"

"We know he is retired," Roderick said impatiently. "He would be at sea in command of several ships if he wasn't."

"Retiring from the navy is not retiring from life," Leona said.

They all looked at her, frowning, expectant.

"That *is* what he is doing, is it not?" Leona said. "He has brought us all here, and he is *pottering* while ignoring all the opportunities he wants for the rest of us. He is only six and thirty years old, not in his dotage. Yet he acts as if he is in his twilight years, as if he has…given up." Her glare was fierce. "His life is *not* over. He should still be having fun."

"*We* are fun," Lucy said. Everyone gazed at her. She sighed. "Some of the time."

"He should have a wife to enjoy his home with," Lawrence said determinedly. "Children, even. At the very least, he should enjoy looking."

Aubrey let out a bark of laughter. "You have a point, Lawrie. You have a point."

"More than one," Delilah said. As the eldest sibling, her opinion counted as the twins' never would. "What is it you are suggesting?"

Leona said, "You all plan to go to the assembly room ball in Blackhaven next month. Make him go with you."

"One can't *make* Julius do anything," Cornelius pointed out.

"One can encourage," said Lawrence.

"One can," Delilah said thoughtfully. She frowned, then nodded as though reaching a decision. "The twins are right. He needs to enjoy himself again and meet new people, not skulk up here alone most of the time, worrying about us. But we must not push likely brides at him. He will be appalled."

"I've never known Julius to be serious about a woman," Cornelius said in apparent surprise. "Have you, Rod?"

Roderick shook his head.

"He was once," Delilah said with odd reluctance. "The young lady threw him over quite suddenly without apology or explanation. Which is why we must be subtle, for it won't be easy for him to trust." She smiled approvingly at Lawrence and Leona. "But you are quite right. I think he is lonely. Worse, he is learning to *like* the loneliness and that is not healthy."

Leona's eyes gleamed as she announced, "Then Julius *shall* go the ball!"

Chapter One

CAPTAIN SIR JULIUS Vale, recently retired from the Royal Navy, had no intention of going to the ball.

Of course, his siblings did not know that. He had allowed them to persuade him into his newest dress uniform for the occasion, partly because he could not be bothered fighting about it, and partly because it still gave him some childish pleasure to trick his brothers and sisters.

Those of them riding with him in the first of the two carriages necessary to convey them all from Black Hill House to the town looked remarkably pleased with themselves. Even Delilah, not the most sociable of creatures, smiled with an air of unusual anticipation. Julius was genuinely glad of that, for no one deserved an evening's pleasure more than Delilah. Except perhaps Cornelius in the following carriage. In fact, even the fragile wastrel Aubrey, lounging beside Julius on the back-facing seat, and Lucy, surely the liveliest of his sisters, chattering away opposite, were entitled to this evening.

As Julius was equally entitled to a night of his own, quieter pleasure.

He barely recognized the town of Blackhaven these days. It had grown enormously since he had last been here over twenty years ago, when it had been little more than a fishing village with a weekly market. Now that market came twice a week, and some of the stalls were permanent. The town boasted a hotel, two inns, a theatre, and a pump room where the gullible bought and drank the fresh spring water rumored to cure all ills, from consumption to barrenness and even senility. To say nothing of the fashionable shops that now lined the high street along with the rather magnificent assembly rooms near the town hall.

Rather to Julius's surprise, their carriage had to wait in line in order to pull up at the assembly building's imposing front door. When they got there, a liveried footman opened the carriage door and let down the steps. Julius alighted first, ignoring the protest of his bad leg, and civilly handed down his sisters. Aubrey brought up the rear as they moved toward the entrance.

Julius limped to one side.

"Aren't we going in?" Lucy asked.

"By all means, go in with Delilah," Julius suggested. "I shall just wait for the other carriage, to make sure they get here."

Lucy exchanged furtive looks with Delilah and Aubrey.

"No, you are right," Lucy said hastily. "We should all go in together."

Clearly, they were afraid he might cut and run as soon as their backs were turned. To hide his smile, he raised his arm and adjusted his eye patch to a more rakish angle. A sprightly lady of middle years, escorted by a good-looking young man, walked toward them. The pair seemed to have come on foot, taking advantage of one of the few dry days this summer.

The lady caught his eye and smiled. Julius inclined his head politely, assuming she would merely pass them and go in. However, he had forgotten the insatiable curiosity and gossip that was the bane of small-town life. Although he had made no attempt to mingle with the local gentry, the town would know that Black Hill was now occupied again. By a scarred, one-eyed Vale with a limp.

"Do forgive me!" The lady seemed to flutter like an uncertain butterfly, her eyes gleaming. "So long ago... But are you not Sir Julius

Vale?"

Julius bowed. "I am."

The lady beamed. "Margaret Muir. You won't remember me, but I was acquainted with your parents. Particularly your father, of course, since he grew up here too. Such a charming man! But it must be twenty years since you left home! In fact, since any of the family was back. So good to have you home at Black Hill. You must know we are very proud of you, our own hero of the great Battle of Trafalgar, and of many battles since."

"Merely one of many men who did their duty," he muttered. Battles had stopped seeming heroic to him a long time ago. Mainly, they were blood and death and the miracle of survival. "But I thank you," he managed, pulling himself together, and gave in to the inevitable. "Of course, I recall you perfectly, ma'am, and your brother, Lieutenant Muir. A pleasure to meet you again. Allow me to present my sister, Miss Delilah Vale, whom you may also recall. And my brother Aubrey, who was in short coats when we left. Lucy here had not even been born."

His siblings duly bowed and curtsied to Miss Muir, and they were all introduced to her slightly embarrassed but amiable nephew, Mr. Bernard Muir.

"I was so sorry to hear of Sir George's death," Miss Muir said, with what seemed perfect sincerity.

"Thank you," Delilah murmured. "You are very kind."

"I hope your brother is well?" Julius managed, dredging up the image of the young Lieutenant Muir from his memory.

Miss Muir's face fell. "Sadly not. He died in Spain, a few years ago now. Bernard is his son," she added proudly.

"Come along, Aunt, we're blocking the way," Bernard said, with a quick, comical waggle of his eyebrows as he herded his aunt to the door.

"I'll bet she was one of the old gentleman's flirts," Aubrey said irreverently.

"She was," Julius said. "But much too respectable for him."

"Here's the other carriage," Lucy said. "Come along, let's go in!" To be sure of it, she grasped Julius by the arm and tugged.

Even with his bad leg, Julius had stood on too many gale-battered decks to be caught off balance, and he held firmly in place until Roderick, Cornelius, and Felicia had joined them.

"What are you waiting for?" Felicia asked, sweeping her hands at them.

"Lucy needed a chaperone," Delilah said sardonically. Although the eldest of the sisters, she was unmarried, and so the widowed Felicia was incongruously the more proper duenna.

Felicia gave a derisory and unladylike snort. Cornelius sighed and tugged irritably at his cravat. Roderick merely strode toward the door, and this time, Julius let himself be drawn inside.

The foyer interior was opulent enough to match the beauty of the outside of the building. Clearly, there was money in the town these days. Beneath the blazing chandelier, a surprising number of people milled between the foyer and the open double doors to the ballroom. Julius was temporarily dazzled by the bright silks and muslins and sparkling jewels. It had been a long time since he had attended such splendid events. And he certainly hadn't expected one in Blackhaven.

Realizing that Lucy was guiding him inexorably toward the ladies' cloakroom, he murmured, "You'll have to let go of me, or we shall all be blackballed."

Lucy giggled and released him, glancing in what she fondly imagined to be a surreptitious manner at her brothers.

Aubrey laughed and strode forward to the gentlemen's cloakroom. "Come on, let's leave our hats."

Julius ambled after him, pausing to allow a lady to pass, which ensured his other brothers had to go ahead or look too much like gaolers. The girls would have hung blatantly on to his arm, so brothers were a definite advantage in the situation.

Casually, he reached out and took the cloakroom door from Roderick, who then followed Cornelius inside. Julius stepped smartly aside, pulling the door closed as he went, and strode straight back to the front exit.

Now for the evening he had promised himself. A long walk home along the shore beneath the stars, followed by a peaceful couple of hours reading in a blessedly quiet house. Providing the twins were in bed.

The sea was calling him like the siren it had always been, so he barely noticed the lively, extraordinarily well-dressed family at the door. He stood politely aside for them, and then, entering just behind them, came...Antonia.

Antonia!

Foolishly, he had imagined that if he ever saw her again, he would not even know her just at first. Not that she could have changed in appearance as much as he, but that his memory would be faulty, endowing her with beauty and character that had never been there in reality.

Yet there she was. One glimpse of her half-averted face, smiling at her companions, and recognition hit him in the pit of his stomach, a storm of old pain and regret and a thousand tangled emotions he could not even name.

Antonia Temple.

She wore a modest ball gown of deep burgundy, and an ivory-colored shawl over her arm. Her companions were a lady approaching middle age and an attractive man in his thirties, who wore an expensive, perfectly fitting evening coat and satin knee breeches. He did not even have a hat, a thwarting of the conventions that might have intrigued Julius in anyone else.

This must be *him*. Macy. The man Antonia had married less than a month after jilting Julius.

She did not even see him. The family in front of her milled between them, heading slowly for the cloakrooms while Antonia and her companions walked straight toward the ballroom.

Without rhyme or reason, as though an invisible thread drew him, Julius followed.

Only as he entered the glittering ballroom, when the music and chatter seemed to strike him like a slap, did he realize the absurdity of his behavior. He paused, wondering if he should just walk straight back out again.

A footman offered him a glass from a tray, and he almost snatched it. At least it gave him something to do while curiosity surged through him.

Why was she in Blackhaven, of all places? What had her life been like over these ten years? Did she have children? Did she ever think of him at all? Would she even know him now?

Was she happy?

She looked happy, damn her. He moved further into the ballroom, watching as her little party took their places at a small table by the wall. From a sconce above, candlelight illuminated her face.

She was still beautiful, her dark hair dressed simply but becomingly. She still smiled often, her expression lively and interested, and yet there seemed to be a serenity about her now that had been quite absent in her youth. Fresh pain twisted in his stomach. No doubt a happy marriage had given her that contentment.

Only…*was* it contentment? He moved nearer. Much of her beauty came from the fine, delicate bones of her face, so in one sense, it would never change. But as she conversed with her companions, gazed around her, acknowledged acquaintances who drifted past their table, it seemed to Julius that she was…unengaged. The inner sparkle he remembered behind her smile was no longer present. Now it seemed merely a social façade. The natural vitality, the sheer joy in life that had so attracted him and still occasionally haunted his dreams, was quite absent.

The girl who had lit up any company had grown *dull*.

Her complete absence of jewels seemed to symbolize that. Her smile implied she was interested in her surroundings, and yet it looked watchful, curiously controlled. She had lost her spontaneity, no doubt in self-interest.

Disappointment crept through him, and then galloped. He turned away, fiercely glad that he no longer needed to care. There was nothing for him in that bare, beautiful shell. There never had been, and only now could he recognize it.

"*There* you are!" Felicia said beside him. She sounded relieved. "Our table is over here."

"Where is Aubrey?" he asked, limping beside her toward the gaggle of his siblings.

"He went outside to see if you had bolted," Felicia said.

He wished he had. He wished he had done it immediately after alighting from the carriage instead of prolonging the joke. Then he would not have needed to see Antonia, to feel this pain of disillusion and loss. Because the great love it had taken him ten years to get over had been based on nothing. She must always have been this shallow and dull, and he too lonely and too blinded by her beauty to see it.

He sat among his siblings, wondering how long he would have to stay before he could slip away. More than ever, he needed the rush of the sea and the release of brisk exercise. Aubrey appeared, briefly, and then vanished again. Antonia and her husband rose and went to waltz together. Julius averted his gaze.

Aubrey returned and threw himself into the vacant chair beside Julius. "I love this town. Do you know the local quack is married to a princess? And the vicar's wife is the scandalous Wicked Kate Crowmore of legend. Lord Braithwaite, the ranking aristo in these parts, who lives in the castle, is married to someone stolen as a child by Romanies—or saved by Romanies; opinions seem to vary—and he has a positive gaggle of beautiful sisters, not all of whom are married."

"No, I did not know all of that," Julius admitted, although he had met the vicar and the doctor, who were both involved with the charitable hospital that currently employed his old ship's surgeon, Dr. Samson. "Why aren't you dancing?"

"I'm waiting for Rod to introduce me to someone. Who is Felicia dancing with?"

Julius followed his gaze. "Bernard Muir, poor fellow. His late father was an officer in the regiment stationed here. Where is Lucy, more to the point?"

"Gave Delilah the slip, but there's a limited amount of mischief she can get up to in one room."

"You are unreasonably sanguine. Or delusional." Julius hauled himself to his feet. "I'll see if I can hunt her down." And then he would leave.

Moving around the periphery of the ballroom, he finally saw Lucy from a distance, re-entering the ballroom through the open doors from the veranda. She was on the arm of a young man he had never seen before. Casting Julius a dazzling smile, she walked onto the dance floor to waltz.

She deserved the amusement, especially if she was to be married. Her betrothal had been arranged since the cradle, by her mother and her crony. And in a moment of more-than-usual idiocy, Sir George had agreed to it. Now that they expected Lord Eddleston to visit later in the summer, Lucy was digging in her heels, and Julius didn't blame her.

They owed Eddleston the courtesy of a visit, but if Lucy didn't like the match, Julius was quite prepared to scupper it.

Delilah, watching from her own conversation, had clocked their younger sister, so Julius swung away from her—and came face to face with Antonia.

She had just risen from her chair and glanced up at him with an apology on her lips that died unspoken. Their eyes locked. He wondered dispassionately if she even recognized him, or if she was just appalled by the blank black covering over his eye socket.

Her expression did not change, but the blood drained from her face and she grasped blindly for the back of her chair, swaying. From instinct, he shot out his hand to steady her. She flinched away with a gasp.

Rigid, he let his hand fall to his side, bowed coldly, and walked away. He had a glimpse of the husband with a faint frown of consternation on his face. And then Julius stepped on to the veranda his sister had just abandoned, and there was blessed fresh air on his skin. It did not cool the fury in his heart.

Whether she recognized him or not, that flinch was an insult. He wished it did not matter. He had only just convinced himself *she* did not matter and never had, so her reaction should neither hurt nor anger him.

The veranda was empty, thanks to the popularity of the waltz, so he leaned against the balustrade, stared blindly over the town that had once been so familiar to him, and forced himself to breathe deeply.

He almost yelled with frustration when the rustle of skirts and a subtle fragrance of flowers betrayed the arrival of other people. Somewhere, more welcome than the waft of rose, was the smell of the sea, and it was calling him urgently now.

He straightened just as someone came and stood beside him in silence. He knew it was her, though why she had bothered, he had no idea. Perhaps she wanted him to keep quiet about their past relationship.

"Your pardon, madam," he said icily.

She must have realized he was asking for more space to pass her without as much as brushing her skirt, but she did not move, even when he turned his scowl on her.

She hadn't been looking at him, though now she cast a fleeting glance up at him. "How are you?"

He let his lips curl, which had worked wonders on ill-behaved seamen who seemed to fear his contempt more than the lash. "Astonished," he drawled.

At last, her eyes met his properly, and a veil descended at once over whatever emotion had been there. "Astonished to find me in Blackhaven? Or astonished that I choose to speak to you?"

"Both. I presume there must be something I can do for you?"

She jerked as though he had slapped her. Then her eyelashes swept down, long and dark against her pale cheek. "Then you presume wrongly."

The breeze catching at her hair, she spun away from him at last. She raised one hand to brush back a stray lock, and he saw that her fingers were shaking.

"Antonia."

Her name seemed to have been dragged from him. He was unsure whether he meant it as a question or a comfort. She paused, still ready for flight, and he didn't know what else to say.

"Why are you in Blackhaven?" he blurted. "Are you ill?" It was, after all, why most visitors came to the town, to take the waters.

"No," she replied. "Are you?"

"No." The door had blown half shut in the breeze. He moved to open it further and saw beyond her to her husband, who was talking with a group of other people near the dance floor, including Delilah and Felicia. "Is that him?"

"Who?" She followed his gaze, apparently bewildered.

"Macy."

Her lips parted. She had a lovely mouth. Vividly, he recalled the softness, the passion, the taste, as if she had kissed him only yesterday. She swallowed.

"No," she replied. "That is Lord Linfield."

He laughed. "A lord? Well worth jilting a mere naval commander for, however proud of his promotion he is."

Something flashed in her eyes at that. Indignation, perhaps, or just amusement. Her smile was bitter. "You are the expert, sir," she said obscurely.

He awarded her another curl of his lip. He bowed very slightly and walked away. He wondered if they had rum in this establishment. And then, with relief, he remembered his flask.

Chapter Two

ANTONIA WONDERED WILDLY if she was asleep and in the midst of a nightmare. She had dreamed so often over the years of meeting Julius again. In her imagination, he always begged her forgiveness, declared that he had always loved her, and provided easily believable excuses for why he had left her. He had looked just as before, handsome and dashing, his gray-green eyes alight with love for her, sometimes with passion, the memory of which still made her body ache in the night.

Occasionally, she had feared he was dead. But never—foolishly, perhaps—had she imagined a reality where he had lost one of those beautiful, far-seeing eyes, or limped so obviously when he walked. Nor had he regarded her with contempt in those dreams, but then, he must always have despised her, or he would never have left her without a word, as though she were nothing and no one.

But no, he was not merely contemptuous, she thought, sinking back down in her seat beside Miss Talbot. He was bitter. As though everything wrong with him was her fault. And that *was* unjust, so much so that emotion fizzed through her veins.

Anger. He had made her angry. The discovery took her by surprise, since it had been so long since she had troubled to be angered by anything. Now, she seized her outrage like a weapon and looked forward to wielding it against him. Even if only to ignore him pointedly.

She snapped her fingers beneath the table, as though banishing the last of her silly, youthful love. Now she was older, wiser, and the mother of a fine son. She neither needed nor wanted Julius Vale in their lives.

Beside her, Miss Talbot was chatting to a group of people, visitors to the town like themselves. Miss Talbot introduced Antonia, and she smiled with as much interest as she could pretend. In truth, she could barely hear the conversation, and in any case, her mind was still on Julius.

Why did he hold her in such contempt? What had she done or said that he should have walked away from their engagement without a word and now despised her with every reluctant glance? Was he just bad-tempered because of his injuries? Because he was in pain? Her heart ached with sympathy for that, despite her determined dispassion.

"Would you care to dance, Mrs. Macy?"

Antonia blinked at the speaker, a pleasant-looking gentleman whose name she could not recall, although they had been introduced. Dragged back to her surroundings, she knew it would be impolite to refuse. On top of which, anything was better than the thoughts in her head.

"Thank you." She rose and placed her hand on his proffered arm. He led her onto the dance floor, where sets were forming for the next country dance.

"Miss Talbot tells me you have come to Blackhaven for the waters," he said while they waited.

"Indeed we have. And you, sir? Are you also a visitor to the town, or do you live here?"

"I live close by, but I am in Blackhaven a good deal, being closely involved with the charitable hospital here."

"How very good of you."

He looked embarrassed. She rather liked the mixture of modesty and awkwardness in his manner. "No, no, just something I could not ignore. Since the end of the war, the hospital has had to expand enormously, mostly because of injured soldiers and sailors coming home." He took her hand as the dance began and, whenever they were close enough, asked her about herself and her opinion of Blackhaven.

She made sure to smile, and her body seemed to remember the steps without effort. Tonight was the first time she had danced in years—Miss Talbot had insisted she do so if the opportunity arose—but she felt none of the fun and exhilaration she remembered from her youth.

Worse, instead of this kind, amiable man whose name she had forgotten, she saw again the dashing figure of the young Commander Vale, who had danced with all the joy of the seaman ashore and swept her along with him. She had been so dazzled, so breathless with love, when he had courted her...

But that had been ten years ago, when the victory of Trafalgar and the death of Nelson were new. At first, she had been flattered by the attentions of the convalescing hero Julius was, for he had been feted and admired by everyone. But her petty social triumph had quickly changed into genuine fascination, friendship, and overwhelming love. She had never known why he had walked away. Sailed away without a word to her...

The dance ended, and her partner said, "Shall we go in search of a glass of wine? Or lemonade, perhaps?"

From habit, she glanced toward Miss Talbot, who, still among her group of potential new friends, was accepting a glass of wine from one of them. Antonia was not needed.

"Yes, that would be pleasant," she said to her partner.

And indeed, it was pleasant to be escorted and looked after. He sent a footman scurrying for wine and found a quiet sofa for them to sit, rather than return at the Talbots' currently crowded table. Antonia wondered if she should be flattered.

"What is it you do at the hospital?" she asked. "Are you a physician?"

"Sadly, I have no such skill. Our chief medical man is Dr. Samson, although Dr. Lampton also gives generously of his time on a voluntary basis, as do several ladies of the town. To be frank, the place was chaotic, with no overall administration. That is my somewhat dull talent. I organize the running of the place, make sure we have enough maids and beds and enough money to fund it all. It is very expensive to run."

"I can imagine. How is it funded?"

"From charity, mostly from the good people of the town, but visitors have also been generous." He looked sheepish. "I'm afraid I importune them shamelessly, especially at events such as these."

She regarded him with somewhat sardonic amusement. "Are you importuning me, sir? There was no need to butter me up with dancing."

He blushed scarlet. "My dear lady, there was no question of that! I only ever ask the gentlemen."

"Dunnett," said a voice behind her.

A shiver of recognition thrilled up her spine to her neck. Even now, his voice did this to her. *Memory. Only memory.*

"Ah, Vale. I did not expect to see you here. In fact, you told us you were not coming."

"My family persuaded me," Julius said, limping around the side of the sofa into view.

He was still dashing, drat the man. He stood straight and tall, and the eye patch did little to detract from his good looks. In fact, it gave him an air at once heroic and vaguely rakish. The scars she recalled from before were still visible from the edge of his jaw, like a spider's web disappearing into his cravat.

Beside her, Mr. Dunnett said with clear reluctance, "Are you acquainted with Mrs. Macy?"

Julius's eyes flickered with brief confusion. "An interesting question. May I have the next dance, ma'am?"

Flabbergasted as she was, her every instinct was to refuse, and yet he had asked her in company, so her bad manners would be noted.

While she hesitated, looking for a reason in his carefully bland expression, Mr. Dunnett blurted, "Really? I mean, are you up to it, old fellow?"

Despite the sympathy in his tone, the words were so brutally insensitive that Antonia cringed for Julius.

He, however, betrayed no more emotion than a slight quirk of his mouth. "Oh, I might not caper around so well at the country dances, but I can just about haul my carcass into a waltz, if Mrs. Macy is willing to take the risk."

Mr. Dunnett's mouth opened, but Antonia could not bear to hear what would come out of it.

She sprang to her feet. "Mrs. Macy does not take risks," she said as lightly as she could manage. "But she is happy to dance." She curtsied. "Mr. Dunnett."

He rose and bowed, his brows still arched with surprise and not a little indignation.

Julius offered his arm, and the world seemed to stand still. For the first time in ten years, she would touch him. It felt absurdly momentous. She placed her fingers lightly on his sleeve, and suddenly noticed the braiding.

"You are a captain now," she said.

"Does that make me more acceptable?"

"Oh, no. I am prepared to dance with anyone."

His gaze flew to her face, and surely there was a hint of surprised amusement in his one, sharp eye. It vanished almost at once.

"So it would appear, Mrs. Macy. I thought you were Lady Linfield."

"I cannot help your thoughts, captain. I certainly never said I was."
She made another discovery, this time on the dance floor. "They are
still in the middle of the cotillion."

"Indeed they are. I admit I was surprised you chose to subject
yourself to more of my company than is strictly necessary."

She opened her mouth to retort, but he was already speaking
again.

"Are you well acquainted with Mr. Dunnett?"

"I never met him before this evening. Are you?"

"Well enough to dislike him. Did he ask you for money?"

"He never asks ladies, only gentlemen, and it is for such a good
cause, you need not sneer. I'm sure many of your sailors would be
glad of the service."

"I'm sure they would. Did you give him any?"

She gazed up at him, perplexed. "I have none to give."

He looked skeptical, standing aside for an elderly lady to pass, and
then continuing their perambulation around the perimeter of the
dance floor. "Why don't you ask Lord Linfield?"

Her mouth fell open, then she closed it with a furious snap. His
meaning was unmistakable, that Lord Linfield was her provider.
Which, in fact, he was, though hardly in the manner Julius was
implying. "How many ways do you wish to insult me in one evening?
If you asked me to dance for the purpose, then please be so good as to
shab off."

His one eye blinked and then a breath of laughter shook him, so
familiar that her temper was swallowed in the pain of memory.

"Shab off?" he repeated. "Hardly a ladylike expression."

"I expect I learned it from you."

"Then I'm surprised you remembered it. Where is Mr. Macy? Is he
happy for you to be cavorting around the country with Lord Linfield?"

"I do not cavort about the country with Lord Linfield. I cavort
about the country with Miss Talbot, who is his sister."

"I see."

"I doubt it."

"Were you always this shrewish?"

"Were you always this *doltish*?"

He laughed with just a hint of savagery. "Apparently."

At that moment, a young lady suddenly swept in front of them, obliging them to halt. She was very pretty, but the array of expressions that flitted over her face were much more interesting. She all but skidded to a standstill beside them, betraying surprise, guilt, defiance, and, finally, sheer fun. She smiled dazzlingly at Julius. "There you are," she said.

"Apparently unexpectedly so. Who are you escaping from now?"

"No one. I am going back to Rod and Cornel. I feel they have had enough peace for one evening." She turned her smile on Antonia with open curiosity. She even dipped a curtsy. "Good evening."

"Good evening," Antonia replied gravely, returning the courtesy.

"All me to present my sister," Julius said with resignation. "Miss Lucy Vale. Lucy, Mrs. Macy."

"How do you do?" Lucy said. She seemed intrigued and quite undecided whether to carry on her way or remain with her brother. There was something very appealing about her, a vitality, an interest in everything that reminded Antonia of Julius when she had first met him. When one looked closely, even her features were similar, though in a more refined kind of way, and her eyes were a more definite green.

"You have a large family, do you not?" Antonia said, remembering. "Are they all with you in Blackhaven?"

"Every one," Lucy replied. "In fact, we are all here at the ball. Apart from the twins, who are only fifteen."

"Goodness," Antonia said vaguely.

"That is more polite than Julius's stated opinion."

"I have heard some of his less polite opinions," Antonia said.

Lucy regarded her. "Just scold him. He is usually sorry—too used to shouting at sailors, you see." With a last brilliant smile at her brother, she glided away.

"She is up to something," Julius murmured.

"Almost certainly. Do you want to follow her?"

"God, no." He paused. "Not unless she leaves the building."

"She is a handful, I perceive." Antonia recalled that there were nine siblings, of both regular and irregular parentage, and that their father, Sir George, was a diplomat, frequently abroad. "She is your responsibility?" she asked tactfully.

"Yes. My father died a year ago."

"I'm sorry."

"Don't be." A rueful smile crossed his face, seeming to surprise him as much as it did her. "He had a merry life. And a useful one."

He did not ask about her parents. Or her husband. Obviously, he had no interest, so why the devil had he asked her to dance?

The cotillion had come to an end, and everyone was milling around the ballroom, returning to chaperones and families, or seeking out refreshment and the next dancing partner.

Antonia found herself watching them, their faces, expressions, and manners. In some ways, this was quite like the public assemblies she had attended in her youth near Portsmouth. There, many of the attendees had been local gentry and worthies, and several army and navy officers from the nearby ports and barracks. There had also been a scattering of the more aristocratic and fashionable, and even the odd exotic foreigner who had arrived by sea and strayed a few miles inland.

She found herself watching a wildly handsome officer of some foreign army, who was wearing his sword. Some gave him a wide berth; others gravitated toward him. He was laughing, his arm around a lively, pretty young woman who did not appear to object in the slightest. Elsewhere, a soberly dressed man seemed anxious to abandon his tongue-tied young partner, and hurried her off the floor so quickly that she was almost trotting. A gaggle of young women, clearly friends, giggled as they walked past, deep in conversation. A man and woman, who looked old enough to know better, gazed too long into each other's eyes, as though forgetting they had stopped talking some time ago.

"Shall we lurch across the floor?" Julius asked, as the orchestra in the gallery above struck up the introduction to a waltz.

It crossed Antonia's mind that he regretted his invitation and was trying to put her off. Or perhaps he had not expected her to accept in the first place. *Hard luck. You shouldn't have asked me, then.*

"By all means," she said sweetly.

Although his limp was pronounced, he had developed his own grace to deal with it. Certainly, as he led her onto the floor, he did not lurch. He took her hand in his and placed his arm around her waist, and abruptly, the world was in chaos again.

He had held her in his arms before, preparatory to tender kisses and sweet caresses that had misled her on so many matters. She wanted to be angry about all that misleading, and yet her brain seemed to melt as swiftly as her body.

Every part of her remembered. Even though this was quite different, merely a dance. No one had waltzed ten years ago—it would have been considered indecent, and still was by some—and he had certainly never embraced her in public.

Julius's embrace. Ten years of longing could not drown, it seemed, in a mere hour or two of his contempt. It was only damnable memory that affected her so. Wasn't it? At least their hands were gloved, but his arm was like warm steel at her waist, and she knew its strength as well as its gentleness. He was as tall as she remembered, his person both achingly familiar and wildly unknown. She could gaze now only into one eye.

Once, she had seen the sea in those profound eyes—all the dangerous beauty of both storm and calm. Now, she didn't know what she saw.

"Why are you dancing with me?" she demanded.

His eyebrow rose. "You said yes. Have you changed your mind? Again?"

The sheer injustice of that deprived her of breath. Or perhaps it was his nearness, the way he guided her backward and around and around and forward again, as every inch of her followed him with insidious pleasure. His limp was nowhere in evidence thanks to the unusual looseness, even abandon, of his steps.

"No. I am quite constant in my opinions and my affections until they are proved to be mistaken. Which is why I will not walk away and leave you standing alone on the dance floor."

"Am I to be grateful not to be humiliated again?"

"It is nothing to do with you," she replied with relish. "Such ill manners might reflect badly on Miss Talbot, whom I wish always to please."

"Excellent set-down," he approved. "If incomprehensible—but then, I believe I am doltish."

"Far be it from me to disagree with a gentleman's beliefs."

A sardonic smile glinted in his eye and faded as they danced on in silence. She had never minded silences with him before. Now, she was far too muddled to know what this one meant or why she cared. But gradually, in the absence of words, she heard only the music, felt only the embrace she had longed for too often over the years. He meant nothing by it, and yet he was *there*, his gaze locked with hers.

Her body felt light and curiously free, yet a sweet heaviness began to gather low in her stomach. She remembered that sensation, too, for she had only ever felt it with him. Older and wiser, now, she knew it meant nothing, but just for these few minutes, she let the sensual pleasure of the waltz engulf her. Her body ached for a greater closeness, to touch at breast and hip, to feel more closely his every movement against her.

This man was her first and only love. In these moments, the ruin of that love hardly mattered. She simply enjoyed him, savored the moment, while desire awakened and streamed through her like new life. Perhaps it showed in her eyes, for his had darkened like the sky before a storm, and his lips parted slightly, perhaps in surprise, or even uncertainty. She remembered those lips on her skin, on her mouth, tender, arousing, loving…

His thumb moved against her hand. He danced her backward and turned her, and somehow she was closer to him. On the next turn, the buttons of his coat brushed against her breast and his thigh touched hers. Heat seeped through her veins. Perhaps he felt it, because his lips quirked in the one-sided half-smile she remembered so well.

Almost afraid to, she forced her gaze from his mouth and back to his eyes, feeling again the shock of the black covering over one—but it was the other that held her, thrilling her with his own naked desire. And then his lashes swept down. When they lifted, his expression was still intense, but she could no longer read it.

"Julius," she began shakily, and the music came to a close.

His hand fell from her waist as smartly as a military salute, as though he had accomplished one task and was ready to move on to the next. It felt like a slap in the face. Another one.

Chapter Three

JULIUS WAS CONFUSED.

Some remnant of chivalry had driven him to rescue her from Dunnett. He had meant to abandon her again immediately, only her damnable self-possession had driven him to invite her to dance, with every expectation that this would embarrass her horribly and she would wriggle out of it.

Neither appeared to be the case. Instead, he could have sworn that waltzing with him moved her as much as it affected him, against his every wish and common sense. In short, he was appalled. Her name on his lips all but crushed him. He wanted, needed, to be away from her, and yet that appalled him too.

He fell back on manners, of a sort, conducting her in now-ominous silence to where she had once been sitting with Miss Talbot. Her hand lay lightly on his arm, yet seemed to burn through his sleeve to his oversensitive skin. Anger curled through him, with himself because she made him feel *this*… Whatever *this* was.

Ten years, and she still made him a fool.

You make yourself a fool. It's only memory. It will be gone in a moment, and so will she. Thank God.

Miss Talbot was not at the table where Antonia had been sitting, but Lord Linfield was, in conversation with a somewhat haughty-looking man who looked vaguely familiar. He had been amongst the noisy family who passed Julius at the entrance to the assembly rooms. Both gentlemen stood up at Antonia's approach.

Julius, who had hoped to melt away, was obliged by civility to await introductions.

"Captain Vale," Antonia murmured, as though she too were anxious for him to be gone. Perhaps he embarrassed her. "Lord Linfield."

Julius bowed and was surprised to see Linfield's eyebrows shoot up with some kind of recognition.

"Not Captain Sir Julius Vale?" he said.

"I'm afraid so," Julius said, while Antonia regarded him with surprise. His father had not been a baronet ten years ago.

Linfield thrust out his hand. "Very glad to make your acquaintance, sir. I knew Sir George, your father—had occasion to work with him several times."

"You are a diplomat also?" Julius didn't know why he was surprised. Antonia's connection to this family eluded him.

"Just back from Vienna."

"One would think you should have had enough of dancing, then," the other man said with a grin that wasn't haughty at all.

"It does appear to be habit forming," Linfield said. "Do you know Lord Braithwaite, captain?"

"Not until this moment. How do you do?"

"And Mrs. Macy, my sister's friend," Linfield added.

Antonia curtsied with her usual grace. The curve of her neck and shoulder was still the loveliest Julius had ever seen. Hastily, he looked away.

"How do you do, Mrs. Macy," Lord Braithwaite said pleasantly, before turning back to Julius. "I'm sure we must have met as children, you know."

"I think I might recall your father," Julius said, as a faint image of a fierce, scowling gentleman passed through his mind. "But I was several years your senior, and I left home at fifteen. Even before that, we traveled a good deal."

"And are you settled now at Black Hill?" Braithwaite asked.

"For the foreseeable future."

"Excellent. My wife will invite you to tea. And to her garden party and all other manner of entertainments, I'm sure." There was an oddly appealing yet shy pride in the way he said *my wife*. It caused Julius a pang that he refused to think about.

"I should advise her to be careful," he said. "I come with eight siblings."

"One good thing about castles is their sheer space," Braithwaite assured him.

"A pleasure to meet you," Julius said to both men, then bowed to them and to Antonia, who was regarding him now with slightly baffled curiosity. Before he looked too long, he murmured, "Excuse me," and walked away.

He was almost relieved to see that his siblings had all vanished from the table. He took out his flask of rum and raised it to his lips. When it was gone, he reached for Aubrey's bottle of brandy and refilled the flask. He caught a glimpse of Lucy dancing, and Roderick sitting beside a very young lady in surprisingly earnest discussion. Aubrey, inevitably, had found the most beautiful girl in the room and appeared to be teasing her.

Assuring himself all was right with his world, Julius stood, picked up the folded hat he had never troubled to leave in the cloakroom, and slipped away to enjoy his longed-for walk home by the sea. Now more than ever it seemed imperative.

Deliberately, he did not glance toward Antonia's table. Linfield had called her his sister's friend, but he was damnably good looking, charming, and successful.

Julius was crossing the empty foyer when he saw Antonia emerge from the ladies' cloakroom and turn at once toward the ballroom. Was this really the last time he would ever see her?

She noticed him. He could tell from the heightened color seeping into her face. But she did not stop, and he knew she wouldn't. He had deliberately killed the spontaneous intimacy of the waltz, and she understood that, even if she did not understand why. Neither did he. None of this made sense. It never had since the day he had been dismissed so summarily from her life.

On impulse, he swerved and intercepted her. For an instant he thought she would bolt, and shame surged up from his toes. But in the end, she paused to wait for him, her head high, an expression of deliberate calm on her face.

She had not been calm during the waltz. And she waltzed divinely, soft, supple, and responsive in his arms…

"Why did you jilt me for Macy?" He didn't mean it to come out as a peremptory bark, and the sound made him cringe inwardly.

Her eyes widened in what looked like incomprehension, quickly followed by galloping fury. "How *dare* you?"

He swallowed. "I'm sorry," he managed. "I did not mean to shout."

"Shout?" she repeated, staring at him. "You are sorry for *shouting*?"

He stared back. "What else should I be sorry for?"

Abruptly, the anger vanished from her eyes, leaving only the confusion that surely mirrored his. Then the ballroom door opened again, and she turned from him and fled.

He strode on to the exit, only just remembering to speak to the doorman, asking him to arrange a message to Major Vale that Captain Vale had gone home. He swept up the empty high street and around to the harbor, greeting the sight and smell of the sea with something very like relief.

The harbor was quiet too, save for the odd splashing of fishing boats and the creak of small pleasure craft tied up along one side. The fishermen would all be in bed, waiting for the small hours when the little fleet would head out, whatever the weather.

Julius ran down the steps to the beach, shuffled down to the wetter sand, and broke into a run. The tide was out, as he had known it would be, and the moon and stars, reflected in the rippling sea, provided, for the moment, enough light for him to see his way.

He inhaled deeply, then tore off his coat and kept running. His bad leg stretched and ached, but not unbearably. He jumped, skidded, and stumbled over the rocks to the Black Cove and kept going. By the time he reached Braithwaite Cove in the shadow of the lowering castle, he was breathing like a steam engine he had once seen in action. He slowed to a walk but didn't pause to rest. His mind wouldn't let him.

There was something he did not know. Something *she* didn't know. Had the last ten years been about mere *misunderstanding*? Was that all their love had been worth? Such a spectacular fall at the very first hurdle?

If so, he was right to be cynical. Love really was an illusion and not worth the time or effort.

And yet, slogging on along the beach for miles and then, painfully, over the rocks to the inland track he almost missed in the dark, he was aware of something flooding through him, something more than bodily weariness. It felt like…life.

IN BLACK HILL House, most of the servants had gone to bed, although the lamp had been left in the hallway burning low. Julius lit a candle from it and crossed slowly to the staircase, his limp much more pronounced now that he had exercised his bad leg well beyond its comfort. He wasn't truly surprised to see two nightgowned figures sitting there on the steps, grinning at him. His youngest siblings, Lawrence and Leona.

"Aubrey wagered us that you wouldn't go," Lawrence said.

"Sadly, Aubrey has lost, then, because I did go."

Their expressions brightened so much that Julius wondered uneasily how much they had staked.

"Was it fun?" Leona asked.

"Of course," he said gravely. "It was a ball. One is keelhauled for not enjoying it."

Lawrence laughed. "Are you all back, then?"

"No, I walked." He glanced at the large clock on the hall dresser. It was two. "But I don't suppose the others will be long now. I suppose it's useless sending you to bed until they come?"

"Pretty much," Leona said. "We saw them again, you know."

He paused on the step beneath them. "Saw what?"

"The horses," Lawrence said. "Heard them, too. The hooves must have been muffled, but we heard them snorting and talking to each other. There were lots of them, like a herd. They went across the fields toward Blackhaven."

Julius sat down on the step. "On their own?"

"Couldn't see anyone," Lawrence admitted, "but we heard men's voices."

"It's probably smugglers," Julius said ruefully. "They've always been around here. I suspect they always will be."

"What do they smuggle?" Leona asked.

Julius shrugged. "Brandy, wine, tea, spices, even silk. Anything that has to pay duty to come into the country."

"Not horses?" Leona asked.

"No," Julius said. "The horses will have been used as pack animals to carry the smuggled goods from the shore."

"But the horses were horse-shaped," Leona said.

"They generally are," Julius said, beginning to smile.

"No," Lawrence said at once, "she means they had nothing on their backs when they were silhouetted against the sky."

Julius gazed at them thoughtfully. "That *is* odd," he allowed. "We should probably look into it. And by that, I mean Roderick and me and the local excisemen and officers of the law, not you." He saw the disappointment strike their faces at exactly the same time, and relented. "At least, not unless you're with Rod or Cornelius or me."

They grinned again, and Leona changed the subject. "Did you dance, Julius?"

"Actually, I did."

They pounced in unison. "Who with?"

He laughed. "No one you know. A lady called Mrs. Macy."

"Oh." Leona's smile faded. "Married, then."

It seemed the twins had joined the family conspiracy to marry him off, or at least to deprive him of the peace he wanted and needed.

"What is her first name?" Leona asked, with much less hope.

"Antonia. Are you two not cold?"

"No," said Lawrence. "Tell us more about the ball."

Julius stood up. "I'll leave that to your sisters."

"Did *they* dance?"

"Lots. So did Aubrey."

"Flirting, I suppose," Lawrence said austerely.

"Almost certainly. But even Rod and Cornell danced at least once before I left. Rest assured, everyone enjoyed the evening and will be home shortly. I, however, being old and decrepit, am going to bed now. Goodnight, smallest siblings."

"Goodnight, biggest brother."

ANTONIA FELT EXHAUSTED by the time the ball ended and she walked back to the hotel with Miss Talbot and Lord Linfield. They were both uncharacteristically quiet.

"I hope you haven't overdone it, ma'am," Antonia said to Miss Talbot as they entered the hotel foyer.

"Oh, no, not in the least. In fact, it did me a world of good, and I have much food for thought. And tomorrow, we shall take those miraculous waters again, so we can dance tomorrow night too."

Antonia smiled, and they climbed the stairs. Linfield, who normally saw them to the doors of their own bedchambers, said a vaguer-than-normal goodnight and entered his room first. Antonia delivered Miss Talbot into the hands of her sleepy maid and walked further along the passage to her own room. Her mind was full of Julius Vale and the expression on his face when she had last seen him. Mostly baffled, but with a flare of...something. Something that she could not read.

She slid her key in the lock, though it turned out to be unnecessary. Frowning, she opened the door and walked in to find a man in her bedchamber.

Worse, he was sitting on the sofa beside her dozing son.

For an instant, she was paralyzed with fear. A fear that was not much allayed when she recognized her late husband's brother, Timothy.

Only when Nurse Suze waddled out of the dressing room, looking outraged, was she able to move.

"Timothy," she said sharply, "what are you doing here?"

"Inspecting the care of my nephew and ward," Timothy said grandly. "And it seems to be as well I did! Not even in bed at this hour."

"*He* woke the lad up!" Nurse Suze exclaimed. "Made him come through here and asked him all sorts of questions when the poor little lamb just wants to sleep."

Timothy cast Suze a black look. "And," he continued, "abandoned by his own mother, who's been gallivanting God knows where."

"He was not abandoned," Antonia said between her teeth. "He was left in the care of two devoted servants—asleep, I might add."

As though he heard her voice, Edward's head jerked up and his eyes opened. He smiled at her, and her heart melted, as it always did.

"I see only one rude old woman," Timothy sneered. "And if that is the standard of his care, I cannot allow it." His hand dropped on Edward's shoulder, but the boy wriggled away too quickly and stumbled sleepily to Antonia.

She crouched and caught him in her arms, hugging him and smiling to show she was not worried and that all was well.

"There were two of us up to five minutes ago," Suze said, "when Miss Roberts saw you all walking along the road, and went to wait for Miss Talbot."

"Go to bed," Edward said happily.

"Excellent idea," Antonia murmured, and rose to take his hand and walk with him into the dressing room, where a truckle bed had been made up for him, surrounded by his favorite toys.

She was shaking with rage as she settled him into bed, tucked him in, and kissed his forehead. Fortunately, he was so sleepy that he merely smiled and closed his eyes, contented now that she was back and lost to the world.

She rose from his bedside and left the room, closing the door tightly behind her.

"I said you may go," Timothy was saying angrily to Nurse Suze.

"I'm going nowhere until I have my orders from Mrs. Macy or Miss Talbot or his lordship," Suze said flatly.

"Wait here a moment longer if you please, nurse," Antonia said, far more calmly than she felt.

Timothy Macy had no right to be here in her bedchamber. Unfortunately, her husband had given his brother legal rights over their son. It was like walking on eggshells trying not to provoke him while giving herself and Edward any life at all.

It was all spite, of course. His threats to take Edward from her were empty. He had no knowledge of bringing up a child, and less desire to. But he still cast her a baleful glare when she countermanded his order.

"If you wish to talk to Edward or about Edward, you are of course

34

most welcome to do so," Antonia said as pleasantly as she could muster. "However, not at three o'clock in the morning, and most certainly not in my bedchamber."

"Good grief, Antonia, we are family," Timothy exclaimed.

"Even family respect privacy, and you cannot imagine Francis would condone your being here."

Timothy blinked rapidly. "Francis was too damned strait-laced."

"I'm certainly sure it never entered his head to walk into *your* wife's bedchamber, whether or not she was there, or whatever the time or day or night. Let us agree it shall not happen again." It wouldn't, for she would issue specific orders that would ensure it. She forced a faint smile to her lips. "I suggest we meet tomorrow afternoon, in the hotel coffee room, perhaps, or at the beach or the ice parlor if you prefer an outing. Think about it and let me know. A note via the hotel staff will find me. Goodnight, Timothy."

He gave in with grace, now that he had made his point of frightening her, and rose, smiling and bowing.

"Goodnight, Antonia. I do trust the boy will not be left entirely to his own devices while you sleep in tomorrow? Or do Miss Talbot's bidding?"

"Nurse is always there," Antonia replied steadily. "*Goodnight*, Timothy."

"Goodnight."

The door clicked shut behind him, and Antonia sank onto the bed. "I am so sorry, Suze. And grateful! Please, go to bed, with my thanks."

"It's my duty," Suze said with a sniff. "Here, let me unhook your gown for you, so you can go to bed."

Much to Antonia's surprise, she did not fall asleep as soon as her head landed on the pillow. Instead, she lay awake, conscious of a knot of excitement in her stomach. And it did not appear to be caused by dread of the next encounter with Timothy, but by the knowledge that Julius Vale—Captain Sir Julius Vale now—was only a few miles away.

Chapter Four

TIMOTHY MACY WAS appalled by the prices charged at the Blackhaven Hotel, which he regarded as being on the edge of the known world. He would look around and see if there was a decent inn in the town instead. One that would not beggar him. For this morning, he made the most of the facilities he would undoubtedly be charged for, and tucked into the very excellent breakfast that he had ordered to be served in his room.

He was only halfway through this repast when a knock on the door disturbed him. "Enter if you must," he said testily.

Jonathan Dunnett strolled into the room. He always looked more like a valet or a bank clerk than a gentleman, but he had a razor-sharp mind of rare deviousness and a positive flair for making money.

"You are such a bear in the morning," Dunnett complained, settling in the chair on the opposite side of the table. "One would think you are not pleased to see an old friend."

"I'd be more pleased to see him somewhere that wasn't a damned wilderness. Blackhaven is almost Scotland."

"I am led to believe there is life in Scotland, too. When did you arrive?"

"Yesterday evening. You were right, of course—my sister-in-law is here, still drudge to Linfield's sister. Though one must admire her for getting them to pay for her child, too."

Dunnett waved that aside. "Their arrangements are of no interest to us. I met the fair Mrs. Macy at the assembly room ball last night. I have a plan that involves her, for which I would like your assistance." He smiled. "After all, we are partners."

"I have traveled hundreds of miles north for this partnership," Macy said, cutting his ham with some force. "It had better be worth my while."

"Oh, it will be. To show my appreciation, I am happy to give you a proportion of earnings from another couple of ventures in which you have had, as yet, no hand." Dunnett reached out, uninvited, and helped himself to a slice of Timothy's toast.

Timothy glowered.

"You have, I believe, some influence over Mrs. Macy?"

"I am her son's guardian. She likes to keep me sweet so that I don't send the pampered little pest away to Eton. Or insist he lives with me."

"Good," Dunnett said, taking a large bite of toast which he chewed and swallowed with apparent relish. "I would like you, in a subtle way, to direct her toward marriage."

Macy shrugged. "She's shown no inclination since my brother died. Her parents are convinced she will have Linfield."

"No," Dunnett said, dusting off his hands. "She will have me." He smiled winningly. "If you have no objections."

Macy paused in mid-swallow, staring at him. "She has no money. You of all people know that!"

"But she has class, the indefinable something that makes her a lady. For a man like me, that makes her the perfect wife. I need a spouse in order to expand my work."

Macy blinked several times. Then he laughed. "Why not? It will certainly remove any chance of her returning to Masterton Hall."

"There is a slight complication, which is why I have requested your help."

"What complication?"

Dunnett sighed. "Julius Vale."

Timothy frowned with impatience. "I dealt with him years ago."

"He has retired to his family estates in Blackhaven. And is interfering with my work at the local hospital. I do not want him interfering with my plans for Mrs. Macy."

Timothy considered. "I see no reason why he should. He must hate her as much as she hates him. That was the beauty of the whole thing. One way or another, we can ensure Antonia falls into your arms." He frowned. "What of the boy, though?"

Dunnett smiled and reached for another slice of toast. "What of him?"

THE VALES' BREAKFAST table was almost as crowded as usual, the only absence being Julius, who had gone to look for hoofprints before the rain came on.

"He thought they were smugglers," Lawrence told his siblings, between mouthfuls of bacon and sausage. "Until Leona mentioned the horses weren't carrying anything. Not even riders."

"Horse thieves?" Roderick said, looking up from his newspaper. "Raided across the border like the olden days."

"They went in more for cattle, didn't they?" Cornelius said, reaching for another piece of toast. "None of our cattle has gone."

"Perhaps they're wild horses," Felicia said.

"Going to Blackhaven for a party?" Aubrey suggested.

"I think we would hear if the streets of Blackhaven filled with wild horses," Cornelius said dryly.

"Perhaps they like horses," Aubrey mused. "It could be an old tradition. The place is wildly eccentric, you know."

"Can a town be eccentric?" Roderick wondered aloud.

"The people in it can," Leona said. "Talking of whom, who is Mrs. Macy?"

They all looked at her, except Lawrence, who carried on eating.

"Julius danced with her," Leona explained. "You must have noticed."

"I met him talking to a Mrs. Macy," Lucy said. "She was rather beautiful, actually, if slightly...tense. But I've no idea who she is. I didn't see him dancing with anyone."

"He did," Felicia said. "But he left early. I'm not sure we achieved anything by getting him to the ball."

They all went back to eating, drinking tea, and reading.

Leona said, "*One* of you must have heard of her. Antonia Macy?"

There followed general shruggings, which was about all one could expect from siblings who were great at making plans and not nearly observant enough to carry them through. She and Lawrence should have gone to the ball. Then they would know.

Then, unexpectedly, Leona found Delilah's gaze on her. "I would not go near that particular lady," Delilah said.

"Because she is married?" Leona said, disappointed. "I was hoping she was a widow."

"Poor Mr. Macy," Felicia murmured.

"Besides, Antonia is the past," Delilah said, setting down her teacup and rising to her feet. "*Not* the future."

"How do you know?" Lawrence demanded. "Perhaps there are lots of Antonias!"

"Let us hope so," Delilah said serenely, and walked out of the room.

Lucy frowned. "I hate it when she does that."

"Does what?" Cornelius asked.

"Knows something that we don't, because she is older, but does not tell us."

"She isn't older than me," Roderick said mildly. "And I have never heard of any Antonia."

"You are a soldier and were nearly always abroad," Lucy pointed out. "Who wants to go into Blackhaven today?"

"We do," Leona said. She had the feeling they were all concealing something, though whether it was anything to do with Julius or not, she had no idea.

EDWARD WAS A curious and precocious child who soaked up information like a sponge. Antonia had already taught him to read, and to write a little. He liked numbers, could point to most countries on the globe, especially those he had been to, and had developed an impressive understanding of plants and the natural world. On top of that, Lord Linfield, who had a fondness for him, gave him the odd casual lesson in Latin.

In short, he was impressively educated for a six-year-old, and Antonia knew Timothy would find nothing to complain about there. His manners were also good, although he had a tendency to pursue conversations to their utmost conclusions, which was not always comfortable.

Inevitably, over a light luncheon in the hotel coffee room, Timothy found the weak points of his nephew's upbringing. "What of the company of boys his own age and his own class?"

"He makes friends easily enough," Antonia said. "There were several children in Vienna with whom he played on a regular basis."

"Foreigners," Timothy said with a curl of his lip.

"Some were British," she said patiently. "And now that we are home, I expect he will have more settled friends."

Timothy pounced. "Then you mean to return to Masterton Hall?" He looked more alarmed than pleased.

"No," she replied. "I shall remain with Miss Talbot."

"Who never stays in one place! Take this bizarre jaunt into the north. It is practically Scotland!"

"Mama, I see a pirate!" Edward whispered loudly.

"Goodness," Antonia said in awed tones, and to Timothy, "Blackhaven was recommended for Miss Talbot's health."

"Vienna also?" he asked sarcastically.

"As you know, she accompanies her brother to all his postings. And I accompany her."

"And the boy accompanies you," he said triumphantly. "Out of the country, even, without my permission. Besides, I don't see how you can be any use to her *and* to the boy."

Antonia counted to five in her head, aware of Edward sliding off his chair. "We manage very well."

"May I go and speak to the pirate?" Edward asked, jumping from foot to foot.

"If you stay where I can see you—and you can see me," Antonia told him, holding Timothy's derisive, disbelieving gaze. "I wrote to you from Dover when we went to Vienna and apologized for the oversight. I saw no reason for you to object, since it would only have put you to the trouble of obtaining nurses and making other suitable provisions for him. And we have already agreed that on any future occasions I shall consult with you well in advance. We have no quarrel, Timothy, and you can see that Edward is healthy, educated, and happy."

His gaze went beyond her, and his eyes gleamed. "With a penchant for strangers."

Antonia jerked her head to the side and saw Edward staring with considerable awe up at a tall man in riding dress. A man with an eye patch. He really *had* seen someone who resembled his idea of a pirate, gleaned largely from an illustrated book he was fond of.

"He is not a stranger," Antonia said, trying to quell the sudden, rapid drumming of her heart. "But an old acquaintance. Excuse me..."

However, as she rose to her feet to retrieve Edward, he looked up and saw her. He started bounding toward her, saying something to Julius, who walked easily beside the boy with his long, if halting, stride.

"Mama, Mama, Captain Vale is a real pirate and has captured many ships!"

"He may well have done so," Antonia agreed, with a serenity she was proud of, "but, you know, he is only pretending to be a pirate. He is really a captain in the Royal Navy."

"Was," Julius said, bowing. "Mrs. Macy."

So, they were to be polite. She just hoped he would not give away the fact that while he and she might know each other, Edward had never met him in his life. And Timothy would pounce on any danger to the boy that could possibly be perceived.

"Captain Vale," she murmured, gazing at him with urgent warning. "Allow me to introduce Mr. Macy."

From faint amusement, Julius's expression turned opaque. His bow was stiff. With a surge of hysteria, she realized he thought this was her husband and had come determined to dislike him. Bizarrely, she rather liked that idea, especially since mischief and the remnants of last night's anger urged her on to deception.

But she could not allow it.

"My brother-in-law," she murmured, and caught the quick, sideways quirk of his lips, almost as if he had understood her temptation.

"How do you do, sir?" Timothy said affably, frowning at Edward, who was tugging at Julius's coat. "Your patience suggests you have children of your own."

"Only younger siblings."

"Ah. I was hoping to find an ally to help my sister-in-law understand the importance of stability to a child's upbringing. It is inevitably a bad thing to be forever hauling them around the country. Even worse, the Continent! Disruptive to education and friendships alike."

"You may be right," Julius said civilly. "But I am the wrong person to ask. My father took us all over Europe with him, and even to Canada once."

Timothy raised his disapproving frown to Julius's face. "Did none of you go to school, sir?"

He clearly expected the response to be "Of course we did," and Antonia tensed. But Julius said, "Not that I can recall. Apart from an English school in Rome for a month or so. We had several long-suffering tutors and governesses, even in Blackhaven, which was a lot less accessible then."

"You are a native of Blackhaven, sir?" Timothy said as though discovering a new tribe in some exotic foreign land.

"I am." Julius's gaze dropped to Edward, who stopped tugging his coat and gave an angelic smile.

"Can we play pirates, now?"

"Pirates don't attack hotels, sadly. We need a beach. I shall meet you there one day. Good day, Mrs. Macy. Sir." He closed his one eye in a wink at Edward and limped back off across the foyer.

With some difficulty, Antonia dragged her attention back to Timothy, as Edward slipped his hand into hers, still gazing admiringly after the captain. She would much rather have done the same.

"Do you stay long in Blackhaven?" she asked Timothy. "Now that you have assured yourself of Edward's wellbeing."

"I have a little business to tend to while I am here," he said grandly. "You may well be gone before me. I hope you will inform me, if so."

"I have already agreed I shall inform you anyway. Come, Edward, let us go and see Miss Talbot and change for our walk."

"Can we go to the beach?" her son asked eagerly. "There might be real pirates there! And ices!"

"Let us hope for a pirate *with* ices," Antonia murmured. "Good afternoon, Timothy."

She crossed the foyer to the stairs, conscious of a massive sense of relief. She had fobbed Timothy off again, and Julius had not seemed so antagonistic. They might even be able to talk to each other one day... If they stayed in the same place long enough.

Miss Talbot was discovered already in her bonnet and pelisse, so Antonia hurried Edward to their rooms to wash his face.

The first thing she saw in her bedchamber was a vase of anemones, and Nurse Suze admiring them.

"Oh, how beautiful," Antonia exclaimed. "They are my favorite flowers! Where did you get them?"

"I didn't. A gentleman left them for you."

"A gentleman?" Her eyebrows flew up, and she took the offered card from Suze.

Captain Sir Julius Vale, R.N. (Retired)
Black Hill House, Nr. Blackhaven.

Heat rushed into her face, and she touched the backs of her fingers to one cheek in a useless attempt to cool it. Anemones symbolized fragility as well as loyalty in love, though she doubted he was aware of it.

"I wonder why he did that?" she asked shakily. A peace offering? An apology? An acknowledgement of friendship?

And would she ever discover which?

IN FACT, JULIUS had been inspired by some half-forgotten tradition of giving flowers to the ladies one had danced with the night before.

That and the sight of the anemones growing wild as he had ridden into Blackhaven. With a jolt, he'd remembered that Antonia had loved the flower, and with that memory came a storm of others: presenting her with a posy of them; her smiling face half hidden in them as she caressed the scentless petals with her cheek; long walks in the sunshine near her home, and barefoot in the sand; stolen kisses in the sunshine and beneath the moonlight; all the pain and joy and hope of first love.

He had been all of six and twenty, but up until then, his passages with women had been either of the merely physical or the distant worship varieties. Antonia Temple had bowled him over utterly. She had not crept or even burst into his heart. She had just arrived there as though she belonged, and the sweetness of her admission that she loved him too still haunted his dreams.

For those few months of his convalescent leave after the Battle of Trafalgar, she had filled his heart and his hopes. She had been the reason behind everything he did and was determined to work toward, his love to come home to forever, the end to loneliness. They had made plans for the future. He had even obtained further leave of absence to be married, and to rejoin his ship in Lisbon in two months rather than sailing immediately from Portsmouth.

For once, he did not allow the memory of what happened next to intrude—his abrupt congé and the fury and misery with which he had sailed from Portsmouth after all. Instead, he remembered her face when she had first seen him last night—her shock, her sudden vulnerability in the face of his rudeness. She had come to him on the veranda.

He had seen in her face from the beginning that the last ten years had not left her unscathed. And yet he had been concerned only with his own hurt. He had not asked and he had not listened, only lashed out like a child in a tantrum or a bad officer in a filthy temper.

In a moment of impulse, born of shame, he'd reined in his horse and picked as many of the flowers as he could hold. Because she had danced with him. And because, for a few short months, she had once loved him. It was acknowledgement and ending. A way to move on. Which was why, when he left them for her with the hotel clerk, he added his card at the last moment.

And then he went to the coffee room to talk to Winslow, the local squire who was also the magistrate, about horses riding roughshod over his land. Winslow scratched his head and frowned and sent for a map, which they pored over, trying to guess the direction from which the horses had come and where they could be going.

"Two nights in a row?" Winslow repeated. "Going in the same direction?"

"Apparently so. And not weighed down with brandy or anything else."

"I'll ask around," Winslow said somewhat doubtfully. "And write to my counterpart over the border. Much damage to your land?"

"Very little. Much of the estate has been badly neglected over the years, so it is not all under cultivation. But it *will* be, so I would rather re-route the horses at the very least."

"Absolutely," Winslow said. "What happened to your man, what's his name? The steward you had in place. Barton!"

"He was too old to be working," Julius replied tactfully. He felt a faint prickling at the back of his neck, as though he was being watched. Ever since, as a very young man, he had been on a ship full of mutinously inclined sailors who constantly watched their officers with a threatening sullenness, he had been sensitive to such observation. "We retired him. He claims never to have seen any horses loose on the estate."

He glanced around the room. The only other occupants were busy about their own conversations over tea or luncheon.

"Do you believe him?" Winslow asked.

"I don't know him well enough to be sure," Julius admitted. A small boy of about five or six was standing staring at him from a table across the room. It had happened a lot since he had lost the eye. Then he looked beyond the boy and saw Antonia.

His heart dived, some mingling of excitement and pain. Was this her son? And who was that pinched-mouthed old stick beside her? Her husband? A family member? If so, she hardly looked pleased by his company. She was tense as a bowstring.

It was none of his business. He dragged his mind and his attention back to the matter at hand.

"I'll speak to Barton again," he said to Winslow. "And maybe keep watch tonight. The moon is still full. And I know smugglers prefer the dark for landing."

"It doesn't sound like smugglers," Winslow said, "not directly, anyway. I'll let you know what I find out. Keep me informed, won't you?"

"Of course." A tug at Julius's coat made him glance down at the boy who had been watching him with such awe.

"Are you a pirate, sir?" the lad asked.

Winslow smothered a laugh.

"In a way," Julius replied. "I confess I have captured and boarded ships and sailed off with their treasure. Though I'm pretty much retired from such adventuring these days."

"I would like to be a pirate. Am I big enough?"

"Not quite yet."

"I suppose I have to learn more, too," the boy said, nodding at the map spread out on the table, "so I can understand the treasure maps and that kind of thing."

"It always helps," Julius said gravely, while Winslow gave another snort of suppressed laughter. "What's your name?"

"Edward Macy."

So he *was* her son. Something twisted inside him, for he could see her in the shape of the boy's face, the set of his mouth. "I'll put in word for you, for when you're older," he said lightly. He turned back to Winslow. "Thanks for your help, sir. I'll call on you with any news. I'd better take Blackbeard here back to his family."

He could not explain his relief in discovering the older man with the pinched mouth and the condescending face was not her husband.

And yet it raised the question, where was he? And why was his brother trying to wrong-foot Antonia on her son's upbringing? Julius rather liked the boy—his courage and his curiosity and the sparkle of excitement in his eyes.

But none of her life or the boy's was his concern. And so he walked away. Again.

Chapter Five

J ULIUS HANDED LAWRENCE his best telescope. "See where they come from, and track where they go as far as you can."

They were in Lawrence's bedchamber, which had the best view of the land over which the horses had been seen.

"I'd rather ride out with the rest of you," Lawrence said mutinously.

"I know. But we have to be sensible. If we don't manage to catch any humans, we need more information to find them."

"Can't Leona or one of the other girls do that?"

"Leona's watching from the other side of the house, in case the horses swerve in that direction. And your eyes are better than anyone else's." It was all true, even if Julius did not want Lawrence to understand that his main purpose was to keep the over-adventurous twins indoors and out of danger, with as much dignity as possible. "We need to know, Lawrence."

Lawrence sighed. "Of course we do." He raised the telescope to his eye and began adjusting it.

Julius clapped him on the shoulder. "Good man."

Lucy, who planned to keep Lawrence company, cast Julius a quick grin of approval, no doubt for his tact, as he limped past her to the door. Felicia was across the hall with Leona, while Delila had settled herself in the drawing room surrounded by books and candles, most of which were not yet lit, since dusk was only just beginning to fall.

"I'll light them in a quarter of an hour," she said. "And the ones outside, giving you time to conceal yourselves first. Are you sure about Aubrey going with you?"

"He has to," Julius said. Although of delicate health since childhood, Aubrey could bear no more coddling, and it was true he seemed so much better up here in the country that they all had cause to hope. "His nature is adventurous."

Delilah smiled lopsidedly. "And it might keep him from more scandalous pursuits?"

"Something like that. Make sure you lock the door when the lanterns are lit."

"I will."

Julius went out, found his horse and his brothers, and swung himself up into the saddle. They set off in silence, since they had already prearranged their hiding places. Cornelius, who knew the land best, was furthest away from the house, then Roderick, Aubrey, and Julius closest.

There was more cloud around compared to last night, but the sky was still light enough to make out the trees, especially with the lanterns lit around the house and the light blazing through the unshuttered drawing room window.

There was a risk that the lights would scare off whoever was behind the horses, but Julius had decided it was more likely they would assume everyone was in the house and otherwise occupied. Besides, at this stage, it was more important to see what they were doing. If they came. And the wait would be long and tedious.

He skulked at the edge of the home wood, holding his horse's bridle and leaning his shoulder against a large oak to ease his bad leg. At sea, when he was the officer on watch, he had walked constantly about the deck to keep himself observant and awake. Here, he did not have that luxury, for fear of scaring off whomever he was trying to catch.

Mostly, he tried not to think of Antonia, dwelling instead on the matter in hand, on his and Cornelius's plans for the estate, and on the charitable hospital in Blackhaven that he hoped to help to some greater degree.

He felt them first beneath his feet, a faint, low vibration of the ground. He straightened, listening intently until he heard it—the dull, soft beating of many hooves on damp, muddy ground to the north.

The horses came careering out of the darkness, unsaddled and unbridled, so far as he could see. He peered more closely, and made out what seemed to be a rope around the neck of one of the front horses. And was that human legs he could just make out running amongst the equine ones?

His own horse whinnied in welcome, the sound lost in the thundering hooves, as he eased himself into the saddle and waited. There must have been twenty or so horses, and at the back, surely, another haltered one.

Julius dug his heels into his horse's sides and broke out from the covering trees. As soon as he crossed behind the last horse, he saw the man clinging to the neck of the beast in front, presumably to avoid being seen as a rider from either the lodge house, which they must have passed, or the main house.

The clinging man had seen him, for he shouted out something, presumably to his comrade ahead, and hauled himself onto the horse's bare back. Julius urged Admiral to greater speed as they thundered past the house. The bareback rider peered over his shoulder and kicked hard at his own mount. It screamed its objection and answered, but Julius still gained on it.

"Halt!" Julius shouted, with more hope than expectation, and, when he was ignored, offered a short prayer to the Almighty. Then he leapt from the saddle, striking the other rider's body with enough force to knock him straight off the horse's back.

They fell together, driving all the air out of Julius's body and sending a shard of agony through his leg. Somehow, he managed to jerk astride his captive and raise his fist.

"Wait! Wait!" the man shouted, thrusting up his open hands in surrender.

Julius lowered his fist. And found himself instantly flying onto his back when his captive bucked, sprang to his feet, and fled in the wake of the horses.

Julius leapt up immediately, ignoring the pain in his leg that, three strides later, refused to take a fourth. He stumbled to his knees and swore.

"Man on foot!" he yelled ahead to his brothers. "Catch him!"

Through the haze of pain, his heart in his mouth, he saw someone—surely Aubrey—jump onto the bare back of one of the horses. Furious with frustration at his own weakness, Julius called to Admiral, who, by some miracle, had chosen not to run with its fellows but to crop at the coarse grass. Eventually, the beast began to amble toward him, and he grasped at the stirrup leathers to try to haul himself upright.

Before he could, his hand was dislodged and Aubrey's frightened face glared at him in the darkness. "Stop, you great, stupid idiot!" Aubrey shouted. "What have you done to yourself?"

"I had him and I let him go! Go after him, damn you!"

"Let him go to hell!" Aubrey said furiously, and then Cornelius was there, too.

Together they hauled Julius to his feet. As he rose, he thought for a moment he had double vision. He could see Cornelius's horse easily enough, but Admiral was nose to nose with another one.

Aubrey grinned. "I got one. Not sure what use it will be."

"Not as much use as the man I let go," Julius said between his teeth. "Damn stupid trick to fall for."

They turned him, resolutely making him face toward the house.

By the blazing lights, he could see Delilah and Felicia running toward him.

"He's fine," Cornelius said, his grumpy voice unexpectedly reassuring. "Will you see if that horse will follow Admiral to the stables?"

By then, Julius didn't know if he was gritting his teeth in pain or in annoyance with himself.

Half an hour later, his leg propped up in front of him on the drawing room sofa, a cup of warm tea between his hands, he scowled at Delilah as she sat down on the edge of the seat beside him.

As usual, she came straight to the point. "They could not have gone after the man you caught, not while you were lying injured on the ground."

"They could have and they should have."

"Is that what you would have done?"

He opened his mouth to snap, *Yes.* And if this had been a naval operation involving his men, it might even have been true. But not with his brothers. Not his family.

He closed his mouth again, then drank his tea. He had spent so little time with his siblings that he had forgotten the warmth, the loyalty that never went away. Why had he not recalled that it was the same for them? He didn't want to be touched by his brothers' care of him, but he was.

Roderick, who had just come in, took a cup of tea from Felicia and said, "They went inland, to avoid Blackhaven, I suppose. Are you hurt, Julius?"

"Only my pride."

"He took a heroic leap and brought down one of the riders," Aubrey said. "Hurt his leg again in the process."

"And lost my man," Julius said, without heat now. "Aubrey is the real hero, for he captured one of their horses."

Aubrey flushed with a pleasure he would never admit. "Unfortunately, we can't question the horse."

"We can up to a point," said Delilah, who had stabled the captured animal and given it food and water. "It's a good horse, strong and well bred, but he's in poor condition. Undernourished, untreated minor injuries and bites. We'll be able to see more in the daylight."

"Why steal an out-of-condition horse?" Roderick demanded, scowling. He valued horses, since they had carried him through innumerable battles.

"Perhaps he wasn't out of condition when they stole him," Julius said thoughtfully. "In fact, we don't even know if he *is* stolen. Though we do know now the horses aren't wild and passing by on their own whim. They are definitely being driven. And in a particular direction." He glanced at the twins, who were sitting on the hearth. "Did you see further than Rod?"

"No, the hill gets in the way," Lawrence said with a frown. "But they came from the west."

Julius sat up. "Did they, by God? I'll investigate that tomorrow. Well done!"

The twins grinned at the praise, and Julius was struck by another wave of understanding. His family had always been so much more than a responsibility to him, but it came to him now that their company was to be cherished. He had left home at fifteen and barely knew them. Neither Lucy nor the twins had even been born then. His contact with them had always been sporadic, except for the letters that had found him in unlikely places all over the world.

Being all together like this was a rarity. They were *fun*, and they were his in a way no one else could or should be. They would not always be here with him. They would find their own paths through the world, their own lives and loves and homes. And that was just as it should be.

MRS. GRANT, THE vicar's wife, was an unexpected delight. Apparently she and Miss Talbot had got into conversation at the ball and formed a connection of humor and ideals. Therefore, Miss Talbot was delighted to welcome her when she called early the following afternoon. Antonia, who had been writing letters for her employer, paused for a cup of tea with them both.

Mrs. Grant was amusing and lighthearted in her speech, for all the world like a dazzling social butterfly inexplicably tied to a staid country vicar and his parish. And yet she gave no impression of being, or even feeling, trapped. At Miss Talbot's prompting, she told them about the various charities in the town, including a soup kitchen run by her husband and various volunteers, and a children's creche at the inn that allowed mothers to work while keeping their children safe and occupied.

"Of course, the hospital is our most ambitious project," she said. "It's so difficult to turn down those who need care of any kind, but it is in danger of collapsing. Dr. Lampton gives his time free, but after Waterloo we had to employ a permanent doctor familiar with long-term battle injuries. And of course we must pay the women who do the nursing and the cleaning. And find food for everyone. It's all enormously expensive."

"I met a Mr. Dunnett at the ball," Antonia recalled.

"Oh, he is marvelous at raising funds. He has no compunction about dunning visitors or…ah…reminding the local gentry of their responsibilities. Did he pick your pocket?"

Antonia laughed. "Sadly, there were few pickings there, but he would not have known had he not asked. Most subtly."

"It is a worthy cause," Mrs. Grant said. "Though I confess there is a fine line between collecting as much as you can and putting people off giving altogether."

"I would like to see this hospital of yours," Miss Talbot pronounced.

"You would? When?"

"Now?" suggested Miss Talbot, who had never been one to waste time.

"Why not?" Mrs. Grant set down her tea cup and stood. "I don't need to be home until four, and we can easily walk, if you would like to."

"Fetch your bonnet, Antonia," Miss Talbot commanded.

Half an hour later, they walked into the hospital building to be greeted by a cheerful matron. "Shall I fetch Molly to show the ladies around, Mrs. Grant?" she asked.

"Goodness, no, Molly is busy," Mrs. Grant exclaimed. "I shall take them."

"Not room five, ma'am," the woman said quickly. "Got a fever in there, and Dr. Samson doesn't know what it is yet."

No wonder they had to pay people to work here, Antonia thought ruefully. Desperate people, probably…

And just plain compassionate people. She met patients who had suffered horrific injuries, some by accident, many in battle who had lost limbs, or eyes or ears. A few women were in the throes of infection after childbirth. One room housed children themselves, weak and ill. Some had no one else to care for them, and the orphanage, some distance away, had an appalling reputation.

It must have been easy to feel oppressed with care and pity, but the women who worked there tended to be cheerful, dwelling on small successes rather than on tragedies.

Male voices echoed from another room, drifting through a half-open door.

"Ah, that is our Dr. Samson," Mrs. Grant said with satisfaction. She knocked on the door, waited for a response, and then stuck her head around. "Good day, doctor. May we bring in some visitors?"

An enthusiastic chorus of male voices made everyone laugh, and Antonia duly followed Mrs. Grant and Miss Talbot into the room.

The first person she saw was Julius Vale, rising stiffly from the edge of one of the patients' beds.

"Captain Vale," Mrs. Grant greeted him with obvious pleasure. "How fortunate to run into you. Ladies, are you acquainted with Dr. Samson and Captain Sir Julius Vale? Gentlemen, Miss Talbot and Mrs. Macy are visitors to the town and expressed an interest in our work here."

The doctor nodded curtly and scowled as though he resented the intrusion. Then, catching Mrs. Grant's eye, he smoothed out his frown and civilly introduced his patients.

"And that is Jenks," he finished, "who served on Captain Vale's own ship. His wound reopened and became infected."

"I though *you* served on Captain Vale's own ship, doctor?" Mrs. Grant said after smiling at the seaman, who blushed furiously under the attention.

"I did, but I retired first. Otherwise, poor old Jenks would have been sewn up a bit better."

A trolley bumped against the door as a woman pushed it in. It was laden with a massive teapot, jugs of milk, a dish of honey, and several mugs.

"Brought you yours here, too, doc," she said cheerfully. "Want a cup, captain? Ladies? Got cake, too, baked by Mrs. Doverton herself. Go on, help yourselves—we got plenty, and it'll only go stale by tomorrow."

The ladies took a slice between them to be sociable and sat on the stools meant for visitors. Antonia, who remembered informing Julius somewhat condescendingly that Mr. Dunnett's attempted fundraising was for a good cause, cringed now to remember it. That he was so well known to the staff suggested that the captain was already involved in the venture, beyond visiting one of his crewmen. She found it difficult to look at him.

Yesterday, he had all but rescued her from Timothy's accusations.

He had given her flowers that he knew she loved.

Miss Talbot was speaking to Dr. Samson. "Do you find this very different from your work at sea, sir?"

"In some ways. Here, I am certainly learning more."

"Is that why you retired from the navy?" Antonia asked. "To learn?"

He sipped his tea and considered. "Yes, partly. There is little room in the navy for a surgeon or a physician to grow, either in his career or in new skills. My position was quite different from the captain's. They wanted to promote him to commodore. A few years more and he would have been an admiral."

Antonia risked a surreptitious glance at Julius, remembering the ambitious young officer he had been. Clearly, he had also been highly capable and successful. She could tell that much from Samson's tone as much as his words. And yet, offered further promotion, he had instead left the life he loved to settle in his ancestral home with his family. She wondered why. Did he ever regret it?

There was no awkwardness in his manner with the injured men. Nor did he have the over-cheerful attitude of many visiting the sick. Instead, quite at ease, as he must have been on the deck of his own ship, he seemed to be making some kind of plans with them, on the assumption that they would get well.

"He's taking people on to work on the land or in his house," Samson said. "Not many people want a one-armed laborer or a disfigured servant. Though many of the patients we get here are just ill through poverty and have nowhere to go when they leave."

As though he felt her gaze, Julius glanced up and caught it. Her heart gave a foolish flutter she told herself was embarrassment, but she refused to look away too quickly.

"The captain provides an excellent example," Mrs. Grant said. "We are trying to encourage other landlords and wealthy people in the town to do likewise."

Captain Vale said something to Jenks, which made the man grin, and put down his cup. Casually, Antonia withdrew her gaze, returning her attention to Samson. But a moment later, someone leaned against the bed next to her stool.

It was *him*. Beneath the scent of horse and sea was something uniquely Julius. She had remembered it at the ball and had no name for it.

"Where is the young pirate today, then?" he asked lightly.

"At the beach with Nurse Suze," she replied. "No doubt looking for shipmates." She drew in her breath. "I hope he didn't offend you."

"Why should you imagine he did?"

"I didn't," she confessed. "He's just a child with a lively imagination. One of his books has a picture of a pirate with an eye patch. Timothy—my brother-in-law—pointed out that his mistake might be considered offensive."

"Not by me or anyone else with—" He broke off, as though thinking better of words, such as *anyone else with half a brain.* "Or anyone else, I'm sure," he finished.

She risked a glance, a quick, conspiratorial smile, almost returned. "Thank you for contributing your point of view. Timothy does not listen to mine."

"Surely he has to listen to your husband's!"

He didn't know. She had not told him, and he had clearly not troubled to find out. Her husband had been a shield, a protection for them both. But she would no longer play such a foolish, cowardly game.

"Hardly," she said, meeting his gaze. "My husband is dead, captain. I would not otherwise discuss my son's education with Timothy Macy. Nor could I have taken the position of companion to Miss Talbot."

SHE HAD ALWAYS taken his breath away. Now she told him quite casually that she was a widow and not the friend but the paid companion of the lady she traveled with.

It explained a good deal but left him speechless at his own lack of perception. How had he ever commanded a ship?

Almost immediately, her own difficulties drowned out his own.

"I'm sorry," he managed. For everything—her loss, and any further pain his own cruel words had caused her. For having to take a paid position when she must have imagined her life and her son's were materially secure. But there were no words he could say here, surrounded by friends and by people whose hurts were much more acute.

Samson drew her into a conversation with one of the other sailors, giving him the chance to slip into the background and observe her. She seemed neither embarrassed nor self-conscious about conversing with a rough, one-armed seaman. It was he who blushed under her genuine interest in his circumstances and his family, though thanks to her friendly, down-to-earth manner, he gradually reverted to his irreverent self.

Samson shooed them all away shortly after that, and as he accompanied the three ladies downstairs, Julius was very conscious of his heart beating too fast. Because she was a widow, because she was free...

And she had rejected him ten years ago when he was whole.

"Does your leg pain you?" she asked quietly beside him.

"No," he lied at once, then, more gently, "Why do you ask?"

"You seem to favor it more than before."

"Oh. Well, I had a minor accident last night. I fell off a horse. It was entirely my own fault. It will recover."

"How did you manage to fall off Admiral?" Samson asked, grinning over his shoulder. "The horse practically embraces you."

"The story involves a lot of other horses and a mystery. I might tell you one day."

"Tell us now," Mrs. Grant commanded. "We love mysteries in Blackhaven, which is fortunate, since we seem to have so many."

"No, no, I won't keep Samson from his work," Julius said hastily, just as Dunnett strode out of his office, beaming and all but rubbing his hands together at the prospect of fresh donations in the shape of Miss Talbot.

Julius should not have grudged him his success in fundraising, and in truth, it was not the success as much as the manner that irritated Julius. And it was true Dunnett gave most of his time and skill voluntarily, keeping the hospital organized and funded and its accounting up to date. He took only a nominal salary for this, and yet some instinct prevented Julius from promising money. Instead, he gave time, and offers of employment at Black Hill to those who recovered and had nowhere else to go.

"Ladies, how charming to see you again!" Dunnett declared. "Has the captain been showing you around our little project? Is it not a worthy cause?"

"Mrs. Grant brought the ladies," Julius said before anyone else could answer. "I am only escorting them home. Ladies?" In a trice, he hustled across the hall and out of the door he held open.

He did not look at Antonia, but Miss Talbot seemed to be amused.

"I really do plan to make a donation, you know," she murmured.

"The hospital will be very grateful," Julius muttered. "Perhaps you could do so via Mrs. Grant or Mrs. Doverton. Or the Lamptons. Goodbye!"

Chapter Six

"**H**OW VERY ODD of him," Miss Talbot said, looking after Julius's speedy but halting progress along the road toward the inn. "Does he have reason to doubt Mr. Dunnett?"

"No, no," Mrs. Grant said at once. "I imagine he thought you would be more comfortable with me, but of course it is entirely up to you how you choose to make your donation. The hospital benefits either way. In fact, you may do it through the bank in the high street."

"I shall speak to my brother," Miss Talbot decided, unusually for her. "Antonia, should we brave the pump room?"

"I believe we should," Antonia replied. "It is, after all, why you chose Blackhaven."

"Indeed," Miss Talbot said, turning again to Mrs. Grant as they walked toward the center of the town. "Do you find the waters efficacious, Mrs. Grant?"

"I've never taken a course of them," the vicar's wife said. "Nicholas—Dr. Lampton—swears most of it is superstitious nonsense, but says there is benefit to everyone in drinking lots of pure, clean water. He is trying to have it piped to all the local wells so everyone in the town can benefit without having to toil up to the stream, but of course the pump room objects because it won't have many sales if the water is free."

"Is it far to the spring?" Antonia asked.

"Not far, just difficult, with a fairly sheer climb before the spring vanishes underground again."

"Then perhaps we shall keep to the pump room!"

They parted in the high street, Mrs. Grant turning right toward the church and the vicarage, and the others carrying on to the market and then left, away from the harbor toward the pump room.

Although it was not warm for summer, several people were sitting outside in the welcome sunshine to consume their water. Cushioned benches and a few tables had been built there for the purpose. Miss Talbot chose to sit on one of the benches, while Antonia went inside and procured two large glasses of water.

When she returned and sat down, Miss Talbot eyed the water without enthusiasm. "At least it does not taste nasty, like the Bath waters. There is just so *much* of it."

At the next bench, an extraordinarily handsome and vaguely familiar young man grinned, as though he had overheard. His companion, a young lady in a most fetching hat with a deliciously wide brim, nudged him then glanced apologetically at Miss Talbot and then Antonia.

The young lady's eyes widened, and with a jolt, Antonia recognized her. Julius's sister, whom he had introduced at the ball.

The girl smiled dazzlingly. "Why, it is Mrs. Macy, is it not?"

"How do you do, Miss Vale?"

"I am most hale and hearty from drinking all this excellent water, which Aubrey makes such a fuss about. Oh, this is my brother Aubrey. Aubrey, Mrs. Macy, who is a friend of Julius."

Antonia felt her cheeks flush, especially because a definite spark of interest crossed Aubrey's face. Hastily, she introduced them to Miss Talbot.

"What a coincidence," that lady said. "We have just been talking to Captain Vale, whom we met at the charitable hospital."

"It is one of his causes," Lucy said. "A couple of his own seamen have turned up there, and of course Dr. Samson is his old ship's surgeon. I wish you had brought him on here with you, actually. The waters might help his leg."

Aubrey hooted, and his sister pushed his glass of water closer to him.

"What is wrong with the captain's leg?" Miss Talbot inquired.

"Oh, it is an old battle wound—quite healed, according to him," Lucy said.

"As healed as it's going to be," Aubrey contributed, lifting his glass. "Only he made it worse, first by walking all the way from Blackhaven the night of the ball, and then by last night's heroics."

Inevitably, Miss Talbot pounced, which saved Antonia the trouble. "Heroics? He said he fell off his horse."

"He *leapt* off his horse," Lucy said indignantly.

"And fell off someone else's," Aubrey added with a grin. He took a mouthful of water. "Did he not tell you about our mysterious happenings at Black Hill?"

"He alluded to a mystery," Miss Talbot recalled, "but divulged no details."

"Well, for two nights in a row," Lucy said, "the twins—who are our youngest siblings—saw horses galloping over the meadow beyond our house. Ten or twenty of them, all together, with no riders or burdens. So on the third night, Julius and Aubrey and my other brothers lay in wait to see what was going on."

"Two of the horses were being ridden," Aubrey continued. "Only when they passed anywhere close to houses, the riders slid down the horses' far sides to be hidden from view. When Julius pursued them, the nearest rider popped back up on the animal's back."

Lucy continued the tale. "Julius caught up and hurled himself from the saddle straight at the other rider. I saw it from Lawrence's window, and it was magnificent! Only my heart was in my mouth, for *both* men then fell to the ground."

"They didn't fall, precisely," Aubrey corrected her. "Julius knocked them both to the ground. With force, obviously, which is why he could barely walk this morning." He scowled. "I'll bet he rode into town, too, the idiot."

"Oh dear, poor man," Miss Talbot murmured. Antonia couldn't speak. Her throat seemed to have closed up. "And the other rider?"

"Used Julius's pain to wriggle free and vanished, either into the woods, or somehow in among the horses," Aubrey said. "Julius was furious."

"I don't know why," Lucy said, a frown forming on her brow. "It was only curiosity, after all. If you ask me, something else is troubling him." The frown vanished, replaced by a smile. "But Aubrey caught one of the horses, so we'll see what comes of that."

"Will you watch again tonight?" Antonia asked, trying to keep the anxiety from her voice, though it sounded a trifle hoarse to her own ears.

"Probably," Aubrey said with a shrug. "But I suspect we've scared them off, whatever they were up to. In any case, how many horses can they have?"

"An intriguing mystery indeed," Miss Talbot pronounced.

Aubrey wrinkled his nose. "Only because I have nothing better to do. Do you stay long in Blackhaven, ladies?"

"Certainly for the rest of the month," Miss Talbot replied. "The rest depends on my brother, who is on leave of absence from the Foreign Office. We are not long back from Vienna and Paris."

"Papa was a diplomat, too," Lucy said.

Miss Talbot smiled. "Sir George Vale. Yes, we knew him quite well. He was something of a mentor to Denzil—my brother, Lord Linfield."

"Really? How wonderful!" Lucy exclaimed. "You must all come to Black Hill one day."

"We would be charmed," Miss Talbot said, while Antonia's stomach knotted with anticipation, though of what, she could not have said.

Aubrey drained his glass and set it down with a grimace. "My duty is done. Come, Luce, we have to fetch the others."

IT WAS THE next day, Sunday, before the idea came to her.

Generally, Sunday was Antonia's day off, though she usually accompanied Miss Talbot to church before spending the rest of the day with Edward. In fact, Lord Linfield escorted them to the parish church, which, surprisingly, was packed to the gunnels, not just with wealthy visitors but with townspeople.

Of course, the vicar, the Reverend Tristram Grant, was a very handsome man in his early thirties, and no doubt attracted much female attention. In fact, Mrs. Grant's husband turned out to be far from the staid country clergyman Antonia had imagined. Instead, he was an inspired preacher with a beautiful voice and a simple, frequently humorous manner that must have appealed to people of all degrees. Edward stopped fidgeting to listen. Even Antonia was distracted from her perusal of the congregation in search of the one head she sought.

But Julius did not seem to be with his family, who took up an entire pew and part of the one behind. She spotted Lucy first, then three grownup brothers, including Aubrey and a tall army officer. There were also two other sisters, whose faces she only glimpsed, and a younger brother and sister of perhaps fifteen, as like as two siblings could be without actually being the same sex.

The front family pew was taken up by the Earl of Braithwaite and his family, who seemed to be as numerous as the Vales, only with the addition of young children. Mrs. Grant also sat at the front with a baby who chattered away to itself and made the vicar and the rest of the congregation laugh.

Antonia felt curiously deflated by Julius's absence, but, refusing to let it dampen her spirits, she concentrated on escaping quickly to the hotel to change and give Edward his reward for being good in church—a walk on the beach to play pirates.

However, almost inevitably, they were held up on the path to the churchyard gate by people eager to speak first with the vicar and then with the Earl and Countess of Braithwaite. As Antonia and Edward edged past, she heard someone say, "I suppose they could be being driven along the coast to supply various smuggling gangs."

"They tend to use sturdy ponies or donkeys," the earl said. "The mystery horses seemed to be much better bred, even thoroughbreds, though not necessarily well looked after."

"A horse-thieving gang?" someone else suggested.

"More than possible," said someone else, "only where on earth were they all going?"

"Horse fairs," the countess said. "There are horse fairs to the south of Cumberland and in Yorkshire this month."

Edward tugged Antonia's hand, and she slipped past with him, her brain rushing ahead. The horses could well be stolen and driven south toward various horse fairs, but where had they come *from*?

Back at the hotel, on impulse, she borrowed Lord Linfield's map of the environs, and as soon as she had changed her best morning dress for an older one she was happy to get covered with sand and stained with salt water, she spread the map out on the bed.

"Have we got ship's rations?" Edward demanded.

"A basket full of them," she assured him, tracing her finger along the coast road from Blackhaven northward toward the Scottish border. Black Hill farm was several miles inland from the coast, but there looked to be several coves on the coast just to the north of it. She folded the map up. "Shall we go further afield, to new beaches?"

"Yes, yes!"

"Well, let's see if we can borrow a gig from the hotel…"

They were in luck. It even had a canopy to protect them from the inevitable rain. Really, for summer, the weather was atrocious, and though they took up a lot of space, she was glad to have two of the hotel's blankets with them, as well as Edward's overcoat and her own traveling cloak. And the basket, also supplied by the hotel.

The horse was a little elderly but good-natured, and seemed to enjoy its outing—as did Edward, bouncing up and down in the gig and pointing to every vessel he spotted at sea, deciding which among them were pirate ships and which were on their way to do battle and capture the pirate captain.

When the road forked, she urged the horse along the lesser track, following the curves around the cliff edges. She felt a funny little jolt when she saw the ancient sign pointing up another track, proclaiming Black Hill. She kept going until she saw a path down to a beach beneath the cliffs, then urged the horse off the track into the shade of some trees. Edward gave the animal a carrot from the basket, and they left it to crop leaves and grass while they scrambled down the path toward the sandy beach.

"This would be a great hideout for a pirate ship," Edward enthused.

It was quite a wild stretch of coast, with tall, jagged rocks stretching far enough out for the waves still to crash over them when the tide was out. There seemed to be no houses, let alone villages, in sight. A few ships sailed past in the distance, perhaps going to Ireland or the Isle of Man, or north toward the islands and the mainland of Scotland. One, only just in sight, seemed to be anchored—fishing, perhaps.

Antonia spread out the blanket and set the basket on top of it, before they sat down to enjoy the pirate banquet.

"Can we go exploring?" Edward asked. "Climb over these rocks and see what's on the other side?"

"Why not? Unless they're too slippery."

The tide had not yet turned, so she merely covered the basket and left it on the blanket before running across the firm sand with Edward.

By the time they reached the rocks, she was breathless and not a little exhilarated. A lady did not run, so there was great pleasure in breaking the taboo.

They clambered up the rocks at the lowest point, until they could see another sandy cove on the other side, and then, without warning, a man suddenly leapt at them from the rocks below.

"Boo!" he yelled, grinning at them with black and yellow teeth. Antonia's heart and stomach seemed to lurch together, depriving her of breath while Edward gasped and caught hold of her skirt.

She glared at the grinning man, who could, in fact, have been a real pirate by his appearance. He wore trousers made of sail cloth and a ragged shirt, with some kind of kerchief tied over his wild black hair. More worrying was the array of weapons at his belt. No pistol, thankfully, but at least two wicked-looking knives.

"What are you doing, scaring the wits out of a child?" she demanded.

"He *should* be scared, and so should you," the man retorted, his grin now more of a grimace. "Scary place around here. Isn't safe, specially not for women and children." He flapped his arms like a scarecrow in the wind. "Back where you came from!"

"Don't be ridiculous. You have no authority over the beaches here."

He laughed. "Got all the authority I need!" He jumped from his perch to stand level with them, and instinctively Antonia backed away, keeping Edward behind her, as the man fingered the long knife at his belt. "You get my meaning, missus?"

His eyes were hard and cold and quite deliberately murderous, but she forced lightness into her voice. "You are not *threatening* me, are you?"

His lips curled back from his rotting teeth into a sneer, but before he could speak, a quite different male voice did.

"He'd better not be," said Julius. He stood on the higher rock to

Antonia's left, dressed very informally in dark breeches and shirt, without coat or cravat. He did, however, have a stout stick in one hand. Perhaps it was that which made his lone figure somehow so imposing. Perhaps it was the steadiness of his one eye and the blankness of the black patch. Or just because he was used to commanding respect in a ship full of press-ganged men, many of whom must have been at least as terrifying as the ruffian before her now.

Relief flooded Antonia. She had never been so pleased to see anyone in her life.

Leaning on the stick, Julius eased himself gracefully down beside her, giving no sign of yesterday's pain.

"In fact," he said without raising his voice, although the words were clipped and sharp, "I suggest he goes speedily back where he came from before the whole beach is crawling with officers of the law."

"You don't scare me, mister," the man sneered, though he took his hand off his knife.

"You don't need to be scared. Just out of my sight. Swiftly."

The man swore, then suddenly leapt back up where he had come from and vanished. His boots clattered against the rocks and thudded onto the sand below.

Antonia wanted to clutch Edward to her and never let him go. But for his sake, she had to make light of the threat, so she only slipped her arm about him, pressing him to her side for the briefest moment.

"Now there's a pirate if ever I saw one," Julius said to Edward, obviously understanding what was required. "I think he was after your luncheon. We'd better go and defend it."

Edward gave a slightly shaky laugh but allowed Julius to take his hand and urge him back over the rocks. Julius turned back to Antonia.

"I'm fine," she assured him, although she seemed to be trembling too much to speak and move at the same time. Somehow, she forced herself to follow, her steps clumsy, although at least she managed not to fall over.

They walked back toward the basket, which now looked lonely on the beach, with the edges of the blanket flapping over it in the breeze. At Julius's instigation, Edward swung between them, laughing, the unpleasant stranger temporarily forgotten.

Only as they tamed the blanket again by sitting on it did Edward say, "What did that man want?"

"He thought he had to protect his treasure from rival pirates," Julius said. "He took the game too seriously, but we saw him off."

Edward thought about that, then grinned. "So we did. Do you think he'll come back with his friends?"

"No. But once you've eaten that cake, we could practice making defenses, if you like. As practice for the next game."

Edward stuffed the cake into his mouth so quickly that he almost choked. Julius smiled faintly and patted him on the back.

The day had taken on a sense of unreality. Antonia had not expected to find Julius on the beach—investigating, presumably, the same suspicions she had formed. If she was honest, she had wanted to impress him by discovering the truth, though she was not too eager to think about why that should be.

"Where should we build our defenses?" Edward asked as soon as he had swallowed the last of the cake.

The captain, clearly, had reconnoitered already. He pointed to the rocky outcrop at the end of the beach farthest from where they had encountered the "pirate"—for which Antonia was grateful.

"Over there," Julius said. "The first thing is to make a wall of sand which protects us. The firm, wet sand, not the powdery stuff. You make a start on that, and I'll be over in a moment."

Edward showed no reluctance to leave them, although Antonia could not help anxiously scanning the beach for any further sign of the pirate or his comrades.

"Where do you think he's gone?" she asked, low. "Do you suppose there are more of them?"

Julius shook his head. "No, he's alone, keeping watch."

"Over what?"

"A boat," Julius said. He pointed in the direction of the next beach beyond the long, tall rocks. "It's hidden in a cave over there, and it's big enough to have needed several men to carry it there."

"Then where are they?"

"At a guess, I'd say driving horses southeastward."

She drew in her breath. "I wondered if they were horses stolen in Ireland and brought here by ship to be sold. It would explain their bad condition."

He smiled approval that stupidly set her heart pattering. "I suspect they've been doing it for years. In fact, I think they used to graze the horses at Black Hill while they recovered from the voyage, then took them southward to the fairs. But since we came home, there are people all over the land, so they have to take the horses more quickly by night."

"There is a ship out there." She pointed out to sea, where the vessel was hardly visible.

"I saw it. It may be the one that transported the horses, probably from Ireland, as you say, and then they were brought ashore over several nights, in that boat hidden in the cave."

"How did you find it?"

"I played here as a boy. I know all the caves and hiding places, and all the secret ways up and down the cliffs."

She had a sudden glimpse of him as a boy, lively, adventurous, imaginative, no doubt commanding his small siblings...

"They don't seem to be very secret," she observed.

"I suppose someone could have discovered them by accident."

She peered at him. "But you don't think so."

"I think it unlikely. Who travels with a shipload of stolen horses if they don't know a way to land them?"

"You mean someone who lives in the neighborhood must have told them..."

He rose to his feet in one surprisingly fluid movement. "That is my fear. Shall we build a castle?"

The afternoon should have been tense and awkward. She was too conscious of Julius, of their past and all the matters unresolved between them. To say nothing of the need to pretend to Edward that the ruffian on the rocks had not remotely frightened her.

And yet, somehow, fun intruded. Edward's laughter was both infectious and precious. He had missed the male perspective on play since leaving Vienna, and Julius, who had already turned in her mind from dashing young officer to imposing, retired captain, now displayed a boyish sense of fun that was beguiling.

And curiously exciting. His sandy hand brushing against hers, the stretch of his shoulders as he dug, the strong column of his bronzed, bare throat when he threw back his head and laughed—it all added to her growing physical awareness. It was almost as if he held her again...

Until they were walking back up the path to where they had left the pony, and Edward had bounced far enough ahead not to overhear.

"It was rash to come here," Julius said abruptly, "suspecting what you did. Don't come this way again until I let you know it's safe."

She bristled. "What do I reply to that? *Aye-aye, captain?*"

"Just 'yes' would be sufficient. Look, he's watching for his fellows to come back, no doubt with significant amounts of money. If they are hiding, they are known, wanted thieves with very little to lose. What would you have done if I hadn't happened to be there?"

"Gone back to the beach and left!" She added stiffly, "Of course we were thankful to see you there, and you turned the afternoon into a very pleasant one for Edward."

"I don't want your damned thanks," he said between his teeth.

"Have I given you any indication that your wants interest me?" she snapped back.

"None," he said savagely. "Though I confess I've wasted an hour or two contemplating yours. What did you want from Macy that I couldn't give you?"

She stared at him, appalled that yet another quarrel had sprung out of nowhere. And yet she couldn't stop her mouth. "Do you know, I cannot remember. I expect it was civility."

He released a short laugh. "*Touché.* Did you get it?"

In cold, daily bucketsful. "You are impertinent," she said. "And I find your constant efforts to blame me for your own shortcomings offensive."

He leapt ahead of her and stood in her path, forcing her to halt. "What shortcomings?"

Abruptly, her anger died before the desperation in his eye. He truly wanted an answer. And she wanted to weep so much that her throat ached.

"What's a shortcoming?" Edward asked, poking his head around Julius's arm.

"A fault, a mistake," Antonia managed. "Keep going, Edward."

Julius said something under his breath and stood aside for her to pass. He didn't speak until they reached the top of the path, when he strode ahead of them and across the track to where the pony waited patiently tied to its much barer-looking tree. Then he put the basket into the gig and said, "Up you go!" before swinging Edward into the air so high it made him squeal with delight and plonking him on the bench.

Without a word, he handed Antonia up beside him. She sought desperately for something to say that would repair this new damage, maintain whatever friendship there had been this afternoon, but all that came out were some lame words to Edward.

"Thank Captain Vale for this afternoon."

"Thanks, capt'n!" Edward grinned.

"I don't know for what, but you are very welcome," Julius said,

74

untying the horse and leading it around in a half-circle, so that it pointed back toward Blackhaven. "Safe journey."

"Goodbye," she said hollowly as he handed her the ribbons. Part of her could not believe she was saying goodbye to him again, still with nothing resolved between them. She almost jumped down to shake him, make him listen to her, force him to tell her what had happened ten years ago.

But he had already turned away, and in any case, there was Edward chattering beside her, curious and precocious and most definitely listening.

Chapter Seven

AMONG MISS TALBOT'S letters the following morning, Antonia found an invitation to dine at Black Hill the next evening.

"How nice," Miss Talbot said. "I admit I am curious to see them all together. I'm sure Denzil will be happy to go."

"So you will not need me?" Antonia said. She wanted, even *needed*, to speak to Julius again, but not quite so soon, and not amongst his entire family, where there would be no privacy. Would he glare at her or ignore her totally? The unfairness of either sparked her anger all over again, which was hardly the mood in which to find any kind of understanding, let alone reconciliation.

"Of course you must come," Miss Talbot said. "Suze will put Edward to bed that evening."

There was no more Antonia could say without drawing too much of Miss Talbot's attention. Besides, perhaps this was the opportunity she needed for a civilized conversation with him, to discover what terrible mistake had parted them ten years ago. The desperation in his eye yesterday haunted her far more than his accusations. And by tomorrow evening, surely, she would have the right words to ask without riling him? Or herself! She still had today and most of tomorrow to think.

As it happened, she did not have quite so long before she saw him again.

In the afternoon, she accompanied Miss Talbot up to Braithwaite Castle to have tea with the countess. In fact, they were greeted by two countesses, since the dowager was also present, a formidable lady of stern features and sharp eyes. The young countess treated her with respect, but did not appear to be in awe of her.

"My husband means to join us," the younger lady said, "but he has been off investigating horse tracks with Sir Julius. Hopefully, he won't be too long."

Antonia's heart jumped at the sound of Julius's name, and something very like panic surged through her. She was not ready to meet him again just yet. In any case, he probably wouldn't even come back with the earl.

But he did. And the two men seemed to be on the best of terms. Julius entered with a faint, sardonic smile on his lips, while the earl came behind, laughing.

Julius saw her at once. The smile died quickly, though his bow was perfectly civil.

"We found the remains of hoofprints," Lord Braithwaite told his wife. "A good number of horses definitely crossed from Black Hill through our land, but no one who could've seen them lives over there. And the sheep aren't telling. Doesn't really help us, though."

"No, we'll have to wait until they come back," Julius said, accepting a cup of tea from her ladyship and taking a seat well away from Antonia.

"You think they will?" the young countess asked.

"We think the horses were unloaded from a ship that's skulking up and down the coast, probably avoiding the scrutiny of the revenue cutters. It's waiting for something or someone."

Antonia barely heard the conversation. She was trying not to watch Julius. There seemed something too deliberate in his relaxed posture, the blandness of his expression. Was he hiding from her? Stupid to imagine he even thought of her. And yet he was so careful about never glancing in her direction that she knew he was.

The knowledge made her heart flutter. His lean, weathered face might have aged in ten years, but it still moved her. She had always loved the still poise of his body, perfectly balanced as though against the rolling of a ship's deck, even when making those swift, sudden movements—as now, when he sprang suddenly to his feet.

"I have taken up enough of your time," he said to the earl. "My thanks for your help."

As he turned to take his leave of the Braithwaite ladies, Miss Talbot set down her empty cup. "Come, Antonia, it's time we were on our way also."

In the ensuing farewells and thanks, it was easy not to look at him. When Antonia finally turned to the door, he had gone, and relief mingled with vivid disappointment. What was the matter with her?

"You will come to our garden party, won't you?" the countess called after them as they left the room.

Leaving Miss Talbot to deal with that, Antonia hurried along the gallery to the grand staircase, which she all but ran down, just to expend the energy that seemed trapped inside her.

A well-trained footman was waiting to return her pelisse. But before she could take it from him, another very different hand did. She spun around to face Sir Julius Vale.

"Allow me," he said.

The footman, dismissed, effaced himself.

Childishly, Antonia thought of snatching the garment from Julius and storming out. Hardly dignified. She turned and slipped her arms inside the pelisse. He did not move away. She could feel his breath on her neck, smell his familiar scent of clean skin and salty sea, overlaid now with a hint of horse. His warmth seemed to burn her.

"What shortcomings?" he asked, just as if there had been no gap in their conversation since the day before. But at least he spoke quietly. "What did I do that was suddenly so unbearable?"

You left me! Yet his words implied—again—that she was to blame, that she had left him. Desperately, she tried to plan her words, to reach some kind of understanding before another quarrel could explode.

"I was told there was a lady in Lisbon," she said quietly.

He did not move. Neither did she. But her body remembered his nearness, the excitement of his touch, the strength of his arms around her. She ached for his touch. She ached for him to deny the lady in Lisbon.

He said, "Who told you that?"

She closed her eyes in pain. "You do not deny it."

He said nothing, and she turned her head to glare at him. It was a mistake. He stood far too close, and his gaze was intense, devouring her. Thrilling her. She did not care about some woman in Lisbon who was no longer with him. She only cared that he had walked away from her.

His lips moved, as though he would speak, and she watched them, unwanted desire curling in her belly, catching at her breath.

And then Miss Talbot's footsteps sounded on the stairs and the footman cleared his throat as he approached the door once more. Julius brushed past her, and the quick, shocking touch of his body made her gasp.

But he only opened the door and went out without a word, leaving the footman to close it again.

"OH, I'VE INVITED the Linfields to dine with us tomorrow," Lucy said casually at dinner that evening.

Julius set down his wine glass and stared at her.

Roderick said, "Who the devil are the Linfields?"

"Lord Linfield is a senior diplomat," Lucy replied, so serenely that Julius knew she was up to something. "He was acquainted with Papa.

Aubrey and I ran into his sister in the pump room on Saturday, and she seemed most interesting and amusing. Didn't she, Aubrey?"

"Oh, most," Aubrey agreed, his mind clearly elsewhere.

"So I thought they would make delightful dinner guests. After all, you did say, Julius, that we should make an effort to become part of the community."

"Lord Linfield is not part of the community," Julius pointed out. "He is merely visiting the town."

"For his sister's health," Lucy agreed. "I am glad to say that he and his sister and her companion have all accepted. Perhaps I should ask the vicar and his wife, too?"

"No, no," Delilah said hastily, "I'm sure there are quite enough of us to frighten them off as it is."

"He was at the Congress of Vienna," Julius said dryly. "I hardly think a family dinner party is going to flummox any of them."

Cornelius grunted. "Do you want us to watch again tonight?"

They had watched last night and the one before. Nothing had happened.

Julius swallowed his beef. "I don't think there's any point. All the animals must be ashore, and I doubt there will be any more activity until the men return from the horse fairs—and they might not even come back if Winslow manages to have them caught red-handed selling stolen horses. Besides, the ship that was anchored opposite seems to have vanished." Which no doubt had something to do with the encounter between him and the "pirate" threatening Antonia and Edward.

Unfortunately, that meant that Julius was left with little to worry about except Antonia's impending visit with her employer and Lord Linfield.

Well, he called it worry. But as he saddled Admiral and went for his usual morning ride, he acknowledged it was more like anticipation. Temptation, even. He had seen it reflected in her face when they were arguing on Sunday, even when they had parted so stiffly. He knew he had hurt her.

Oh, she fought him, with spirit, and she tried to hide her own weakness as any good fighter would, but he had seen it. It had been there at the hospital, too, and even at the ball. And most certainly at Braithwaite Castle yesterday when she had asked about "the lady in Lisbon."

To have an old affair flung in his face should have angered him. But he could not have hurt her if she did not care for him. Or at least remembered that she had once.

Perhaps she regretted her decision in Macy's favor. Perhaps she regretted it as soon as he had sailed. He had certainly never gone back to find out. And she had never written. He had, twice, and she never replied. According to Delilah, who had found out for him, she would have already been married to Macy by the time she received his second letter.

He didn't honestly know if her presence in Blackhaven was a painful curse or a blessing of infinite possibilities. She churned all his emotions, almost unbearably. But for the first time since he had walked off his ship, he seemed to *feel* the blood flowing through his veins. His nerves tingled with life, and his brain hummed with plans for everything—mostly for the house and gardens, and even the land that he had delegated to Cornelius.

He would not think of Antonia, but he knew she was there, hovering in his mind, woven into everything.

THE RAIN WENT off as Antonia accompanied her employers in the carriage to Black Hill. There was a more direct road than the one she had taken along the coast, so the journey was not long—fortunately, perhaps, for Antonia's nerves. Her stomach felt knotted like a sail rope, just because she would see him again, and had no idea whether he would be distant, quarrelsome, or friendly, or in some new mood she had not encountered since meeting him again.

She made up her mind to respond to friendly overtures and to ignore the unpleasant. She would not let him hurt her again. And even if he did, she determined he would never know it.

It should not be difficult. He had a positive gaggle of siblings, at least two of which seemed disposed to be friendly. *In any case, I am the companion. He has no reason to notice me, either in public or private.*

As the carriage turned up the drive to Black Hill House, Antonia found herself admiring the gracious manor house, and the grounds that were only partially tidied. One side of a terraced, formal garden was a riot of color and floral scents, the other more of a meadow, with tangled flowers and thorns with bits of stone poking through.

"I understand they have only recently returned to find the place badly neglected," Lord Linfield said. "I believe Sir George placed his trust in the wrong people. Now they are home, one of the brothers has taken over the running of the land, and the rest are doing their bit with the house and gardens."

His sister and Antonia both gazed at him in surprise at such knowledge, and he flushed slightly, although he pretended not to notice.

A couple of children bounded up to the carriage, running beside it until the horses pulled up at the front entrance. The boy opened the carriage door and let down the steps, and Antonia saw that he must have been nearer sixteen years than the twelve she had originally thought.

"Welcome to Black Hill!" he greeted them. "I'm Lawrence, and this is Leona."

Leona bore a startling resemblance to her brother, especially perhaps because her hat had been pushed to the back of her head and was held on only by the knotted ribbons at her neck. Her skirts were not full length, and bore earth and grass stains, of which she appeared refreshingly oblivious.

"Welcome!" she echoed, jumping back so that her brother could hand the ladies from the carriage.

"Miss Talbot," young Lawrence said with a bow. "Mrs. Macy. My lord."

"Thank you," Antonia said gravely, and received a wider grin from both children.

"Here's Simon, our groom," Leona said. "He'll help with the horses. Come inside!"

As bemused as the Talbots, Antonia allowed herself to be swept into the house.

"Ah, I see the twins found you first," Lucy said, greeting them at the front door in a gown of floral-embroidered muslin. "You found us without difficulty?"

"Well, our coachman did," Lord Linfield said wryly, while a man-servant took their hats and outdoor clothing.

"This way! We thought we would have tea, since it is still early." Lucy led them into a bright, rather charming room with wide, tall windows overlooking the gardens.

Another lady, perhaps in her mid-twenties, rose from an old but comfortable-looking sofa to greet them.

"This is my sister, Felicia—that is, Mrs. Maitland. Fliss, Miss Talbot, Mrs. Macy, and Lord Linfield."

"How do you do?" Felicia said pleasantly. She had something of the same mischief in her eyes as Lucy, although overlaid with something much more restless. "Welcome to Black Hill. Please, sit and be comfortable while we have tea, and then, if you like, we can seize the blink of sunshine and show you our half-garden." She turned to the twins, apparently not remotely surprised by their grubby appearance. "Today is a civilized day. You must change."

They sighed and left.

"And wash," said Julius from the passage, causing a flutter in Antonia's stomach and protests from his young siblings that ended in laughter. He strolled in just behind the tea trolley, dressed in a dark coat and neatly tied cravat.

The perfect host, he bowed over the ladies' hands in welcome, and then shook hands with Lord Linfield. He certainly paid no special attention to Antonia, but nor did he glare at her or ignore her. Only once did she catch what might have been an ironic glance as she took a discreet chair, close to Miss Talbot but slightly behind her. A good companion was discreet and did not put herself forward. Perhaps he still thought of her as the pampered daughter of a country gentleman.

By then, they had already met Major Roderick Vale and Miss Delilah Vale. Aubrey sauntered in as they were finishing tea, and it was decided to take a stroll in the garden. Here, the twins joined them looking scrubbed and clean, and they devoted themselves to escorting Antonia, rather to her surprise.

"Do you like gardens?" Leona asked on one side of her.

"I do. But I have had little chance to cultivate one recently."

"Why is that?" Lawrence asked from her other side.

"I have been traveling with Miss Talbot. We had no garden in Vienna or Paris, and when we got back to London, the gardeners did everything."

"Felicia had a lovely garden in Sussex," Leona said. "I was sorry to leave there."

"To come up to Blackhaven?"

"Oh, no, before then, when Felicia's husband died and she had to sell the house to pay his debts. I shouldn't have told you that, should I?"

"No, probably not, but I won't blab."

"We knew you wouldn't, since you're a friend of Julius's," Lawrence said.

"Did he say that?" Antonia asked with another flutter in her stomach.

"No. Delilah, I think. We keep forgetting what we can say to each other, the family, friends, outsiders. It always seems to be different."

"And we don't really understand why," Leona added. "The truth is the truth, after all. I hope you don't mind, for example, that we are illegitimate."

Antonia blinked. "It is hardly my place to mind, and if it was, I wouldn't. If you see what I mean."

"Perfectly. So is Delilah. Some people look down their noses at us because of it, but Julius says these people are unworthy of our regard, and they were quite happy to entertain Sir George, who was our father."

"Did you live with your father?" she asked.

"Oh, yes," said Lawrence. "Our mother died in Bavaria shortly after we were born. She was a countess, but her family didn't care for us. Where is *your* husband, or do you not like him either?"

Antonia closed her mouth before it could drop too far open. "My husband died several years ago," she managed at last.

"Aha!" Leona's eyes sparkled at her brother. "She is a widow, just like Felicia. Did you have to pay his debts, also?"

"No," Antonia said. "He didn't have any. And I think that may be one of the questions you shouldn't ask people who are not your family."

"You're right, of course," Lawrence said quickly. "Are you offended?"

She regarded him, and then his sister. They looked like scrubbed angels, and far too like Edward at his most manipulative. "No. But you don't need to pretend such childish bluntness, either. You can ask me anything you like honestly, though I reserve the right not to answer."

They exchanged guilty glances, though Antonia had the impression they were not actually displeased.

"Sorry," Leona said. "We've found it the best way to extract information from people who are usually far too stunned not to answer. It worked better when we were younger."

Antonia's lips twitched without her permission, and an answering smile began in Leona's eyes. "What information is it you really want to extract?"

"How it is you know Julius?" came the prompt reply.

She was almost ready for it. "We met at a ball more than ten years ago and lost touch after he sailed."

"But you were good friends?" There was an odd anxiety in the girl's expression, mirrored in her brother's.

This was more dangerous ground. Julius had clearly told them nothing about her, but she was tired of hiding. "It seemed so," she said lightly. "In fact, we were engaged to be married."

That shocked them—so much that they stopped in the middle of the path. Fortunately, everyone else was ahead of them. Antonia walked on, pretending to admire a gorgeous red rose.

"Was he awful?" Leona said behind her, in a very small voice.

"I'm not sure what you mean," Antonia said, searching in vain for a change of subject. "This rose is lovely."

"I mean, why did you break it off?" Leona said, refusing the distraction.

It obviously never entered her head that Julius could be the one who had done so, only that he had given her cause. Well, she had never suspected he would do such a thing either, until he did. If a man broke an engagement, the lady's reputation was essentially ruined.

The eldest Vale sister peeked back around the corner from the next path and then came toward them. "Don't monopolize Mrs. Macy," she said. "Surely it is Lord Linfield's turn?"

The twins took the hint and ran ahead, although Leona glanced back, her face troubled.

"Sorry," said Delilah. "You've been 'twinned.'"

Antonia summoned a smile. "Don't apologize for them. They are delightful."

"And ruthlessly inquisitive. Especially about Julius, since he is the brother they know least and admire most."

"I suppose that must be true of all of you, since he spent so long at sea. You must be very glad to have him home at last."

"Yes. It is good to be together. To support each other."

There was such significance in Delilah's voice that Antonia met her gaze. Yes, definite hostility. She didn't even trouble to hide it.

Antonia was a mere companion. She should lower her eyes submissively and take whatever shame anyone chose to heap upon her. But she had had enough of Vales blaming her.

She held Delilah's gaze. "If you wish me to go, of course I shall. Only, I wish you had not invited me in the first place."

"I didn't. Lucy invited you." If Delilah was surprised by her response, she gave no sign of it. "But of course I am not so rude or inhospitable as to ask you to leave. I ask you only to leave *him* alone."

Antonia didn't know if she felt more astonished or furious. She tilted her chin. "Make the same request of your brother. If you dare."

Delilah did not back down, though a frown twitched her brows, as though she were finally surprised. "It isn't a question of daring, Mrs. Macy. We are all here to pick up the pieces, but I don't want to do it again. Come, let us catch up with the others. It is almost time for dinner."

Antonia walked beside her in stunned silence, trying to think.

We are all here to pick up the pieces, but I don't want to do it again. Meaning Delilah had done it before. Which surely meant Julius had been in pieces before. Over Antonia.

Then why had he left her in the first place? Without even seeing her to explain?

Taken with the oddity of his behavior toward her since they had met again in Blackhaven, it implied someone had lied to her. Or to him. She wanted to march right up to him and demand the truth. She even began to do so, only the sight of him talking to Miss Talbot reminded her with a sudden jolt of her own position and his.

Nothing was the same anymore.

She waited for her chance while they drank sherry before dinner, but he did not come near her. Dinner was pleasantly informal, with everyone going into the dining room together and sitting wherever they landed—except for Julius at the head of the table, and his widowed sister Felicia at the other end. Antonia found herself between the twins, who only told her funny stories about their lives and asked questions no more prying than how old her son was.

In between times, Lord Linfield entertained the company with funny stories about the late Sir George. Which seemed strange, because until they had come to Blackhaven, Antonia had not even known that Linfield ever met Julius's father. And yet now he seemed to be lighting up the entire family's happiness with his memories, showing a side of the man they had clearly never seen. Even Julius, whose feelings about his father had been somewhat ambivalent in his youth, was smiling, a rare softness in his expression.

When the excellent meal was finished, Felicia led the ladies away, leaving the gentlemen to their port. Julius chose to hold the door for them, and Antonia's heart sped up again as she followed the other women. She hesitated in the doorway, wondering if she dared. When else would she have the opportunity?

With quiet amusement, he said, "Are you finding the courage to ask me something indelicate, like 'where is the cloakroom?'"

She flushed. "Of course not. I know perfectly well where to find it. But I would appreciate a moment of your time. There are things I have to say. Things I have to know."

Something flared in his eye that could have been anger. Whatever it was, she knew he would refuse. She dropped her gaze, defeated for the moment, and walked blindly past him. The door closed.

He said, "This way," and walked past her to another room, where he held the door for her.

Her heart hammering, she walked into a book-lined room full of comfortable sofas, a large walnut desk, and a long window overlooking the countryside to the sea in the distance. It smelled of old books. She stood just inside the door, twisting her skirts between her fingers until she realized what she was doing and forced herself to stop. Too late, for he had seen her discomfort, though it seemed he chose not to mock her.

"Please, sit down. What is it you want to say to me?"

She stayed where she was and opened her mouth to ask the questions that had torn her apart for ten years. Yet what came out was, "I did not thank you for the flowers."

"You are welcome," he said gravely.

Unexpected laughter, closer to hysteria, threatened to rise up from her toes. "They are lovely, still—but that is not really what I wanted to say."

"I know."

"Do you?" She moved away from him, further into the room. With her back to him, it was easier. "Ten years ago, I think someone lied to me. Or perhaps to you. Did you really leave for Portsmouth without a word to me or my parents and just sail away?"

She felt rather than heard his movement as he walked around her and stood facing her.

"What word did you want?" he asked.

She stared at him, no longer able or willing to hide the hurt. "Any word," she whispered. "A reason. A farewell. Even an insult would have given me a clue."

He did not blink. His eye was fierce, all but devouring her. "You didn't know, did you?" he said hoarsely. "Dear God, you didn't even know that I had been to your house, let alone that they sent me away."

"*Who* sent you away?" she demanded.

"Your father. Both your parents. When I called to take you walking—as we had planned—I was shown into your father's study, and he told me all three of you agreed that I was not a suitable match, that the lifestyle of my family was not such that they were prepared to allow you to live among them. That my own behavior was not proper enough. That you had said our engagement had been a mistake and was at an end."

"My father said that? My mother…" Her head was throbbing, and she rubbed at it, frowning, trying to comprehend the enormity of such terrible lies. "And you…left?"

His crooked smile dawned, and she wanted to weep. "Well, I refused to go until I had seen you. It took both footmen, the butler, and your father to throw me out, but yes, I left. Will you laugh if I tell you I climbed halfway up to your bedchamber window before they called the constables on me?"

She shook her head. "No, I won't laugh." In fact, a tear had escaped the corner of her eye. She wiped it away with her fingers. "Why did you not write to me?"

"I sent you a note before I left, and another when I was at sea. I received no answer."

There was pain in his voice that caught at her heart, piercing her own sense of misery and betrayal. She met his gaze. "I received no note, no letter. Not even a reply to the one I wrote to you, asking why you had left. They hid them from us. My own parents…"

His hand came up, as though he could not prevent it, wiping another escaped tear from her cheek. She gasped at his touch, and the words almost exploded from his lips.

"You weep! And yet you married Macy within the month. Delilah found that out for me."

"What else could I do?" she retorted. "I thought you had gone back to the lady in Lisbon they told me about. I was ruined—at least according to my parents. Since it was what they had already told me, they had to tell the world too that you had jilted me... And I confess, with you gone, I didn't greatly care what I did. I suppose I was ill. I *felt* ill for a long time, and when I began to pay attention again, I was already married. Dear God, how could they do that to us? To *me*?"

He stretched his hand out, cupping her face.

"I am so sorry," she whispered.

"So am I." He dipped his head and closed his mouth over hers, an instant of fierce gladness, and her tears flowed over their lips. Even through the unbearable emotion came a spark of recognition and arousal. And this was *so* not the time or the place.

He parted their lips and let his forehead rest for a moment against hers. "We shall talk again. But not like this. I never left you, Antonia."

Oh God, would the tears never stop? "You have to go now, or I'll flood you."

His breath hissed. It might have been laughter or admiration or some mixture of the two. "Shall I send Miss Talbot to you?"

"On no account," she said in alarm, stepping away from him with reluctance and yet a dawning relief that felt like very wobbly happiness. "I despise watering pots. I shall be right as rain when you've gone and I have washed this wretched face. Julius?"

He paused by the door and glanced back over his shoulder. "Yes?"

"I never left you either."

He smiled, and the gleam in his eye melted her. She swung away so that he would not see, so that she could control herself once more, and the door closed softly behind him. By the time she counted to twenty, she was smiling and the tears had been driven back where they belonged.

She went in search of the cloakroom and a basin of cool water.

Chapter Eight

A S JULIUS RETURNED to the dining room, he seemed to be walking on air. He felt as if some massive weight had been lifted from his shoulders, a burden he had grown so used to that he had barely noticed it. Yet he had carried it through a decade at sea, during battles and boredom, crises and celebrations, and even through the family reunions and their return to Blackhaven to restore the house and lands.

Now, he felt infinitely lighter. A huge surge of energy made him want to run, to leap across the table and shout and laugh, because she had loved him after all.

He did not even care what that meant for the future, only that it was healing the wounds of the past that he had hidden for so long. It seemed he needed that very badly. And he thought she needed it, too.

Later, he would find out everything about those ten years, about what her life had been like and how he could help. Right now, as he threw himself into his chair and reached for the port, he wanted to burst into song, to make his brothers and Linfield as happy as he.

He contented himself with a large grin, a brimming glass, and an exuberant toast that made them all laugh, his brothers with a certain air of surprise. But it was Lord Linfield who interested Julius, all the more because Antonia had been part of his household for some time. He and his sister had even taken in the child, which was a highly unusual arrangement.

Despite the sneaking jealousy, Julius knew there could be nothing improper in the relationship. A gentleman did not make his mistress his sister's companion, not unless he was far too lofty to care for either the rules of Society or the reputation of his sister. And Linfield, recently ennobled for his diplomatic services at the Congress of Vienna, was certainly not that. Still, the man might well be pursuing Antonia honorably—how could he live in the same house, see her every day, and not be smitten? And Antonia…

No, he would not allow his wayward thoughts to go there. These moments in the library with her were too new and too precious to reach beyond. He would savor this strange new freedom she had given him, as though it were permission to enjoy his life. And quite suddenly, he did.

His brothers were relaxed. Even Cornelius had a faint smile on his lips. They had made interesting new friends.

And Julius wanted to see her again. Now.

He sipped his port, savoring the anticipation until Linfield at least had reached the bottom of his second glass.

Julius rose. "Shall we rejoin the ladies?" he suggested.

Aubrey, clearly, would rather have lingered with his brandy, but Linfield stood at once, still amiable and amusing. He had that easy social grace and lightness of manner that had characterized Sir George. Julius could not help liking him, but he wasn't entirely sure he trusted him any more than he had trusted his erratic parent.

ANTONIA, MEANWHILE, WAS learning more about the family from Lucy.

By the time she had joined the other ladies in the drawing room, her face was fresh and clean of tearstains, and she was once more calm and serene. As she took her place beside Miss Talbot, she was sure no one would know that her whole world had just changed.

Anger with her parents simmered beneath the surface. Whatever their reasons, their actions were a betrayal she did not think she could ever forgive. Since her marriage, and more particularly since her widowhood, she had grown somewhat apart from them, though without any intention, let alone quarrel. Perhaps, in her heart, she had always blamed them for Julius's departure, as well as for the misery of her marriage.

But her anger was subdued, very much secondary to the wonder of her reconciliation with Julius. He had still loved her. He had not left her. His kiss, soft and gentle, lingered on her lips and in her heart. Even now, she felt the butterflies in her stomach, sweet and secret and arousing.

Beside her, Miss Talbot was deep in conversation with Delilah and Felicia about some important matter raised at the Congress that had not yet been resolved. The twins had vanished to the stables, where they were apparently caring for the horse captured from the thieves.

Lucy sat down beside Antonia. "It must have been very exciting in Vienna."

"Oh, it was. Exhausting, too, because most of the diplomacy seemed to be carried out in ballrooms. Miss Talbot and I had to excuse ourselves from parties on several occasions—a luxury poor Lord Linfield did not have."

"Have you been with Miss Talbot for long?" Lucy asked, tactfully not saying the word *companion*.

"About three years now, since my husband died."

Lucy's gaze was steady and almost too curious. "That must have been hard for you."

In many ways, it had been easier than his being alive. "It put us in a difficult position," Antonia said lightly. "My husband's estate was left entirely to his brother, in trust for Edward."

Lucy's eyes widened. "With no provision for you?"

"The right to live in his house for my lifetime, or until I remarried. But I had no income, no resources of my own. It was most fortunate for me that Miss Talbot was then looking for a companion, in order to make her travels with her brother more acceptable."

"Fortunate indeed," Lucy said. She seemed about to make some criticism—no doubt one Antonia had already railed about in her head, such as the poor marriage settlements negotiated by her father, or the infamy of her husband in making her no better than a poor relation in her own home. Then she said abruptly, "Was yours a happy marriage?"

Under no circumstances was Antonia prepared to discuss that. "By most standards," she said meaninglessly, and turned the question around. "Why do you ask? Are you contemplating matrimony yourself?"

She expected a flutter of embarrassed denials from the younger woman, or perhaps even breathless confidences. Instead, Lucy wrinkled her nose and grimaced.

"I've been betrothed since my cradle," she said unexpectedly. "And now I might have to do something about it. He's coming to Black-haven to meet me."

Antonia blinked. "You haven't met him before?"

"Never. Our mothers came up with the notion when we were born on the same day only a few years apart. Our fathers even drew up prospective settlements—subject to renegotiation in the year of our actual marriage. But after my mother died, no one seemed to take it seriously. Until now."

"It seems very...old-fashioned," Antonia said, struggling to find neutral words that were sympathetic. After all, it was none of her business.

"Antiquated," Lucy agreed heartily. "But Julius says that in the circumstances, we owe him a meeting."

"Perhaps he is right?"

She sighed. "Oh, he is, I'm sure, but I don't have to like it. Or him."

"Well, if you didn't like him, surely Julius would not *force* you to marry him?"

"He could certainly make it confoundedly difficult to refuse," Lucy retorted. "He has a somewhat jaundiced view of love matches, and I suppose I can see his point. Felicia married for love, and look where that got her. And there is some woman in Julius's own past who made him miserable. In any case, he sees no reason why he should make a marriage of any kind, so *I* don't see why I should have to marry just because my mother was sillier than his."

Antonia choked on a sudden laugh that she tried to cover in a cough, and Lucy's eyes twinkled appreciatively.

"Well, she *was* silly, by all accounts," she said. "Silly enough to put Sir George off any further marriages after she died. I don't really remember her. She passed away when I was only two. But in her portrait she is very young and beautiful."

"You have a different mother to Julius?"

"Julius and Roderick were born to Sir George's first wife, the others to his second, I to his third." She met Antonia's gaze. "I expect the twins told you they are illegitimate. Their mother was a very sophisticated countess who more or less willed them to my father, much to the count's relief." She smiled. "I will say this for Sir George—he treated us all the same."

Was there a warning in that confidence? Surely not. A mere companion's view of anyone was of no consequence. But Antonia had the feeling Lucy was sharper, more perceptive than she appeared from her insouciant manner, and she had probably sensed the tension stretched between Antonia and Julius, if not the tangle of old love and bitterness. Perhaps she sensed the possibilities, too, but Antonia would not think of those.

"When will he come, this suitor of yours?" she asked.

"Next month, perhaps. Or August. Julius is waiting for a letter."

"No one can force you to marry," Antonia blurted. "Just say no." *God knows I wish I had.*

Suddenly Lucy's eyes were serious. "The thing is," she said, pleating the delicate muslin of her gown, "I'm not sure that is quite fair either. I am a bit of a trial to Julius. He has taken on all of us, you know, even Felicia's debts. He gave up the sea for us. None of us thought he would ever leave the navy, but he did, and not because he is too injured to serve. And in return… Well, we fiddle about with the house and the garden, but only Cornelius is really contributing. My betrothed is a wealthy man, and the settlements are generous."

"Julius—Captain Vale—would never allow you to marry for such a reason alone!"

"No, but should *I* allow it? Should I grin and bear it?" She gave another quick, apologetic smile. "That is why I am vulgarly curious about your marriage and anyone else's. I want to know what I might choose to bear."

"Perhaps you should wait and see if you can bear the gentleman in question first."

Lucy's eyes dropped. Although she nodded, Antonia had the sudden suspicion that there was even more to it. That there might well be someone else Lucy would like to marry.

But further questions vanished into thin air as Julius strolled into the room with Lord Linfield and his brothers. He looked so handsome, so uniquely, desirably imposing that Antonia's stomach dived and her whole body flushed. She could not bear to look at him, so she pretended to be distracted by Felicia ringing for tea, and then by the setting sun showing gold and pink and orange over the fields to the sea. Gradually, her cheeks cooled, while the twins entertained everyone with a clowning duet on the pianoforte that they had perfected.

Everyone applauded, laughing. Felicia poured the tea, and Lucy played a more conventional air while they drank and nibbled delicious morsels of cake.

"How well you play," Lord Linfield complimented Lucy. "With lightness and feeling."

She blushed prettily. "Oh, you are too kind. It is Roderick who is the real musical talent of the family."

"Whatever you are after, Lucy, the answer is no," Roderick said, and a ripple of laughter echoed around the room.

Antonia smiled, thinking there was probably much more to Roderick Vale than the bluff soldier he portrayed.

A movement beside her made her glance up, and her heart lurched. Julius sat beside her.

"Would you care for a stroll before the sun sets completely?" he asked quietly.

Warmth seeped into her face. "That would not be wise, would it?"

"You would not have mentioned wisdom ten years ago."

"I barely knew what it was ten years ago. The company is settled."

"I was not inviting the company."

There was challenge in his eye, but also understanding and a glinting smile that undid all her resolve.

"It will only be five minutes," he murmured, "and we'll leave the doors open. Do you want your cloak?"

She hesitated only an instant, then rose to her feet. "I have my shawl."

Before she could reach for it, he lifted it from the back of her chair and placed it lightly around her shoulders. He did not touch her, but somehow she was so aware of him that it felt as if he did.

Miss Talbot glanced up, and he said, "I'm taking Mrs. Macy for some air."

"Don't let her catch a chill," Miss Talbot said mildly, and turned her attention back to Roderick, who had now been persuaded to the piano.

Antonia did not know if anyone else saw them go out through the French window. She was afraid to look. She could almost feel Delilah's gaze burning into the back of her head.

"They care a great deal for you," she blurted. "Your siblings."

"I care for them," he admitted, offering his arm.

She placed her hand on it and suddenly could not breathe for the upsurge of memory and longing. To be this close to him, to touch him...

As they walked, she gazed with genuine appreciation at the spectacular sky. The breeze stirred her hair, bringing the scents of the night, cut grass mingling with honeysuckle and a hint of roses, even the salt sea in the distance. His every movement at her side was a shock and a delight. She had never wanted to be anywhere more than here at this moment.

And that was frightening.

"Why did you give up the sea?" she asked, almost desperately.

"I didn't. I left the Royal Navy for many reasons, most of them to do with being bored and tired of death and injury."

"Are they so severe?" she asked, rocked by another fear she had not previously considered.

"Not my own," he said. "I have been lucky. Many of my sailors and friends were not so fortunate. Besides, the strategy and the tactics of battle no longer interest me. They come with a price in blood I am no longer willing to pay, which makes me something of a liability to my country and my comrades."

"And so you came home to be a gentleman farmer?"

He smiled deprecatingly. "Something like that. I have money to invest in the land, and Cornelius has the knowledge. He was a land steward for several years. And the house is big enough to accommodate us all when necessary." He glanced down at her. "What happened to your home?"

"Masterton Hall?" She gazed over the softly muting colors of the sky. "I have the right to live in it if I choose. I don't choose. It belongs to Edward, but Timothy has control."

"I see."

Perhaps he did.

"And the Talbots? You are happy with them?"

"I don't know what I would have done without them. They don't just tolerate Edward, you know—they are kind to him. They like him."

"He is a likeable child."

"I think so."

His gaze grew fixed, drawing hers back to him.

"And I have seen something of the world with them," she babbled. "I always wanted to travel."

"I remember," he said softly. His gaze dropped her lips, and the butterflies in her stomach soared. "I remember so many things about you, it's like a deluge… I would like to kiss you."

"Don't," she said shakily. "You have only just stopped hating me."

"I never hated you. Only myself."

"I don't think that's true."

He stopped, and his head blocked the fading light and color from the sky. "I find it does not matter anymore. I care only for the present." He cupped her cheek, and she had to stop herself turning into it. "Your face and your skin are the same, and yet you are indefinably different. Does my missing eye appall you?"

"Only for the pain you must have suffered."

He closed his eye. "Not pity, Antonia. Please not pity. Kiss me as a man, not a wounded sailor."

"Are they not one and the same?" she managed.

His mouth quirked. She could see the texture of his lips, the tiny nick at one corner, feel his breath on her skin. "Let's find out," he muttered, and her stomach dived as his mouth touched hers.

Slow and gentle, he dropped tiny, brushing kisses on her lips until she parted them in a silent gasp. And then his mouth took hers.

Was this how it had been before? This wild, aching tenderness, so deeply, utterly sensual that her blood seemed to ignite and she melted in pure, helpless wanting? Her hand came up of its own volition to touch his cheek in wonder, then his hair, the back of his neck, where she clung as the kiss deepened and she pressed involuntarily against him.

Oh God, she remembered that hard strength, the thrill of his arousal growing and pushing against her. It moved her unbearably that he still wanted her. He held her close in his muscular arms, kissing her and kissing her until she gasped, from lack of air as much as from overwhelming desire.

He raised his head at once, and they stared into each other's eyes. It felt like recognition, though of what, she was far too befuddled to think. Her breath was short and shaky.

Some movement caught her eyes, and she jerked her head around in time to see Delilah whisk herself around the corner of the path.

"They're just coming," she called to someone else.

Dismay splashed Antonia like cold water. Of all the people to have seen… But a breath of laughter hissed between Julius's lips, and he did not immediately let her go. Instead, he took her face between his hands and dropped a short, gentle kiss on her lips.

"That was our warning," he said.

I have already had mine. She does not like me. She swallowed. "We should rejoin the others."

"Of course." He stepped back, and she felt a foolish sense of panic. She had no idea what his kisses meant, or even her own. Was this really about the present? Or just exorcising the past?

She was grateful for his arm beneath her hand as they strolled back toward the drawing room window. It felt like a connection to those moments of intimacy, which she could not regret even if Delilah cut her for the rest of their lives. Surely, the woman would not blab about the indiscretion she had witnessed?

Of course not, she realized. Any threat to Antonia's reputation was likely to inspire Julius to chivalry, and that, Delilah would like even less.

Was it guilt now that made her heart beat too rapidly? It did not feel like shame, although with the breeze cooling her flushed cheeks and her lips tingling from his kiss, she felt sure everyone would know what they had done beneath the cherry tree. Beside her, Julius began to talk, telling some lighthearted story from his adventures at sea. Her heart warmed all over again, because she realized he was giving her time to recover and making it sound as if he had been telling this story the whole time of their absence from the company.

Chapter Nine

"THAT WAS A very pleasant evening," Miss Talbot pronounced as the coach carried them back along the dark road to Blackhaven. "A charming family. Eccentric, perhaps, but I always like that in people."

"A trifle...irregular," Lord Linfield said thoughtfully. "Sir George really was a shocking old rake."

"Well, I'm not sure if I was a new wife that I would care to have my husband's by-blows thrust upon me, as well as several legitimate children."

"No, but from the children's perspective—and their birth is hardly their fault—it was the only decent thing he could do. And they all appear to accept it."

"Do you?" Miss Talbot asked.

"Of course," Lord Linfield said after a moment. "Besides, it is none of my business. Did you enjoy the evening, Mrs. Macy?"

Antonia was glad she sat in the shadows to hide the color rushing into her face. "Very much," she managed.

She was hugging those secret moments of passion to herself, sweet and thrilling. And yet they were not completely secret, for Delilah had seen them. Julius hadn't seemed to think this mattered. He even found it funny. But to Antonia, Delilah's observation felt like a thorn amongst the unexpected beauty.

Still, she had no idea where any of this was leading. And that, God help her, was exciting.

JULIUS STOOD GAZING out of the open library window, through the darkness toward the sea. For once, he was not thinking or planning, just *feeling*. And that was rather intoxicating.

The door opened and Delilah said, "Oh! I didn't realize you were in here. I came to douse the candles, since I sent the servants to bed."

"I'll put them out when I go." Some faint hesitation in her manner made him glance over his shoulder at her. "Is everything well?"

"Yes, of course." Her fingers twisted on the door handle, then she came into the room. "It *is* her, isn't it? *That* Mrs. Macy?"

"The lady I was engaged to, yes."

"Is she pursuing you again now that her first choice of husband is dead?"

He winced, then let out a short breath of laughter. "I think, rather, she was in pursuit of the truth. We had a conversation this evening that we should have had ten years ago. She never sent me away. In fact, she was at least as hurt as I, and pushed into what I think was an unpleasant marriage, besides. It was her parents who lied to me, and to her, and hid our letters so that she would marry Macy."

Delilah stared at him. She never suffered fools gladly, and she had that look in her eye that said she was not about to start. "Is that what she told you?"

"It is what we deduced," he said with a stab of irritation.

"Oh, Julius, don't fall for the lies again! She has Linfield and his sister eating out of her hand, *their* servants caring for *her* son while she still receives a salary—and through them, access to the best of Society. Now she has seen that you have a fine estate here. Macy left her with nothing, you know."

He scowled. "Of course I know. And you are misinterpreting everything."

"Am I?" she challenged.

"Yes. You don't know her, Delly."

"I know what she did to you ten years ago."

"What was done to both of us."

She stood beside him, gazing up at him with all the annoyance and all the care of which he knew she was capable. More than that, there was fear in her eyes that jolted him.

"Don't be foolish, Julius," she begged. "She married Macy a bare three weeks after she dismissed you. One does not find oneself married accidentally. She snared him and his wealth as easily as she caught you. Only he at least protected his family from her machinations."

"By leaving her dependent on a brother whose face would curdle the milk?"

"Exactly! Why would he have done that unless he had reason not to trust her?"

"Don't, Del," he said between his teeth. "You don't know her at all."

"I know what she did to you ten years ago," Delilah retorted. "You had me frightened to let you sail away. Even Papa was anxious."

She and Sir George had come from London to meet his betrothed, and instead found him at his worst, newly *un*-betrothed, shocked, and shattered. He didn't want to dwell on that time, when despair had alternated with moments of blind, reasonless hope. Sailing had been his only escape.

"And you imagine this is history repeating itself?" he said.

"It does, you know," she said, her expression gentling.

"Perhaps. But not consistently." He gave her his crooked half-smile. "Believe it or not, I was never a fool. I am used to reading people's characters. Instead of hating her, consider why I loved her in the first place." He bent and kissed her cheek. "Goodnight, Delilah."

THE FOLLOWING MORNING, Edward accompanied Antonia and Miss Talbot to the pump room. Since the weather was cool and cloudy, with a hint of rain in the air, they all went inside.

Antonia's heart gave a little lurch of pleasure, for seated by the window were Julius and Aubrey. They both rose and bowed.

"Won't you join us?" Aubrey suggested, which Edward did with alacrity, all but dancing in front of Julius.

"Captain! Did you see that horrid pirate again?" he demanded.

"No," Julius said, "but I'm keeping watch for him. Aubrey, this is Master Edward Macy, an excellent shipmate. Aubrey is my brother, who captured one of the pirate's horses."

"Pirates have horses?" Edward asked, frowning with incomprehension.

"Only for land-bound activities," Julius assured him with a quick gleam of his eye aimed at Antonia.

Her heart melted.

"Allow me to fetch your waters," he said, while Aubrey handed Miss Talbot into a chair.

Even Edward received a small glass of water, which he eyed with some disfavor. "Do they not have lemonade here?"

"Sadly not. The water is meant to make you feel better."

"I don't feel bad," Edward argued.

"'Thank you' would do," Antonia murmured, mortified.

Edward grinned. "Thank you," he said, and took a dutiful sip. "It doesn't taste of anything."

"Be grateful," Miss Talbot murmured.

"Do you feel bad?" Edward asked Julius.

"Lord, no."

"He only comes to make me drink it," Aubrey said. "He thinks because I was once a weakling child, I still am."

"Only your head is weak," Julius retorted. "And I can do nothing about that. As for your bodily strength, the water can do no harm."

"My argument exactly," Miss Talbot agreed. "And I must admit I do feel considerably less tired since coming to Blackhaven. In fact, I have decided to be 'at home' this afternoon, in the hotel, if you or any of your family are still in town."

"Thank you," Julius said.

Feeling his gaze upon her, Antonia glanced at him. There was a smile in his eye that melted her bones. She could not help the blush rising to her face, because she was sure he was remembering last night's kisses. And she had been able to think of very little else. She dragged her gaze free, urging Edward to drink his water before reaching rather blindly for her own.

She was almost relieved when the Vales took their leave, although as soon as Julius's back vanished through the door, a ridiculous desolation swept through her.

This was foolish beyond belief.

MISS TALBOT'S "AT home" had been arranged shortly after the ball when she discovered some old acquaintances from their days in Vienna. Lady Launceton was the niece of one of Lord Linfield's colleagues.

"Jeffrey Daniels," Miss Talbot reminded Antonia. "His daughter married young Corner, who is now quite a shining light in the Foreign Office."

"Oh, yes, of course I remember them."

"Then you must recall the extended family that came with them— or at least the dog. The niece inexplicably married some mad Russian. Only it isn't actually inexplicable at all, because the Russian inherited her family's property and became Baron Launceton."

"I remember the dog," Antonia said. "What brings them to Black-haven?"

"The waters, of course. Lady Launceton is *enceinte*. Charming girl." She broke off in sudden alarm. "Oh, dear, you don't suppose they will bring the dog here?"

Antonia laughed at the possibility. In truth, she did not much care, for there was every possibility Julius would come.

Lady Launceton and the mad Russian were in fact the first to call—without the feared dog, but *with* the most beautiful young lady Antonia had ever seen. She vaguely recalled noticing her at the ball, for she was extraordinarily eye-catching, all dark hair and pale skin and large, brilliant eyes. Individually, her features were perfect, yet somehow the arrangement of those pretty features raised her looks to breathtaking beauty.

"My sister, Miss Henrietta Gaunt," Lady Launceton said.

Henrietta smiled in a friendly, entirely natural kind of way that was almost as surprising as her beauty.

Miss Talbot introduced Antonia, adding, "And of course you must know my brother, Lord Linfield."

"Of course. We met in London during the Season, too," Lady Launceton said. She seemed to have the same open, unaffected manners as her young sister.

Antonia rang for the hotel servants to bring tea, while Miss Talbot asked Henrietta if she had enjoyed her first London Season.

"Oh, yes. I met many very kind and interesting people."

Antonia, who had quite expected something about fashion or dancing, was surprised all over again.

"Miss Gaunt was much sought after," Lord Linfield added. "I daresay you don't even remember dancing with me."

Henrietta smiled. "Of course I do! You waltz better than most men in London."

"Well, I was in Vienna," Linfield said modestly, and not entirely seriously.

As a friend, Antonia was glad to see he was not drawn by her beauty to flirt with so young a girl. More unexpected was the realization that Henrietta was not trying to flirt with him or with anyone else who called. Which was modest of her, but Lord and Lady Launceton must surely have been looking for a great match for her. Perhaps Linfield, recently ennobled with little inherited wealth, was not good enough.

Antonia, as usual, kept in the background, pouring tea and offering scones and cakes, while she covertly watched the door and alternately longed for and dreaded the arrival of Julius.

Instead, Timothy arrived, graciously welcomed by Miss Talbot.

"Edward is with his nurse for an hour," Antonia said at once, presenting him with a cup of tea.

"I know you make every provision for him," Timothy replied, causing her to peer at him to see if he was quite well. He smiled blandly. "I am not an unreasonable man, merely a fond uncle. And caring brother-in-law, of course."

"Of course. Have a scone."

Materializing beside him was Mr. Dunnett from the hospital, beaming at her. "Mrs. Macy, what a great pleasure to see you again. May I sit beside you?"

"Of course," she said warily. "Do you care for cream and sugar in your tea?"

Timothy, smiling benignly, drifted away.

"You must miss having your own home," Mr. Dunnett said.

"Not really," she said lightly. "I am quite content."

He looked surprised, then smiled. "Of course. You would say so, being a good friend to Miss Talbot."

"Miss Talbot has been a good friend to *me*," she said, trying to keep the rising tartness from her voice.

"I have been thinking of buying a home, with a little land," he said.

"Indeed? Near Blackhaven? Is there much available?"

"Why, no, a little closer to civilization."

"I'm sure the hospital will be sorry to lose you."

"Well, I believe I have set them on the right path, and now I must look after the comfort of my own life."

"I wish you well," she said, mainly because she could not think of anything else, but it made him smile as though she had delivered a fulsome compliment.

Lady Braithwaite arrived, with a young gentleman in spectacles and three young ladies whom she introduced as her youngest sisters-in-law. The gentleman, Mr. Hanson, was the local member of Parliament, and married to the earl's middle sister, Maria.

Mr. Dunnett kindly offered to ferry them cups of tea and offered plates of cakes and scones, and Antonia was happy to accept. The sitting room was full of people, including Mrs. Grant and the doctor's wife, Mrs. Lampton, a couple of army officers from the local barracks, and several visitors who were staying at the hotel. Antonia rang for more tea.

It had not long arrived when, without warning, Julius, Aubrey, and Roderick strolled into the room.

Antonia's heart immediately sped up. Somehow, the Vales filled the space, as if there was no one else in the room.

To avoid watching Julius, she turned back to Mr. Dunnett. "Are you not a native of Blackhaven, then, Mr. Dunnett? Where is if you are from?"

"Surrey, originally."

"And will you return there to seek your new home?"

"No, I believe not. I am drawn to look somewhere entirely new. Where would you recommend?"

She was startled. "I could not begin to give such advice! Would you oblige me further, Mr. Dunnett, by taking this cup to Miss Talbot?"

That lady was flitting happily among her guests and seemed to have talked herself dry. Mr. Dunnett duly obliged, and she poured cups for the Vale brothers. Roderick had paused to talk to Lord Launceton, "the mad Russian," and Aubrey, with a quick grin and a murmured greeting, swept up two cups of tea and sauntered off to join them. No doubt the beautiful Henrietta was the attraction.

Julius sat in the chair just vacated by Mr. Dunnett. "When you are free, come for a walk on the beach with me."

Surprise sent the blood rushing into her face. She aimed desperately for some kind of propriety. "I am free on Sunday afternoons. Edward—"

"I cannot wait that long. I have already gained permission from Miss Talbot, who is planning to nap when everyone is gone and will not need you."

She wanted to be angry at such high-handedness, but his words filled her with too much pleasure. *I cannot wait that long.* But their last misunderstanding had lasted for ten years. She would not risk another.

She looked at him. "A walk with what purpose?"

Something flared in his eye and melted into a smile. "An assignation, of course. Will you come?"

Panic swept over her, because of the risk—she was a mother, with a respectable position she could not afford to lose—and yet she so wanted to go, with a strength that took her breath away. Then, with relief, she realized he was teasing.

"A brisk walk will be most pleasant."

He smiled, one of his rare, full smiles that took her back ten years and yet dazzled her in the present. "Then I shall await you in the foyer."

He rose and sauntered across the room to speak to Lady Braithwaite and Lord Linfield. Miss Talbot's callers were drifting away. No further tea was required, and she had no idea what to do with her hands—or with her eyes, which she was determined not to turn in

Julius's direction.

Timothy, she was glad to see, had left without troubling to speak to her again. Mr. Dunnett made a point of taking his leave of her before thanking Miss Talbot for her hospitality and departing. The Braithwaite ladies left escorted by Roderick, and thereafter everyone else drifted away, too. Carefully, Antonia did not look at Julius as she rose to collect the abandoned crockery for the hotel servants to take away.

"Leave that, my dear," Miss Talbot said. "The staff will see to it. Go and fetch your bonnet and take your walk. Edward will be fine with Suze for another hour."

It was true that she normally spent this time with Miss Talbot, usually reading to her or some other quiet activity that required the absence of children.

"Is there nothing I can do for you, ma'am?" she asked.

Miss Talbot smiled. "Yes. Enjoy your walk. I like Captain Vale."

Warmth rushed under her skin. Was her employer promoting her friendship with the captain? Did she imagine he was courting her?

The assignation comment had been a jest.

Hadn't it?

Well, for her own sanity, she would treat it as such. Still flushed, under Miss Talbot's tolerant gaze, she walked to her own room and found her hat and pelisse. A quick glance out of the window convinced her to pick up her umbrella—really, this summer was barely a summer at all—and she left the room, deliberately ignoring her passing reflection in the glass.

Julius did indeed await her in the foyer, where he was examining a notice about some gaming event. He seemed to know as soon as she approached him—which she did feeling ridiculously self-conscious— for he smiled at the notice before turning to greet her, just as though they had not met by arrangement.

"Mrs. Macy. Allow me to escort you." He bowed and offered her his arm. "It is a town of gossip," he murmured. "I am looking after your reputation. As far as may be consistent with an assignation."

"I don't believe a public walk along the town beach at five o'clock on a summer afternoon truly constitutes an assignation."

"No? What is it, then? A mere appointment sounds so...businesslike."

"Don't you have business to discuss?" she asked innocently.

To her surprise, he appeared to be seriously considering the question as they left the hotel. "Not business," he said at last. "But certainly, we have much to talk about."

"Such as?"

"Your life in the last ten years. Mine. What the future holds."

"One can hardly know the latter," she pointed out.

"But one can influence it, to some extent, at least."

This part of the high street was too busy for personal conversations, so they walked largely in silence, with Julius nodding occasionally to acquaintances. She remembered that she had never minded silences with this man. Uniquely among the young gentlemen of her acquaintance ten years ago, he had never tried to impress with his own cleverness or wit. He had seemed more interested in *her*. Just being in her company had appeared to give him pleasure, a need to savor without necessarily filling every moment with chatter.

Not that there had been *no* chatter. She remembered long conversations, not all of them serious, for they shared a sense of humor, a love of the ridiculous that made life such fun.

It was that sense of fun that he had been missing when they met at the ball and the hospital. Perhaps in her, too. Perhaps it was creaking back into life for both of them.

The street was quieter as they approached the harbor and the steps down to the beach. He took her hand to help her down the stairs, and when her feet were both on the sand, he spoke as if the words burst out without permission.

"What was he like? Macy? Did you love him?"

Chapter Ten

"**W**E HAVE A problem," Dunnett murmured, sinking onto the sofa beside Timothy in the hotel foyer. His gaze rested on the front door, through which Antonia had just departed with Julius Vale.

"A minor one," Timothy replied with a hint of impatience. "You wanted me here to exert a little pressure. Why don't we simply exert it and have done?"

Dunnett sighed. "You have no subtlety," he complained.

"I think you will find I do," Timothy said, stung. "And knowledge besides. You cannot imagine the Vales care for this reunion any more than we do?"

"Is Vale the kind of man who can be influenced by his family?" Dunnett asked.

"He can be manipulated," Timothy said. "We proved that before. All we will need is my pressure on Antonia, and a little family hint to Vale."

"From whom?" Dunnett asked, frowning.

Timothy smiled with blatant smugness. "From the lady currently over there in the tearoom, looking at least as displeased as you. Miss Delilah Vale."

WHAT WAS HE like? Macy? Did you love him?

With Julius's words, the reality of life seemed to slap Antonia in the face once more. She was not a naïve young girl unexpectedly given a second chance to love. She was a widow, a mother, a woman of experience she did not wish to think about, let alone speak of to him.

"Don't ask me. You will despise me whatever answer I give."

"I could never despise you." He sounded surprised by the very idea, though after a moment, when she said nothing, he added, "I admit I tried for a time, but it never worked."

The tide was out, leaving a largely empty beach where they could walk and talk in privacy. She took his proffered arm once more. There should be no more misunderstandings between them, only truth.

"I did not love him," she admitted. "To be honest, I did not even like him much. My parents chose him, and I barely noticed him. Yet I made vows to love and honor him. The best that can be said is that I grew used to him. I don't think he ever got used to me."

"Then it was not a happy marriage. I thought I would be glad of that, or at least triumphant. But I am neither. Only sorry."

She shook her head. "Don't be. He was not a cruel man, or even a bad one. We just were not...suited. He had no...fun. No passion. Though he was proud of me, in his way. He liked to show me off. I mistook that for liking me, so I tried to be a good wife in return. Until I realized he did not even see me as a person, merely a possession that his brother did not have, that he thought other men envied. He was proud of Edward, too. But I don't think he knew how to love. It was not in him."

Julius's hand closed over hers on his arm, his grip strong and oddly comforting. "I'm sorry. I hate to think of you in such a situation."

"I needn't have been," she said honestly. "I brought it on myself. And since Edward came out of it, I cannot truly regret it. When Francis died... It was a short, sudden illness. I felt numb, and then, God forgive me, relieved."

She tried to smile. "I was punished for that, too. You know how I was left, materially. Timothy talked of living in Masterton Hall himself. He certainly arrived whenever he wished and started redecorating, changing rooms around. And then he thought he would rent it out, with only a small suite of apartments set aside for me, and Edward until he was sent away to school. Edward was three years old at this point.

"I had begun to apply for paid positions almost as soon as I knew how Francis had left us, but no one wanted a governess, a housekeeper, or a companion who came with a small child. I was desperate until I heard from Miss Talbot. She was desperate, too, because her old companion had left her suddenly to care for a sick relative, and she needed to travel immediately with her brother. She agreed to take Edward, too, even dragged along their old family nurse to help care for him while I was busy. Without her, I don't know what I would have done."

"Could you not have gone back to your parents?"

"I could have," she admitted. "In fact, I was on the verge of it. But I was reluctant. My father would always take Timothy's side in any matter that arose."

"Why?" Julius asked blankly.

She glanced at him in surprise. "I don't know. Men assuming other men always know better than women?"

His frown deepened. "You are his daughter."

"I was his daughter when he lied to me and sent you away."

"Do you suppose Timothy convinced him to do that, too?"

She blinked. "I have no idea. I can't imagine why."

"You came with a decent dowry, as I recall. Whatever happened to that?"

She shrugged. "Somehow my father let it all go to Francis without any provision for me."

"So Timothy inherited that as well? Or will it go to Edward?"

She frowned. "The latter, I imagine, but I honestly don't know. Either way, I have no more control over it than I have over the rest of Edward's inheritance."

"I hate to think of you so…dependent," he muttered.

"Oh, so do I, but since there is nothing I can do about it, I merely keep Timothy as sweet as I can, and thank God for my place with Miss Talbot." She met his gaze with a smile. "What of your ten years, Julius? Adventure, heroism, and success. With some painful new injuries."

"That sums it up nicely."

She pushed his arm in mock annoyance. "No, it does not! What actions did you see? When were you promoted to captain, how did you come by your injuries? How badly do they pain you? Whom have you loved?"

She hadn't meant to speak the last question aloud, but it came out anyway. His gaze grew intense, if unreadable, and for a few moments, she thought he would not answer at all.

Then he said, "Are we back to the lady in Lisbon again? There was such a lady. She was a widow, sweet and generous, and I was fond of her. She married someone else, even before the Trafalgar campaign. I was glad for her. I certainly never saw her again."

There was relief in that, but then, she had already decided the lady in Lisbon was merely yet another of her parents' lies. Now, her heart warmed because he had told her.

He shrugged off the memory. "After you and I parted, there were innumerable sea battles, sieges, and blockades, which I shall not bore you with today, mostly because I don't want to think about them just now. I was promoted to captain about five years ago. The leg was a saber injury fighting off a boarding party, the eye some flying wood splinters in an explosion. I was lucky both times. The eye gave me the most bother because of the terrible headaches, which rarely trouble me anymore, and my vision has adjusted well. It isn't pretty, but covered, it does not seem to frighten women and children. Is it the women you really want to know about?"

"I want to know it all. But I will settle for whatever you care to speak of."

Unexpected anger flashed across his face. "Don't do that."

"What?"

"Be so damned submissive. You were never like that."

He was right, and the knowledge appalled her. "That is true. I wasn't. I had too much spirit, too much certainty, and no responsibility. Life has taught me otherwise. Changed me, if you like."

He pulled away, and hurt pierced her heart. But he threw his arm about her shoulders, hugging her to his side. "Not all battles are fought at sea with guns and sabers," he said unsteadily. "I know that. But please, *never* be afraid of me."

"I'm not."

His face lightened and he released her, glancing quickly around to see if they had been observed. But there was only a couple with a small pug heading toward the harbor, their backs to Antonia and Julius. He took her hand, drawing her toward the rocks from where they would be less visible.

"Then you came this afternoon because you wanted to?"

"Do you imagine Miss Talbot instructed me to come?"

A smile flashed across his face and vanished. "I would not put it past her. But no. I…I would like it if there were no debts between us, no blame."

"You mean begin with a fresh slate, a fresh page, so to speak."

He thought about it, then shook his head. "Not that. You can't forget the past, and I find I don't want to. I regret my mistakes, my blindness, but I don't regret you, Antonia Temple."

Warmth swept through her. "I don't regret you either."

He lifted her hand and softly kissed her fingers. He was smiling. "Then this really can be an assignation."

"I have no idea what that entails," she said loftily.

"A tryst. A lovers' meeting." He turned her hand and kissed the inside of her wrist, and then her palm, before he folded her fingers over as though to seal the kiss. "I have the most powerful urge to court you."

"C-court me?" she repeated.

"If you are willing." He must have read the surge of desire in her eyes, for he stepped closer, and she flung up both hands, her palms against his chest, wrestling with gladness and regret and loss.

"Julius, we cannot go back," she said. "We are no longer the people we were. Specifically, I am no longer eighteen! I have a *child*. You have a dependent sister who does not like me."

"I have lots of dependent sisters. If you mean Delilah, she does not know you except to blame you for the state she found me in before I sailed ten years ago. She is fiercely loyal, but she is not cruel. When she knows you—"

"You cannot speak for her. Or for Edward."

"I have not proposed marriage," he pointed out. "Only a courtship. To learn each other again and see where that leads. That is surely not wrong or frightening? For us or our families."

She shook her head, dumbly. The trouble was, she could not think properly when he stood so close, caressing her palm and her wrist until the skin seemed to sing.

He said, "For the sake of your reputation, I shall be discreet. For instance, I will step behind this useful rock and make sure no one else can see us before I take you in my arms. Or kiss you."

She gasped as he wrapped his arms around her and dropped his mouth over hers, a leisurely, unhurried kiss that grew and deepened. She clutched his coat button and one lapel and tried to say, "This is unfair!" But the movement of her lips against his felt so exquisite that she forgot her original intention and just kissed him back.

She had always loved his mouth, his kisses, never quite understanding how she could feel them right down to her toes, and especially in the pit of her stomach and lower, where everything grew deliciously hot and heavy and sweet. His hands swept down her back, over the swell of her hips and rear, and drew her more closely against him.

With another gasp, she found the will to tear her mouth free. She *was* Edward's mother, and she could never let her good sense vanish in a moment of foolish self-indulgence. Julius's arms loosened at once, though he did not release her or step back.

As though gathering strength, she let her forehead rest against his shoulder, while her hands slid down from his neck to grip his arms. Where was her wretched hat?

"It did not feel like no," he murmured against her hair.

Her fingers tightened. "I cannot think when you are so close. I..."

"That is a promising sign."

A choke of laughter escaped her. "Is it? You cut up my peace, Julius. A peace that was hard-won."

His lips moved against her hair as he spoke. "Shall I go away?"

Emotion shuddered through her. She raised her head, staring up at him with sudden, breathtaking understanding. "*That* is what I could not bear. To let this chance pass, to never know if I feel so *alive* because you make me remember my youth. Or just because you are here and you are *you*. Oh God, I'm not making any sense."

She tried to turn away, but he caught her chin, turning her face back up to his. "It makes sense to me," he said softly, and kissed her lips. "And if we part again, it shall be as friends."

At that moment, she was fiercely, and quite unreasonably, determined that they would never part again.

He let her go and, rather like a conjurer, plucked her missing hat and umbrella from the rock beside him. "I'm afraid a couple of your pins have loosened."

"The hat will hide it," she assured him, cramming it back on her head and stuffing a stray lock beneath it. "Do I look like a hoyden?"

He smiled. "You look beautiful. Like a perfectly respectable companion who has not been recently embraced and ruffled."

Laughter caught in her throat. She took his arm, and they strolled together out of the protection of the rocks. An elderly lady, supported by a younger woman and followed by two maidservants, was walking in their direction.

"Just in time," he murmured. "Would you come sailing with me, Antonia?"

"You have a boat here?" she asked in surprise.

"Well, I have a rowing boat tied up at the harbor, but I know a man who will lend me a larger vessel until I can buy it from him."

"I would love to sail with you in either," she said.

"We can take Edward, if you like."

And she smiled because he could not have said anything that pleased her more.

DELILAH HAD COME into Blackhaven driving the small gig, in order to buy thread to repair various bedroom curtains. Having made her purchase, she would have gone straight home, except that she caught sight of three of her brothers crossing the high street and entering the hotel.

Miss Talbot had mentioned being "at home" this afternoon. Delilah did not much care for such gatherings, which tended to be mostly women who looked down their well-born noses at a mere by-blow. And somehow they always knew. Blackhaven would know.

On the other hand, she had been thinking she should speak to Antonia Macy again, both because she regretted being quite so rude and because she should at least try to find out if Julius was right to forgive the woman. On the other hand, if she turned up now, her brother would think she was spying on him.

She decided to have tea in the hotel and think about it.

She did not mind sitting alone in public. At thirty, she believed she was long past the age of needing a chaperone, and she certainly had never wanted one. Besides, she had had tea here before, both alone and with her sisters.

When she entered, she was immediately shown to a corner table, where she ordered her tea and watched people pass by in the foyer, going out and coming in. Normally, she amused herself by imagining stories about whoever interested her. Today, she had too much else on her mind, mostly the memory of Julius's disintegration ten years ago when Antonia Temple had jilted him.

Growing up, Julius had been her adored big brother. Roderick was too close in age to herself to become a hero to her, but Julius was, which had made his sudden human weakness curiously shattering.

It had not lasted, of course. He had hauled himself out of his trough of misery and reported to his ship for duty. But the blackness in his eyes had haunted her for months. She had hated the unknown Antonia for what she had done to Julius. She hated her now for coming back and threatening to do it all again. Delilah did not trust her.

Roderick and Aubrey sailed out the front door without noticing her. And without Julius. She almost hurried after them to ask where he was. Then she knew she would have to call upon Miss Talbot. She finished her tea, thinking what she would say—and was suddenly jolted by the sight of Julius and Antonia arm in arm, walking across the foyer toward the door.

So Antonia had not taken Delilah's warning seriously. She supposed she hadn't really expected it, especially not when Julius was disposed to believe Antonia's lies.

If they were lies.

She shifted uncomfortably in her chair. One way or another, she needed to know the truth.

She rose, collecting her reticule and her parcels and made her way out into the foyer. Two men, whom she had barely noticed before, sat on the nearest sofa. The older of the two rose and, rather to her surprise, walked quickly to intercept her.

"Excuse me, ma'am. We have not been introduced, but am I correct in believing you to be Miss Vale?"

She regarded him coldly. "I am."

He bowed with perfect respect. "My name is Macy. Timothy Macy."

She could not stop her brows flying upward in surprise.

"My brother was married to the lady who left the hotel with your brother Captain Vale only five minutes ago. Forgive me, but I could not help noticing that the sight appeared to distress you."

And that, quite definitely, was none of anyone else's business. "You are mistaken," she said abruptly. "You will excuse me."

"Of course," he said, standing aside at once. "I merely hoped you and I might be allies in a common cause. Are you sure you cannot spare me a moment of your time?"

He spread out his arm, indicating the sofa he had just risen from and the other man, who now rose too. Delilah glanced between them, knowing she should walk away. But as usual, curiosity won.

"A moment only, sir, for I am expected elsewhere."

"Of course," he replied, but she was already walking toward the sofa, where Mr. Macy hastily introduced the other man. "Mr. Dunnett, who administers the hospital. Dunnett, this is Miss Vale."

Delilah had heard of him. Julius did not like him. She nodded curtly and sat on the edge of the sofa, her back rigidly straight from habit as much as tension. Dunnett sat back down in his old place, and Macy drew over a nearby chair to sit opposite.

"Allow me to be frank, Miss Vale," he said. "My poor brother made a bad choice in his bride. You might say he was driven to his grave by his disappointment. In short, the woman is a menace, and it grieves me to see her dig her claws into such a great man as Sir Julius. I think it grieves you also."

Delilah fought with her instinct to stand and walk away. "You are aware," she said, "that my brother and your sister-in-law are old friends?"

"They were engaged," Macy said wryly, "before she decided my brother was richer."

It was so much what Delilah had always believed that the old anger surged forward again. How could anyone treat Julius so? Did no one but her see the loneliness and vulnerability in him, along with all his honor and goodness? But yes, Antonia must have. That was how she manipulated him.

"Then she needs another distraction," she snapped.

"I have one in mind," Macy said, glancing significantly at Mr. Dunnett, who beamed at her. "But I might need your help in deflecting her from the captain."

Delilah stared at him. She did not trust him or like him. But Julius's relationship with Antonia had to be nipped in the bud before he was hooked once more.

She nodded curtly. "What is it you want me to do?"

Chapter Eleven

"**P**LEASANT WALK?" MISS Talbot asked with studied innocence when Antonia joined her for dinner that evening.

"Yes, thank you," Antonia replied, willing herself not to blush at the memory. Somewhere, deeper than the physical delight of his kisses, there was a heady warmth because he would court her, an excitement that she of all people could truly make him happy. But she could not think so far ahead. She would live for the moment, take each day as it came. "Pleasant nap?"

"Short and sweet," Miss Talbot replied. "I really do feel much stronger these days, so you don't need to pander to me quite so much. I am more than happy to spare you from time to time, should there be other amusements you wish to pursue."

Antonia drew in her breath. "Miss Talbot," she said firmly. "I think you are reading far too much into a simple walk along the shore with an old friend. I have no intention of neglecting my duties, or what I consider to be my friendship with you."

Miss Talbot's cheeks turned a little pink with pleasure. "I am glad you think of me as a friend. I am. For that reason, I can say to you, don't sacrifice any chances for me!"

"Sacrifice!" Antonia exclaimed. "Chances?"

"Yes, my dear." Miss Talbot leaned forward and covered Antonia's hand with her own. "You are a young woman, beautiful, charming, and kind. There will be many chances, whether or not you choose Sir Julius. Actually," she added, sitting back as her brother entered the room, "if I were ten years younger, I would set my own cap at Sir Julius."

"Give it a shot," Lord Linfield said cheerfully. "Fascinating family, and I'd be glad to call him my brother-in-law."

Miss Talbot sighed and exchanged speaking glances with Antonia, who laughed with sheer good humor.

THE FOLLOWING DAY, Antonia and Edward stepped into a rowing boat, with the help of Captain Vale, and were rowed out of the harbor. Edward was positively bouncing with excitement, and Antonia had to hang on to him before he fell over the side or overturned the boat. Without spoiling the boy's fun, Julius managed to convey the danger of the sea and the ways pirates avoided falling into it. Edward giggled, but he did sit still, and no longer wriggled when he pointed out other vessels.

It was a delightful hour of lighthearted conversation and banter. Antonia enjoyed the glide, roll, and dip of the boat beneath her. More secretly, with pleasant little flutters of desire, she enjoyed the sight of Julius in his shirt sleeves, casually pulling at the oars. His muscles flexed beneath the fabric of his shirt in a way that seemed to tie her stomach in knots, and yet it seemed so casual and natural.

Even Edward seemed to notice such ease. "Did you have to row yourself when you were a captain?"

"Well, no, I always had oarsmen with me in the longboats. But I've rowed since I was a boy, just for fun."

"May I row, Mama?"

"You may learn," Antonia said, "when we find a suitable pond or a lake. And a boat!"

"There are several small lakes around Blackhaven," Julius said. "Including one at Black Hill."

Edward almost bounced, but contented himself with gripping the edge of the bench and grinning hugely, before being distracted again. "Look at that big ship! That would make a grand pirate vessel!"

"That's what I thought," Julius said. "Shall we go and inspect it?"

"You mean go aboard?" Edward squeaked. "Will they let us?"

"Oh yes."

Antonia understood. "This is the ship you want to buy?"

"If I can justify it to myself. There is a small crew on board, so we can sail along the coast for a little, if you like."

Antonia had not meant to be away all day, even though Miss Talbot had given her permission—in fact, had told her not to come back before dinner. But since her own experience of ships was limited to the Dover to Calais packet, and one short trip up the River Danube, she owned herself to be intrigued.

"Whose ship is it?" she asked, as they drew to the side of it.

"It currently belongs to Captain Alban, once the bane of the Royal Navy as little better than a smuggler with piratical tendencies, until he made himself heroic by running French blockades, harassing French ships, and even turning up at the odd sea battle. He lives near Blackhaven with his wife and young family and is no longer quite so adventurous, so this ship is surplus to his requirements."

"Is he on board?" asked Antonia, who recalled the name.

"Oh, no. A ship should only have one captain at a time."

Their approach had been spotted from the ship, and while Julius tied the rowing boat to the side, a seaman swarmed down the ladder to take Edward on his back.

"Don't let go," Antonia said nervously, and then had to concentrate on negotiating the ladder herself, no easy task in skirts. Julius came right behind her, a comfort, and yet she wasn't sure she wanted him to see her graceless and occasionally immodest clamber.

Edward, who had had to stay in their cabin during both his Channel crossings because of Miss Talbot's seasickness, was utterly delighted to scamper about the deck, looking at everything from the massive sails above him to the wheel.

Antonia followed him, listening in fascination to Julius's explanations, watching as they raised the anchor, unfurled the sails, and began to glide over the sea. She had to hold on to her hat while salt spray was blown against her face, but she didn't care. Julius was in his natural element, and for the first time she began to understand his love of the sea with more than just her head. She felt the power and the awe and a peculiar sense of freedom.

She glanced up at him, smiling, and found his attention already on her. The jolt to her heart thrilled her, and yet that too seemed natural. One of those rare moments of total happiness washed over her. Such instants did not always have a reason, but for her, now, this one did. He stood beside her, a beloved stranger whom she seemed to have known forever. The contradictions did not bother her. And when he turned to answer Edward on his other side, his hand brushed against Antonia's. She followed her heart and curled her fingers around his. His hand closed at once, and even the deepest kiss had never felt so sweet.

It was a magical day, watching the town of Blackhaven and the towering castle drift by. Julius pointed out the Black Hill and his own land and house in the distance, the beach where they had played at pirates, and the cove next to it. Then she realized Julius was gazing further out to sea and a ship sailing on a parallel course.

Something in his stare made her say, "That's the same ship, isn't it? The one we think brought the horses?"

"Yes," he said. "It appears to be back. If it ever went very far away."

"What is it waiting for?"

"The return of the men from the horse fairs, I suppose." He took a glass from his pocket, and she smiled because even ten years ago, he had always had it with him. He pointed it toward the other ship.

"Are we going to chase it?" Edward asked excitedly.

"No." Julius turned the glass toward the shore. "No, we are going to have tea."

"On board?" Edward asked.

"Sadly, I didn't think to order provisions." Julius called orders to the seamen, who immediately began hauling ropes and sails. The ship began to rock and turn in a large, graceful arc, sailing back toward Blackhaven and closer to the shore. "But we can have tea at Black Hill. Someone should meet us on the shore."

Antonia wasn't sure she wanted to leave the ship just yet, let alone face Delilah's disapproval. But Julius nodded toward the horizon and some ugly black cloud. "I think there's a storm whipping up, and I'd rather have you safe ashore before it hits. Can you feel the wind has quickened?"

Now that he mentioned it, she could.

"Don't worry. We should have time." He didn't sound remotely anxious. In fact, she rather thought he was testing the speed and maneuverability of the ship, filling the sails with the stronger wind to rush toward the beach and then furling them and dropping anchor as close in to the shore as was safe.

This time, Julius climbed down the ladder first, with Edward on his back. As soon as Edward was safely delivered to the rowing boat, Julius came back for Antonia, but she was already halfway down the ladder, feeling much more agile than she had on the way up. They waved and shouted farewells to the amiable seamen, who grinned and waved back while Julius untied the boat and pushed it hard away from the ship's side.

"Do they come with the ship?" Antonia asked.

"They could do, though I cannot really afford to pay a standing crew."

"Will they find other ships?"

"Alban probably has space for them somewhere."

"But you couldn't sail it yourself, could you?"

"Not very easily," he admitted. "But there are benefits to employing seamen in the house and grounds."

She laughed. "You have thought this all out, haven't you?"

"To a degree."

They were halfway to the shore when they felt the first drops of rain. The boat bobbed a bit more wildly, but both wind and tide powered them in roughly the right direction. Julius's skill did the rest. Just before they reached the shore, the blackened sky opened and hurled its deluge.

"A downside to piracy," Julius said cheerfully to Edward, who at first found it all very amusing. By the time Julius jumped out and hauled the boat up on to the beach, they were all soaked through and Edward was shivering with the cold. Julius helped them both out of the boat, picked Edward up bodily, and seized Antonia's hand.

They began to run up a half-hidden path clearly well known to Julius. Another man, apparently a servant, met them a few moments later and took Edward from Julius, leading them to a shabby but blessedly closed carriage. He deposited Edward in it, then leapt up onto the box while Antonia and Julius piled inside too.

The horse set off at a bumping trot that made Antonia wince and Edward giggle. Julius rummaged beneath the seats for blankets and threw the first over the lad. Antonia wrapped it around him and hugged him to her side for greater warmth, though she was afraid of just making him wetter. They were all soaked to the skin.

Julius placed the other blanket around Antonia, his hands gentle as they held her shoulders for a moment.

"Sorry," he said, tossing his dripping hat on the bench beside him. "I mistimed it. Should have paid more attention to the sky and less to our mysterious ship. But we should be home in a trice and get you into some dry clothes."

After the bumpy track came a smoother road, and the horse picked up speed. The rain was still pounding on the carriage roof and flung at the windows by the rising wind. The horse galloped up the drive to the front door of the house. A servant erupted down the steps and threw open the carriage door, and they all bolted into the house.

"Ah," said Felicia, rushing across the hall to them. "No one warned you against excursions with Julius! Come with me!" She whisked Antonia up the curving staircase to the floor above and along a wood-paneled passage.

"You must be Edward," she said over her shoulder. "I'm Julius's sister, Felicia."

"I'm pleased to meet you, ma'am," Edward said politely. He was looking around him with interest, completely oblivious to everyone else's hurry.

Felicia threw open a door to a warm bedchamber. "The maid will bring hot water in a moment. I'll just see what I can find for you both to wear."

Antonia hauled off Edward's wet clothes and wrapped him in a towel, by which time a maid had brought the hot water, with which Antonia sponged him down before wrapping him up again. He was no longer shivering, but asking lots of questions about the house and who lived here.

Felicia reappeared with clothing. "Sorry, I had to steal the boot boy's Sunday best! It will still be too big for you, but it will be warm."

Ten minutes later, Antonia too was in warm, dry clothes borrowed from Felicia, who then took them downstairs to a cozy sitting room where a fire had been lit. Julius rose from one of the chairs at the hearth, a glass of brandy in his hand. He looked warm and dry but rather gloriously rumpled in casual old clothes and toweled hair he had forgotten to brush.

"And here is the hot chocolate," Felicia said, as the footman brought in a laden tray.

It was unexpectedly comfortable, drinking hot chocolate and eating warm scones and cake by the fire, while the wind and rain battered at the windows. Antonia spared a thought for the crew of the ship they had just left, but Julius maintained that they were experienced seamen and would be fine. He was more concerned for the fishermen whose livelihood depended on going to sea in all weathers, and in much smaller vessels.

The twins appeared, asking about Captain Alban's ship and whether or not Julius meant to buy it. A little later, Roderick and Lucy came in, apparently as delighted as the twins to discover Antonia and Edward. Cornelius arrived, damp-headed and anxious about the weather's effects on their crops, and Edward engaged him in precocious conversation about the possible harm and recovery. He was always interested in something, and all the Vales seemed to accept that.

He was also fascinated by the twins, who took him off happily for a tour of the house. The rain showed little sign of easing.

"You should probably just stay the night," Lucy said. "There's no point in getting cold and wet again, and I can see you are worried about Edward."

"No, no, I'm sure he's strong as an ox," Antonia said, not quite truthfully, "but I do hesitate to take your coachman and horses out in the storm. Either way, it seems we are doomed to put you out!"

"We are not in the least put out," Felicia assured her. "We are all glad of your company, and Edward is a delight."

"I think we shall have to go, though," Antonia decided with some reluctance. "Miss Talbot expects me back by dinnertime, and the storm will only make her worry more."

Julius said, "I'll send a man to Blackhaven on horseback with your message. He doesn't mind the weather, and it will be quicker than the carriage going by road."

Antonia hesitated, but in the end she was much too comfortable—and too afraid of taking Edward out in the cold again—to protest. She thanked him gracefully.

DINNER WAS DELIGHTFULLY informal, and Edward, much to his joy, was allowed to join them. Everyone talked across the table, even from one end to the other, in a dizzying variety of topics, banter, and argument. Even Delilah, who had joined them for dinner, spoke politely to Antonia, though without a great deal of enthusiasm. If anything, she seemed distracted.

Edward, though he insisted he would like to stay up longer, almost fell asleep at the table, and the twins showed Antonia to the room she had changed in. It now had the remains of a fire in the grate, and a truckle made up at the foot of the big bed.

"Felicia thought Edward would be more comfortable with you in a strange house," Leona said.

"That was very thoughtful of her."

Lawrence ruffled Edward's hair, which earned him a sleepy grin, and Leona gave him a brief hug before they danced off and Antonia helped her son into bed.

He was exhausted, poor mite, but showed no signs of fever or illness. She pulled the covers over him, kissed him, and sat on the edge of the bed to wait until he was asleep. It took about half a minute. She waited another couple of minutes then rose and returned to the drawing room.

The Vales were discussing general plans for the house and grounds. Julius, standing by the window and looking out at the storm, was nodding in agreement. Antonia sat on a vacant sofa and Roderick offered her a glass of wine, which she accepted.

"Is Edward settled?" Felicia asked her.

"Instantly!"

"Of course, he must be used to traveling," Lucy said. "He was in Vienna with you, was he not?"

"Indeed. And Paris. It is something of a bone of contention between his uncle and myself. But truly, I think Edward is more sociable and better educated than most boys of his age."

Delilah lifted her head from whatever she was sewing and glanced at Antonia. Her eyes looked troubled. Then she bent once more to her needle.

Julius sat next to Antonia, and immediately comfort and warmth spread through her. How could one be so soothed and yet so physically aware of the person next to them, not even touching? But then, the whole evening had felt dangerously comfortable, especially after the magic of the day spent with Julius. It seemed the enchantment went on.

Perhaps it was the wine.

As darkness fell, the rain lessened but still spattered against the window in smaller blasts. A maid drew the curtains while the footman brought tea.

Conversation was general, so there was no tête-à-tête with Julius. She barely looked at him, yet her awareness grew more and more intense. His legs were long and strong, and she imagined them without clothing, muscular and sliding along hers.

She blinked to dispel the shocking vision, feeling her cheeks burn. Marriage had not cured her of that kind of desire, the belief of something tender and wonderful, given and received. She tried to remember the unpleasant if blessedly few passages of intimacy with her husband, in the hope the memory would act as a shower of cold water.

It didn't. Instead, her wretched imagination placed Julius's face over her husband's, Julius's naked skin under her hands, his mouth lowering to hers, and it became a completely different act in her imagination. She had no hope of summoning Francis's memory.

She drew her hand across her face, hiding her gasp for breath, and all but jumped to her feet. "I believe I am as exhausted as Edward and will bid you goodnight. Thank you for your rescue, and for such a delightful evening."

Inevitably, the men all rose too, and Felicia waved away her thanks.

"If it was delightful, you made it so," Roderick said, with unexpected gallantry.

Julius said, "I'll light you up to your room."

Not you, please not you... But no one else offered, and to object would be to make more of it than he meant. And so she smiled, curtsied to the company, and left.

A light burned in the hall, but she was afraid to look at him until he lit one of the candles at the foot of the stairs. The glow flared upward, casting his profile into sharp blades and shadowed hollows. Her mouth felt dry; her body burned.

She walked quickly up the staircase and along the passage to her door. She swallowed hard, and turned with as natural a smile as she could manage.

"Thank you, Julius. I left the lamp turned low for Edward, so I shall be fine now. Goodnight."

She grasped the door handle tightly behind her, so that he would not see the trembling of her hands. But his gaze seemed riveted to her face, dropping only from her eyes to her lips. Her heart drummed mercilessly. Slowly, as if he could not help it, he raised the backs of his curled fingers to her cheek.

"Are you well, Antonia?" he asked softly. "Have I offended you?"

She almost laughed. "Goodness, no. It was a lovely day, and your family is most kind." Her voice was a little shaky, but with luck, he would not notice.

His knuckles glided gently across her cheek like silk, and then his hand opened and slid around her nape.

She gasped at the sheer, devastating pleasure of his touch. "Good-night, Julius," she said firmly.

"I suppose it must be so…"

Was there a question there? Was he asking…?

His fingers moved against her nape, his caress almost distracted. His gaze devoured her, searching and finding, surely, her answer to the question he had not quite asked. The tension stretched between them like a bow.

His lips quirked. "My door is the one at the end. If you change your mind."

He bent his head, and she almost moaned with her need for his kiss. If his mouth touched hers, she would be lost and fiercely, helplessly, glad of it. His cheek, rough with stubble, brushed against hers, and he kissed her neck, just below her ear.

Involuntarily, her mouth opened at the sudden pleasure. And then his hand fell away, and he stepped back and strode away.

She almost stumbled into her bedchamber, breathing so loudly that she was afraid of waking Edward. A few deep breaths and she felt able to turn up the lamp a little. She went across to Edward and touched his hand and his forehead. They were pleasantly warm, quite without the tight, hectic heat of fever. And he was sound asleep.

Relieved, she walked to the window, wishing she could open it to cool her cheeks, her very blood. But she could not let in the rain and wind, so she merely slipped behind the curtain and gazed out at the darkness.

The window looked across the countryside to the sea. After several minutes, she heard the sounds of everyone else going to bed—footsteps and hushed voices and murmured goodnights.

She smiled and almost felt ready to retire, too. God knew she was tired enough. If only she could stop remembering that Julius was under the same roof. *My door is the one at the end. If you change your mind.* At least she had managed to hide what was truly on her mind! She hoped.

She took one last look out to sea. The light of a ship bobbed faintly, just within her view. In fact, the light flashed twice and then went out.

What if that was the horse ship? Signaling to someone on the shore? Specifically to the nasty man who had accosted her and Edward on Sunday.

Why on earth would it be? Many ships passed this way every day, sailing up the coast from the south or across from Ireland or the Americas to the west. It might even be a ship in trouble because of the storm.

She hesitated, aware that her urge to bring the matter to Julius's attention was not clear-cut. She both feared and longed to see him again this evening. Now. Forever.

Oh God, I am mad.

But if it was Lord Linfield, or anyone else of her acquaintance who was interested in the mystery, would she not tell him? Why should she not tell Julius? Was it not simply a kind of cowardice to wait here and do nothing?

She moved slowly toward the smaller bed and again touched her son's skin. Still healthy and peaceful. She snatched up a candle, lit it from the lamp, and hurried from the room.

Chapter Twelve

THERE WAS ONLY one door at the end of the passage. Antonia hovered near it in sudden indecision. She breathed in and out twice, to be sure, and then scratched softly at the door.

She had barely touched it when it opened. For an instant, Julius stood in the center of the glow coming from her candle in front of him and from the light within the room. He was once more in his shirt sleeves, but this time he had no waistcoat and no cravat either. His eye patch was still in place, adding an air of darkness, of unreadability, to his face.

She opened her mouth to speak, to blurt out what she had seen and suspected about the ship, but he gripped her wrist while he snatched the candle from her and whisked her inside his bedchamber.

In fact, it wasn't that bad. It appeared to be a mere sitting room. A rather masculine one. The walls bore paintings of ships and the sea. A bookcase was full of clearly well-thumbed books. One or two seemed to have water damage on the spines. An old leather armchair sat by the fireplace, but from the squashed state of the cushions in front of the hearth, that was where he had been sitting—or sprawling—most recently. She liked to imagine him lounging so casually. It felt intimate, at once comfortable and sensual.

She tried not to see the open door to the bedchamber beyond.

"I was looking out of the window," she said in a rush. "There's a ship—I'm sure it's the same one. I think it was signaling the shore."

"So do I," he said.

Her mouth was already open to justify her opinion, but at that she shut it again and swallowed. "You do? Then…then you saw it, too?"

"I had to have a room with a view of the sea."

"Of course." She should have realized that. So stupid… "Then I'm sorry to disturb you."

"Don't be. I am not disturbed. Or not in the way you mean."

Her eyes slid away from his. "Will you do anything? About the ship?"

"Not tonight. I don't think they'll risk the longboat in the storm. I think any signaling was all one-sided, from the ship."

She nodded, and could think of nothing else to say, except words that stuck in her throat. The past had come alive and fused with the present, and… And she really had to go.

"Goodnight, then," she managed, and all but bolted back toward the door.

"Antonia."

His voice stayed her, and she stood quite still, her back to him.

"Is the ship really why you came?"

She closed her eyes. "Yes. I couldn't *not* come, just because it was you." Laughter caught in her throat. "Oh dear, I'm not making any sense, am I? Again…"

She did not hear him move, and yet suddenly he spoke right behind her.

"Marry me, Antonia."

The words seemed to embrace her, warm and healing and unbearably sweet. And unbearably painful, because she was no longer the naïve young girl he had asked ten years ago. Whatever lies her body tried to tell her, she had been married and knew better.

She opened her eyes but did not turn. "Whatever happened to courting?"

"That was yesterday. I have moved on."

In spite of herself, laughter bubbled up. He touched her shoulders, and all the old awareness was reignited.

"If you had not come, I would have been good, let you take your time. I would have waited. I still will, if you ask it of me. Even though I can feel your desire, almost as urgent as my own. We have waited ten years, Antonia. Let it be now. A marriage between *us*. Which we can let Mr. Grant confirm at a date of your choice."

He moved his hands down her arms, and his lips touched her nape, making her head twist with pleasure.

It was now or never.

"I am afraid you won't like being married to me," she blurted. "I am not…"

"Not what?" he asked, his breath still hot on her skin.

"Physical," she whispered. "I have been married, and I know. You are *very* physical. And I am not."

There was a pause. She waited for the disappointment to hit her, to hurt. And yet she would bear it because she loved him. But he had to know.

"Oh, my dear," he said softly, turning her into his arms. "What rot."

He bent and took her mouth in the gentlest, most sensual kiss she had ever known. His lips caressed; his tongue glided and seduced until she sought it with her own.

"Is this not physical?" he whispered into her mouth. He slid one finger slowly down the length of her spine, making her arch into him. "Do you not *feel* it?"

"That is *kissing*."

His smile flickered as he kissed her again. His hand moved over her hip until she pressed against his thrilling hardness. He released her mouth before she was ready, eliciting a tiny sound of protest, but he caressed the length of her lips with his and softly kissed the corner of her mouth before gliding over her cheek to her ear and her neck, down her throat to the hollow where her pulse galloped against his lips.

"Do you not like this?" he murmured, sweeping his hand from her thigh up her side to settle on her breast. His mouth, hot and tender, moved lower. "And this?"

Whatever she had been meaning to say came out only as a low moan of pleasure and need. He freed her breast and kissed there, too. Heat and exquisite delight rolled over her in waves as he teased her nipple with lips and tongue. She tangled her fingers in his hair, to cling, to feel it.

"I *know* you like this," he whispered, straightening. He moved his hips against hers, caressing her with his whole body as he took back her mouth in a deep, arousing kiss that ended too soon. "And there is so much more you will like... Will you let me show you?"

They both knew the answer, but she could not find the words. So she kissed him instead, and that was sweet and heady. His fingers busied themselves with the hooks and ties of her borrowed clothes. She let out a gasp of triumph as she found her own way under his shirt to his hot, naked skin. In a welter of desire she had never known, she was literally swept off her feet and into his arms.

She tried to object when his uneven step reminded her of his injury, but he then kissed her again more fiercely. When he set her down in the bedchamber, where a few candles burned, her clothes all slid to the floor. Involuntarily, she tried to cover herself with her arms, but he caught her wrists, and her embarrassment died in the glow of his devouring eyes. There was power in this, and unexpected new pleasure.

"God, you are beautiful," he said unsteadily. "I have imagined this for so long. You here with me, naked and loving."

"I do love you," she said. "I always have."

He threw off his shirt in one swift, startling moment, and reached for her. At last she had his bare skin against hers, hot and smooth, his hands sweeping down the length of her back and over her rear. He lifted her again, laying her on the cool sheets. She heard her own breath quick and shallow as he stripped off the last of his clothes and came for her.

The sight of his nakedness astonished her, but there was no time to fear it. He closed her hand around his hardness, letting her feel its amazing heat, the velvet softness of the skin. But now he caressed her ever more intimately, slipping his fingers between her legs, and the clamoring of her body rose with wild new pleasure. She had never in her wildest dreams imagined a man stroking her there, or felt the rushing of such ecstasy. She reached up blindly for his mouth, gasping and writhing.

He slid inside her, and she could not believe this was the same act as her husband had occasionally performed. When he began to move, the pleasure intensified once more. There was only Julius, his face above her, his body joined with her.

"Now we are one," he ground out, stretching within her. "And you do like it."

"Oh, I do," she gasped, and this time they fell into bliss together.

JULIUS'S HEART SANG.

He had wanted her for so long, latterly mostly in his dreams and in his moments of harsh honesty. Until today, when everything had cleared in his mind and he read her own desire. He loved her. He had always loved her, always wanted her, and now with a strength that surpassed even his more youthful lusts.

When he had heard her soft footsteps approach his rooms, his heart had almost stopped. He had wanted to tear open the door and drag her inside. Instead, he had stood on the other side of the wood, listening to her breathe, knowing he must let her take her own time and that she might well change her mind and retreat again.

The ship was largely an excuse. He appreciated that. What had truly astounded him was her belief that she was not "physical" enough to please him. The thought of her gritting her teeth and letting him slake his lust appalled him, though it was clearly all she had known with Macy.

He wanted to please her. For her own sake, he wanted her to know all the joys of love, and resolved to teach her, even at the expense of his own raging desires. Moreover, it had to be *now*. He would not have her waiting and fearing what was to come—some dreadful wedding night like her last.

And so his vague hopes of seducing her had become a determination to pleasure her. And he had. He was as proud of that as of all his naval battles. The joy she had given him was a bonus, an unexpected wonder that thrilled through him still as he held her loosely and tenderly in his arms.

His lethargic body wanted to sleep. His mind insisted he stay awake and savor every moment of Antonia naked in his arms after their first loving. There would be many more. Many, many more.

Fresh arousal seeped through him. He quelled it as best he could, for her sake.

Her lips brushed his shoulder. "Is that how it is meant to be? For married people?"

"For lovers, married or not."

She swallowed. "I thought it was because I did not love him. But I think it was because he did not love me. He had no love."

He did not want to talk of Macy here, but this seemed to be something she needed. He stroked her hair, spreading it across his face and inhaling it. It smelled of the sea. "I'm sorry he hurt you. And yet so glad we have been given this second chance. I will not leave you again."

She smiled, raising herself on her elbow. "Nor I you. Except for right now, when I must go back to my own chamber."

"Stay." He kissed her with lazy passion and rejoiced in her instant response.

Curious and tender, she traced the edges of his eye patch with her fingertips. "When we are married, will you stay with me all night?"

"Every night. Unless you kick me out." He caught her probing fingers, dragging them away from his missing eye. He would not allow such ugliness to mar the moment.

She let him. She even kissed him. "Perhaps you could kick me out now, in a gentle kind of way, just to make me go."

"Don't go."

"You are no help." She dropped her forehead on his. "I don't want to leave Edward for too long."

"He will be fine, you know." Still, he loved her all the more for her care of the child. He even rose with her, draped Felicia's gown over her head, and gathered the rest of her clothing into a ball while she collected hairpins from the floor and the bed.

He opened the door for her and listened for sounds of wakeful siblings. Finding all quiet, he took her in his arms again for another long, tender kiss. And then, reluctantly, he released her. She left him with a quick, mischievous smile, which somehow increased his own happiness as she vanished into her own chamber. Quietly, he closed his door.

Stark naked, he fell back into bed and slept, with his heart still singing.

THE MORNING DAWNED dry and fair. The earth, battered by wind and rain, smelled sweet as he strode around the grounds, releasing the excess energy of his body, even though he didn't want to go too far and miss Antonia at breakfast.

In the end, he met her and Edward in the garden, and any possible awkwardness was covered by the boy rushing at him with glee and pounding him with questions about the storm and the scattered flower heads and a few sad-looking plants. Clearly, Edward had suffered no ill effects from yesterday's soaking. Nor had Antonia, judging from her glowing face. She was wearing her own gown again, duly cleaned and dried, and her beauty hit him afresh, along with gladness, the memory of last night's passion, and a sudden resurgence of lust.

Still, there was a new, quieter pleasure in giving her his arm and letting Edward dance ahead of them along the path and into the house. It already felt familiar, like a harbinger of their life together.

Delilah, Felicia, and Aubrey were discovered in the breakfast parlor. Cornelius was already out inspecting the fields. Julius would have to go and see what damage there was to tenants' property. There would be much to do, though what he really wanted was to escort Antonia back to Blackhaven.

"You are welcome to spend the day with us," Felicia said when they had sat down to their chosen platefuls. Julius spotted genuine liking there and was glad. Felicia, the most sociable of his sisters, had missed female friendship.

"Oh, you are kind, thank you," Antonia replied. "But I have already neglected my duties shamefully. I must get back to Miss Talbot."

Only for a little. And then she need never leave him again. Now that happiness was upon him, he yearned for it with an urgency that took his breath away. The years of anger and loneliness might never have been. They were worth it for *this*, for her...

He dragged his gaze away from her before he embarrassed them both, and encountered Delilah's gaze instead. No, she still didn't like Antonia, but there was something else in her eyes he could not read. He would speak to her later.

Aubrey went to order the carriage and offered to escort Antonia.

"Then I can get my water drinking over with at once," he added with a quick grin.

"Do you want company?" Delilah asked him.

"I'm happy for it, but there is no requirement," Aubrey replied. "I have some things to do in town."

He was clearly up to something. Julius silently wished him well.

A few minutes later, he rose to accompany Antonia into the hall, where a servant waited with her duly dried and repaired hat and pelisse. Julius handed her into the waiting carriage, secretly running his thumb along her palm, and was gratified to feel her fingers cling to his for a moment before she released him.

Reluctantly, he stepped back to make way for Aubrey and Edward, with whom he shook hands, and then the horses trotted forward, carrying her away from him.

But not for long.

With effort, he swung around and strode for the stables. Time to examine the damage around the estate and confer with Cornelius.

IT WAS AFTERNOON before he found the time to ride over to the shore, tie up his horse, and climb warily down the hidden path to the beach where he had seen the longboat. He kept a careful watch for the lookout who had threatened Antonia and Edward. But though he found signs on the beach of someone living there—the remains of a fire, a few bird bones half buried in the sand—the man himself appeared to be absent.

So was the ship that had been anchored opposite.

Had they completed their business, whatever it was, and sailed already? Was all this effort and threat and secrecy really worth it for a few unhappy horses? Julius did not underestimate the difficulty of transporting the animals, let alone unloading them via longboats and persuading them up a treacherous cliff path. Surely there were simpler ways, even if the horses were stolen?

After a careful survey of the empty beach and the rocks, he made his way to the cave. Lifting the trailing weeds, he was triumphant to see the boat still there. He listened very carefully, but none of his senses picked up any human presence. He stepped inside, letting the covering weeds fall back behind him.

Little light now penetrated, so he had to feel his way around the boat. Jumping up, he hauled himself inside, but found nothing more than a rather ill-smelling bedroll. This was where the lookout slept, so he was still somewhere around.

Hastily, he eased himself out of the boat again and cracked his shin painfully against something solid and wooden. Muffling his curse, he bent to feel a large crate, but it was nailed shut. He shuffled on and found another, and this time, the lid lifted easily, as though someone had recently inspected the contents. He reached inside and closed his hands over cool wood and metal.

His blood chilled, for he knew that shape. The crate was full of them. Rifles and pistols.

Chapter Thirteen

ANTONIA WAS UNCERTAIN how much to tell Miss Talbot. Her heart full, she wanted to blurt out the amazing news that she was once more engaged to marry Captain Sir Julius Vale. But last night was a haze of wild happiness, and his proposal was all part of that, carried more urgently, no doubt, on the tide of the emotion surging between them. Afraid to break the spell by too eagerly breaking the news before he was ready, she held her tongue, and largely let Edward explain about the ship and the storm and staying the night with Captain Vale, whose brother and sister were twins.

Antonia said only, "I'm so sorry about staying away so long. I just couldn't bring myself to take Edward out in the cold and wet again."

"Of course you could not. You did exactly the right thing and seem none the worse for your adventures. Now, shall we totter round to the pump room before we decide on something more interesting to do with our day?"

"Of course," Antonia agreed.

There was no sign of Aubrey by the time they reached the pump room, although, of course, he might easily have come and gone if there was no one congenial to detain him. He gave Antonia the impression of a young man in constant search of trouble or entertainment, probably both, and he could probably conjure them from very little.

They were just about to leave again when Timothy walked in, once more with Mr. Dunnett. Now there was an odd friendship.

"What a fortuitous meeting!" Mr. Dunnett said, beaming.

"But hardly surprising," Miss Talbot said tartly. "We come here every day to take the waters."

"But I have never caught you before to thank you for your very generous donation to the hospital."

"There is no need, I assure you. And I'm afraid you must excuse us, for we have a few errands this morning."

"Ah. I was hoping for a moment of Antonia's time," Timothy said.

Antonia's heart sank. "Edward is with Nurse Suze."

"I do not doubt it," Timothy said with an apparent attempt at generosity.

"I can spare you five minutes, Antonia," Miss Talbot said. "I shall wait for you outside."

It was a kindness in her, giving Antonia the opportunity to deal quickly with whatever this was, just not too long. Antonia bowed to the inevitable.

Both men rose with Miss Talbot, and Dunnett hastened to open the door for her, though, rather to Antonia's surprise, he closed it again behind her and came back to the table. She blinked from him to Timothy. What on earth was the point of privacy from Miss Talbot if Dunnett remained here?

"I am pleased to tell you, Antonia," Timothy said smoothly, "that I have today received an offer for your hand in marriage."

Whatever she had expected, it was not that. Her jaw showed an unladylike tendency to drop. Could Julius really have spoken to Timothy? Already? Timothy had no say in her re-marriage, although she supposed it concerned him so far as it would affect Edward.

"F-from whom?" she stammered.

Timothy's eyebrows lifted. "Why, from Mr. Dunnett. Who else were you expecting to offer for you?"

"No one." She stared in disbelief. "Mr. Dunnett and I are barely acquainted."

"Ah, but Dunnett and I are old friends, and he knows a great deal about you from me."

She could only imagine—in which case, why on earth was Dunnett offering for her?

"I admire you hugely," Dunnett said with great seriousness. "Hugely, I assure you. It is time I married, and I am persuaded you will be the perfect wife for me." Perhaps he read the lack of enthusiasm in her stunned face, for he added hastily, "And of course I shall do all in my power to make you happy."

Antonia swallowed and summoned the barely recalled phrases from her youth. "I thank you for your offer. While entirely sensible of the honor, I am afraid I must regretfully decline—"

"I don't think you quite understand, Antonia," Timothy interrupted, his voice sharp. "I have given my blessing, since it solves all our problems."

"What problems?"

"That of Edward. And that of you gadding about the Continent with strangers."

"The Talbots have been good friends to me," she said in sudden panic. "And you know there is *no* problem with Edward."

Timothy curled his lip. "You say that when you took him away from these so-called friends in order to spend the night in that even more ramshackle establishment at Black Hill? The house is full of old Vale's by-blows, and who knows who else's!"

Antonia tilted her chin. "I can only assume you have never been there, for you are entirely mistaken."

"You are quick to their defense," Timothy sneered. "Can it be you are so quick to reject Dunnett because you expect an offer from the man who left you at the altar ten years ago?"

"He did not leave me at the altar," she said between her teeth.

"And my offers are none of—"

Timothy did not let her finish. "In any case, you would be foolish to take such an offer seriously. He was overheard saying he might well propose to you, win your acceptance, and then leave you as revenge— for what, I can only imagine."

"Overheard by whom?" she asked.

Timothy waved that aside. "It hardly matters. He was talking to his sister. The eldest one. She is a bastard, too."

Delilah. Something clawed in her stomach. Now, the story was almost believable. And yet she didn't believe it.

"The Vale family does not concern you or Mr. Dunnett. Nor does it weigh on my answer to Mr. Dunnett. Now, if you will excuse me, Miss Talbot—"

"A moment," Timothy barked. An attendant walked past their table, moving on when Dunnett shook his head at her emphatically. Timothy lowered his voice, but his eyes were like steel. "I believe there is no question of your turning down Mr. Dunnett. Unless you now want Edward to go away to school."

She blinked in confusion. "What?"

"I have made my decision," Timothy said coldly. "Edward will live in the house of a man I trust, or he will go away to school."

"Timothy, you can't!" she burst out. "He is six years old!"

"I can and I will. Unless you marry Dunnett."

"I have no other choice than Mr. Dunnett?" she asked desperately. She even cast him a hasty smile, adding, "Kind and honorable as I know he is."

"None. He is the only man I know and trust prepared to take you on. You and another man's child. The banns will be called on Sunday. You may run along now to Miss Talbot and give her the good news. She will be looking for a new companion."

"I THINK THEY stole the horses in Ireland and shipped them over here to the horse fairs, then used the money to buy guns to arm another Irish rebellion."

In his study, Mr. Winslow, the magistrate, regarded Julius with some consternation. "Would a few horses pay for so many guns? Besides, Ireland is quiet just now."

"Ireland is never quiet. Resentment merely burns under the surface from where it bubbles up every so often. And people die. I shan't debate the rights and wrongs of their cause with you, but I cannot sit by while so many weapons are transported over my land. I have seen enough of war to wish it on nobody else."

"They may have come *off* the boat with the horses," Winslow suggested.

"No, they definitely weren't there when I first found the longboat," Julius said.

"Either way, we need them in safe custody. I'll send to Colonel Doverton at the barracks to have them removed."

"You *could* do that," Julius said. "Or we could wait and see who collects them and arrest them all at once."

Winslow suddenly sat up and began rummaging through the papers on his desk. "Wait. I had a report from the excise fellows... A revenue cutter found a vessel skulking in one of the inlets only a few miles up the coast. It seemed to have sustained damage in the storm last night. They were trying to repair it. The excisemen searched it and found nothing on board." He found the papers he was looking for and skimmed down the page. "The captain claimed to be sailing to Liverpool to collect various cargos for Glasgow and the islands. Livestock, among other things."

Winslow's eyes gleamed as he glanced up at Julius. "I wonder if we *could* catch them all together?"

"The ship, the crew, and the guns," Julius said. "A perfect haul, if we can manage it. The Royal Navy would have been useful but…maybe we can manage it without them. Do you happen to be on good terms with Captain Alban? I have a loan of one of his ships, and if he brings another, plus the revenue cutter…"

"I'll go and see Alban right away. And see if we can't get Doverton's help to keep watch."

"How long will it take them to repair the ship?"

Winslow consulted his letter. "A couple of days at least, probably longer."

"Only they won't want to leave the guns unattended. I wonder where the men who brought them are hiding out?"

"Somewhere not too far away from their cargo," Winslow said uneasily. "I think you and your family need to be very careful."

"And any observation will have to be subtle," Julius warned.

"Absolutely." Winslow glanced at his watch. "You'll stay for tea, Vale? My wife will be disappointed if you don't."

What Julius really wished to do was go home, change, and drive in to Blackhaven to visit Antonia. Perhaps he could take her to dine at the hotel, along with Linfield and his sister, of course.

Later. Civility compelled him to accept Winslow's offer, especially if they were pursuing the guns business together. "Thank you," he said. "I should love to."

A COUPLE OF hours later, he strode through his sitting room, smartly dressed in his new civilian evening coat and pantaloons. Energy thrummed through him. He wondered if Antonia would agree to calling the banns on Sunday…

A knock at the door halted him as he bent to pick up his hat. "Enter!" he commanded, and Delilah walked in.

"Oh, you are dressed to go out. And very smartly, too. What event are you gracing with your presence tonight?"

Despite her wry tone, he gathered that she was pleased for him.

"I don't know yet," he confessed. "I was hoping to dine with Linfield, but I may be too late."

The pleasure vanished from her eyes. "By Linfield, I gather you mean Mrs. Macy."

"She is usually there with Miss Talbot," he said evenly.

"You only saw her this morning," Delilah said. "Do you have to pursue her quite so assiduously?"

"I don't *have* to, no."

His naval lieutenants would have recognized that tone and known to step back. Delilah, however, was his sister.

"Julius, you are making a spectacle of the woman and harming her reputation into the bargain. For goodness' sake, leave her alone for a few days."

He regarded her with rueful understanding. "Disingenuous, Delly. Don't pretend you give a fig for Mrs. Macy's reputation. Though I hope you will come to."

Color seeped into her cheeks, but she did not back down. She rarely did. "I care for yours. I don't want you making a fool of yourself. More than that, I don't want her ruining your life a second time."

This was a conversation he had planned for tomorrow, after he had spoken to Antonia again. But today would do just as well. Delilah would have to understand.

"There is no question of that," he said. "We understand the lies told to each of us ten years ago. And you should know, I have asked Mrs. Macy to marry me, and she has accepted."

Delilah spun away from him. Her fists clenched at her sides and then slowly unclenched. "I'm afraid you must be told that she will not marry you. She is already engaged to another, much richer man. She must be stringing you along for reasons of her own. Revenge, no doubt, because you sailed away from her before. Remember, she did not see your agony then."

"You make her sound like a monster," he said impatiently, striding past her to the door. "Stop being ridiculous."

She caught his arm. "Can't you see it is *you* being ridiculous? Julius, she is going to marry Mr. Dunnett!"

He blinked and then laughed, which seemed to surprise her. "Dunnett isn't rich, and she barely knows him."

"Oh, he is a lot richer than you know," she retorted. Two spots of angry color seemed to be burned into her cheeks. "I had a very enlightening conversation with Mr. Timothy Macy just the other day. She used your interest in her to inspire Dunnett to propose. But I suppose she couldn't tell you that while she was at your mercy in a boat in a storm and then a guest in your house!"

The idiocy was no longer funny. "I did not constrain her to come with me, and you have gone beyond ridiculous to offensive on so many points that I don't know where to begin. Just *never* imagine I shall tolerate it. Goodnight."

She snatched her fingers back from his arm, looking as though he had hit her, but he was too irritated to do anything but walk away.

Although he did not believe a word of it, he was annoyed to have his euphoria interrupted by such malicious silliness. It was not like Delilah to behave so—she was neither stupid nor spiteful. Therefore, she must have been somehow induced to believe the nonsense. Macy was no doubt convincing when he chose to be. After all, Julius had a suspicion he was behind his forced parting from Antonia ten years ago.

He scowled as he climbed into the carriage, but as they bumped and slogged over roads still muddy from the storm, ever closer to Blackhaven, he found his mind's image of Antonia gradually banished all annoyance. Excitement at seeing her again was at the forefront of his thoughts. After years of fighting loneliness, anger, and regret, entirely unexpected happiness beckoned. He realized that he had never stopped loving her. She deserved happiness, and he yearned to provide it.

As he leapt from the carriage outside the hotel, he was filled with the memory of their night together, and delightful imaginings of many such nights, plus days of laughter and friendship, even children who would plague and entertain Edward...

He strode across the foyer, feeling as if all the energy would burst from him if he could not see her now.

"Will you ask Miss Talbot and Lord Linfield if they will receive me?" he said to the clerk at the desk. "If they have not yet dined, I shall be happy to wait for them in the dining room."

"Captain Vale, is it not?" the clerk said. "One moment, if you please, and I shall inquire."

Rather to Julius's surprise, the man scuttled off himself, leaving the desk unattended. Julius paced the floor, his sense of anticipation as urgent as any schoolboy embarking upon his first assignation.

At the sound of footsteps, he spun around, but saw not Antonia, nor even Linfield, but Timothy Macy strutting toward him.

Julius felt his lips curling with distaste, but, recalling the prime reason for his presence, he contented himself with the minimum nod required by civility.

"Sir Julius," Macy said cooly.

"Macy."

"I am told you have been asking for Miss Talbot and Lord Linfield."

Julius's eyebrows flew up. "I cannot imagine why."

Macy flushed slightly, but snapped back. "Because if, as I suspect, your true purpose is to bother my sister-in-law, I must decline to accommodate you."

"When you acquire such power, Mr. Macy—though I cannot imagine how you ever could—then I will reconsider discussing the matter. You will excuse me."

"I will not." Macy stood his ground. "I cannot allow you to harass my sister any further."

"I may return that compliment, at least. Miss Vale *is* my sister."

Macy's flush deepened, but he thrust his chin forward aggressively. "The matter is entirely different. I merely imparted some information to Miss Vale. You are pursuing Mrs. Macy with offensive advances."

"I am rarely offensive," Julius said, "though I believe I might make an exception in your case."

"For God's sake, man, can you not take a hint? Mrs. Macy is engaged to marry Mr. Dunnett and declines to see you ever again. If you dare to force the issue, Mr. Dunnett and I will take legal action on her behalf."

"I am seeing a pattern here," Julius said softly. "And I do not like it." He raised one arm to block Macy from sidestepping him, and without another word strode toward the dining room. The clerk at the desk was pretending not to see him. Julius suspected he had been instructed to inform Macy as soon as Captain Vale asked for any of Linfield's party. Presumably Macy had spun him some plausible yarn also.

Julius had no idea whether or not they were in the public dining room, but it got him out of Macy's way while he looked. He refused to start a brawl where Antonia's name might be bandied about.

He saw her at once, at a quiet table in the corner with Lord Linfield, Miss Talbot, and another gentleman he did not know. Except, of course, that it was not Dunnett! Macy must think him an imbecile to fall for such a tale.

She was beautiful, graceful, everything he had ever wanted and more besides. His heart ached, because despite the faint smile on her lips, he could tell she was distracted. He hoped she was thinking of him, though she had grown so used to hiding her feelings that it would be hard to tell until she looked across the room and saw him.

"Are you dining tonight, sir?" a waiter asked him.

"No, I believe I am too late," Julius replied, "but I'd like you to give a message to Lord Linfield that I shall await him in the coffee room if he and his party have no other engage—"

He broke off, for Antonia looked up and saw him.

There was no mistaking the utter dismay in her face, or the fear and misery chasing after it.

The blood ran cold in his veins. Dear God, was Macy right after all? Was he so obsessed, so selfish, that he had not seen this before? Had she been too afraid to refuse him? For an instant, his own fear and utter shame held him paralyzed.

Until he remembered that Antonia was afraid of no one. She had never been some submissive, milk-and-water miss. He recalled her standing up to the thieves' watchman on the beach only the other day. Relief poured through him along with a different anxiety altogether. Something was wrong. Very wrong.

"Pass the message, if you please," he said abruptly to the waiter, and turned on his heel. Her white, frightened face haunted his every step.

The coffee room was empty, which at least meant he could pace relentlessly without disturbing anyone else.

Would she even come?

In fact, he heard Miss Talbot's voice sooner than expected. "I shall wait right here at the door. If you are sure."

"Perfectly," Antonia said, low but determined.

She walked in and pushed the door behind her, not quite closing it. She looked white and was trembling.

He strode toward her, his hands held out. "Antonia, what is it? What is wrong?"

She stepped back, raising both hands as though to fend him off. He was so stunned that he stopped dead, staring at her, trying desperately to read the expression in her pale, determined face.

"I am afraid what we talked about yesterday cannot be." Her voice was steady and yet sounded as toneless as if she were reading something she did not understand. "It grieves me, but I hope you will

THE CAPTAIN'S OLD LOVE

understand there is no other way. I am betrothed to Mr. Dunnett and must ask you not to contact me again. I wish..." At last, her voice cracked and she finished unsteadily. "I wish you every happiness with someone else. Goodbye."

With disbelief, he realized she was leaving, which at least galvanized him into action. He all but sprinted after her out the door in time to see her taking Miss Talbot's arm. "Antonia, for God's sake, speak to me."

"I have said everything I can say," she all but whispered, and he had the feeling she was held together by the frailest of threads. Fury that someone should have done this to her warred with helplessness.

"Five minutes," he said. It came out as a bark, like an order issued on deck, which was not remotely what he intended, and understandably, she did not turn to face him. But Miss Talbot did, glaring at him over her shoulder as if he did not know his own lapse in courtesy.

Then, to his surprise, she mouthed, "Later." And he was left gazing after their backs as they walked back toward the dining room.

At the foot of the stairs, Macy and Dunnett stood together, looking unbearably smug.

Chapter Fourteen

ONE THING WAS clear to Julius as he strode unevenly along the road. Macy and Dunnett were in alliance. Together, somehow, they had won Antonia's obedience, and it was breaking her heart.

Julius would not stand for that. Which was what turned his steps now toward the hospital. He needed to know who Dunnett was, and how he was connected to Macy. Why was Macy so eager for Antonia to marry Dunnett? Delilah had implied he was rich, but if that was true, he did not seem the kind of man to take a low-salaried position administering a charity hospital.

He had hoped to find Samson, his most trusted source of information, on duty. But the woman who let him in said Dr. Lampton was here for an emergency, since it was Samson's day off. "Do you need him, sir?" she asked.

"No, I don't, though you might tell him I'm here when you see him." Julius strode directly over to what he knew to be Dunnett's office and tried to open the door. "This is locked."

"Yes, sir. Mr. Dunnett always locks it."

"Why? Does he keep money in there?"

"I couldn't say. Records, mainly, of patients and donors, who gives what and when. He says it's private."

I'll wager it is. "Do you have the key?"

"Oh, no, sir. Only Dr. Samson has it." She frowned. "And maybe

Dr. Lampton."

Julius sighed. "Where is he?"

Dr. Lampton was discovered in the room used for single patients who were not expected to live.

"Out," he growled at Julius as soon as he stuck his head in the door.

Julius, who had met the doctor before, did not take offense, and waited in the passage, pacing once more as though on the deck of his ship.

At last, the door was flung open and Lampton scowled at him. "What do you want?"

"The keys to Dunnett's office."

Lampton's scowl deepened impossibly, then vanished as he rummaged in his pocket and came out with an entire ring full of keys, which he tossed wordlessly to Julius before retreating back into the room and closing the door.

Julius returned to Dunnett's office and, after trying several likely-looking but wrong keys, managed to let himself in.

The room was immaculately tidy. The old but large desk in the middle of the floor was quite clear apart from basic writing materials. Rows of ledgers occupied a bookcase behind. Ignoring them, since they were on open display, Julius turned to the tall cabinet beside it. This turned out not to be locked either, but contained only records of the patients who had passed through the hospital, their ailments, and the results of their treatment. Some showed where the patient had gone when they left.

Interesting, but hardly what he was looking for.

He closed the cabinet and carried the first two ledgers to the desk. He was still poring over the figures when Dr. Lampton came in bearing two cups of tea, one of which he set down by Julius's elbow before perching on the edge of the desk.

"What are you looking for?" Lampton asked.

"Whatever it is, I'm not finding it. How is your patient?"

"Hopeful. You know, you really won't be doing us a favor if Dunnett takes a pet at your interference and leaves us. He brings huge amounts of money into the hospital, much more than we ever received before he came."

"I'm gathering that. He has regular donations coming in every quarter from people who don't even live here."

"And from those who do." The doctor sipped his tea.

Julius closed the ledger in front of him with a snap. "And all this money is in the bank? Who has access to it?"

"Board members and Dunnett himself."

"Who is on the board?"

Lampton shrugged. "Myself, Tristram Grant, Colonel Doverton, and Braithwaite for a little aristocratic weight. Samson keeps an eye on supplies and orders what we need. Dunnett pays for it from our healthy bank balance. It's all working remarkably well, so I beg you not to bring it all tumbling down."

Julius became aware he was drumming his fingers on top of the ledger and forced himself to stop. "Who is Dunnett?" he asked abruptly. "How does he come to be here?"

"He came to the town about a year ago—for the waters, like everyone else, or so he said."

Julius pounced. "So he said? You don't believe him?"

Lampton hesitated, which seemed to be rare for him. "I do recall a vague impression at the time that he might be running away from something. But I had no reason and certainly no evidence. He came to one of our fundraising events, gave generously himself, and joined in our persuasions to everyone else. We made twice as much as usual on that day. Naturally, we were delighted with him, and began to draw him more into the life of the hospital. Now we employ him, though his salary is hardly large. And we can afford to pay a full-time physician as well."

Julius met Lampton's searching stare in silence.

"I don't trust him," he said at last.

"I was afraid you were going to say that. But don't confuse trusting and liking."

Julius grimaced. "You're right. I don't like him. He always reminded me of a seaman on board my first ship who could persuade any of his fellows to do anything, even the midshipmen who always ended up taking the blame. He died of an infected rat bite, and only then did it transpire he had been stealing from everyone for months."

"That sounds more like an allegory than truth."

"Oh, it's true. But I admit Dunnett keeps the books meticulously. Every penny received is accounted for and paid into the hospital bank account. And every amount spent, large and small, seems to be listed with care."

"And yet?" Lampton prompted.

"And yet he is a rich man, apparently. Where does his money come from?"

"Investments, he says. Made a little on the Exchange. A lot, I gather, when most people lost during the Waterloo panic."

Julius pushed the ledgers away from him and reached for his tea. "Thank you," he said belatedly.

Lampton inclined his head with wry humor, and for a few moments they drank in silence.

"Do you know Macy?" Julius asked.

"I know Mrs. Macy. Kate Grant likes her."

"Timothy Macy is her late husband's brother and seems to be a great friend of Dunnett's."

"Then maybe you should ask him your questions."

"I would if I thought he would answer me at all, let alone with the truth." He eyed Lampton over the rim of his cup and broke the habit of a lifetime. "He doesn't want me to marry Mrs. Macy."

"And what does Mrs. Macy want?"

"To marry me. Or, at least, she did until they got at her. Now, apparently, she wants to marry Dunnett."

Lampton's eyebrows flew up. "Well, beyond execrable taste, can you blame her?"

"You mean, being one-eyed and lame, I am not much of a catch?" Julius asked sardonically.

"No. Meaning what have you done to offend her?"

Unexpectedly, there was a hint of steel in Lampton's eyes. Aware of last night's seduction, Julius almost blushed. But he hadn't offended her then. He hadn't offended her at all. She had left him this morning, as happy as he. And this evening, she was afraid.

"You are asking the wrong question. I'll answer the one you should have asked and tell you that if he has hurt a hair on her head or one shred of her feelings, I will break his arms and legs."

"You do know that I am an overworked physician?"

"You need not attend him. Who, besides Dunnett, accesses the hospital's bank account?"

"In theory? Board members. But none of us has reason to access it, since Dunnett runs everything so smoothly."

Julius drew in his breath. "Will you come with me tomorrow morning to look at those accounts? Or look at them yourself and tell me if anything is wrong?"

"Thank God," Lampton said, straightening his long body. "I thought you were about to suggest breaking in tonight, and there I cannot oblige you. I am going home to my wife and children. You may call at my house at ten tomorrow morning, and if I'm free, I shall come with you. If I'm not, we'll press-gang Grant."

DELILAH PACED THE drawing room floor in conscious imitation of her brother. It didn't seem to help. Her stomach was knotted and her chest painful. She was very afraid she had made the wrong decision.

Despite the urgings of Mr. Macy and Mr. Dunnett, despite her distrust of Antonia Macy, she had had no intention of spreading their lies in whatever cause. The very idea had made her feel grubby and treacherous.

And yet as soon as Julius told her about his proposal of marriage, she had blurted it out, her one aim being to remove his blindness where Antonia was concerned. These accusations might not be true, but he had to open his eyes for long enough to see what *was* true, that Antonia had never been worthy of his love or trust, and she certainly was not now.

But it had not worked. She had been prepared for his disappointment, grief, even anger. Instead, any disappointment had been with her. Besides that, there was only irritation.

He had not believed a word of it.

Of course, he was quite right not to. He usually was, and that was the root of her true unease.

Could he be right about Antonia, too?

Macy had shown he was quite happy to intervene in Antonia's affairs. Perhaps he had done so already to secure her for his brother ten years ago. In which case, Antonia was as much a victim as Julius—and Delilah was playing into the hands of their enemies.

She needed to know what had transpired from their meeting tonight. She could not sleep before then. Her siblings were all either out or asleep, and she felt very alone with her own fears and shames.

At last, she heard the horses trotting into the yard, and rushed to the window. He was already out of sight. She went to the drawing room door, waiting impatiently for him to appear. One of the stable lads must have dealt with his horse, for he didn't take long to come in.

She knew his leg was paining him by his halting advance across the hall and his slow ascent of the stairs. Even in the dim candlelight, she could see the lines and shadows of exhaustion on his face.

Impulsively, she went to him. "What is it?"

His eye widened as though he were surprised to see her. She braced herself for anger and accusation, and certainly he frowned. "You were right. She is determined to marry Dunnett, and I don't know why. Do you? Beyond the grudge you bear her for ten years ago?"

"No," she said honestly. "I did not ask. I just wanted her away from you."

"Something is going on between him and Macy. And she is the victim. She and Edward. That isn't right."

"No," Delilah whispered. "It isn't."

"She wouldn't tell me."

Delilah swallowed. "She might. I believe she will be at the garden party at Braithwaite Castle tomorrow."

JULIUS WAS GLAD of so many tasks ahead of him. They kept him busy, prevented him brooding pointlessly while he waited for the next chance to see Antonia. To *save* Antonia.

He rose early as usual and took his morning ride in the direction of the coast. He found no sign of the damaged ship, which was presumably still being repaired further up the coast. He did find Hatton, the constable, yawning near the cliff edge, waiting to be relieved.

"Morning, captain," he said, springing to his feet and tugging his forelock.

"Good morning. Anything happening?"

"No, sir. The fellow what sleeps in the cave came back quite late— think he'd been to the ship up the coast—but he was on his own. He hasn't appeared yet this morning."

"Nothing else?"

"Not yet, sir."

Julius nodded. "I hope your colleague turns up soon. You look like a man in need of sleep."

"That I am, sir."

"It will be worth it," Julius assured him, hoping it was true. Certainly, it seemed to cheer Halford.

Julius rode home in time for breakfast with Cornelius and Lucy, both of whom were looking forward to the afternoon at Braithwaite Castle.

"It is meant to be a garden party," Lucy said, "but everyone knows it will rain, so Lady Braithwaite has several events happening inside too—an exhibition of art, music, poetry, dancing... Lord Tamar, the painter, is her brother-in-law, and she says they are hoping Sacheverell the poet will attend also to read his latest work. Oh, and children are invited, so the twins will be welcome."

It crossed Julius's mind that Lucy was up to something. She might just have needed relief from boredom, of course, but there was a certain sparkle in her eyes that spoke of mischief. He added it to his list of matters to attend to, comforting himself that she would spend most of the day in public with the family, and went off to change out of his riding clothes.

He drove the gig into Blackhaven, and by ten o'clock was knocking on Dr. Lampton's front door. He was shown into a sunny parlor where Mrs. Lampton—known locally as the princess—and a young boy were playing with a happily gurgling baby.

"Good morning, Sir Julius." Mrs. Lampton came to meet him, holding out her hand. "Nicholas was called away, but he claimed he would not be long, and that we should keep you here by means of tea and breakfast and anything else you would like."

Julius accepted the tea and found himself drawn into the family's beguiling circle. There was an easygoing affection between them that seemed to expand to include visitors, and intensified when Dr. Lampton came home. The boy, Andreas, regaled him with the latest doings of the baby, and the doctor laughed.

He drank his tea quickly, his attention focused on his family. Julius guessed that he was kept too busy to see as much of them as he would like, so that he made the most of every moment. He saw the glances of amusement and understanding between the doctor and his wife, their casual yet intimate touches. It was like a glimpse into the parallels and possibilities of his own life. Andreas was the doctor's stepson, as Edward should be his...

Lampton set down his cup and rose. "Shall we go?"

Hurriedly, Julius dragged himself back to the present, thanked the princess for her hospitality, and waved to Andreas and the baby.

At the bank in the high street, the clerk was happy to show the hospital's accounts to Dr. Lampton.

"Is Mr. Dunnett unwell?" he asked anxiously as he led the way into a small office at the back.

"Not that I am aware," Lampton replied. "I'm just carrying out my trustee duties."

"Of course, sir. And may I say I hope you will see a large and immediate return on the hospital's investment?"

"Investment!" Lampton stared at him. "What investment?"

The clerk, clearly alarmed at Lampton's expression, backed to the door. "I'll bring you the book, sir."

"I think you had better bring us the manager as well," Lampton said.

"I take it," Julius said, "Dunnett is not authorized to invest hospital money?"

"We talked about it," Lampton said, dragging his fingers through his hair and throwing himself into the chair at the desk. "Since so much more money was coming in—thanks largely to Dunnett himself, it must be acknowledged. But we felt we could not yet take the risk. It was something for the future, if donations continued to be as high as they were."

Julius paced.

The clerk reappeared and placed a large book on the desk in front of Dr. Lampton. "Mr. Bell will join you directly," he said, bowed, and hurried out.

Lampton had already flipped open the book, turning rapidly to the newest page. He lifted his gaze to meet Julius's. "Five pounds. We have five pounds. The rest was transferred yesterday to a broker in London."

ANTONIA BARELY SLEPT. Before her eyes, whether open or closed, she saw only Julius's face as she sent him away. Like Antonia, he was used to hiding his hurts, but he could not conceal the pain she was inflicting upon him. Knowing what he had suffered ten years ago—because she had endured it, too—made the deliberate cruelty even harder to bear.

And yet what was the alternative? Timothy had every right to send Edward wherever he wished, and he would not be the only child sent to school so young. But she could not, *would* not, tolerate the bewilderment, the loneliness, the sheer misery he would face. The cruel neglect, the lack of love, the harsh discipline…

No. She would find a way out of it, even if it meant fleeing the country, but for now she could not risk Edward. She must do everything Timothy or Dunnett told her.

Her own loss, her own misery, was a constant pain, like a backdrop to every other thought and emotion. From time to time, the sheer injustice of it caught at her breath, but until she found a way to fight and win, she would play their incomprehensible game. She just prayed she would find that way before she was irrevocably tied to Dunnett. Another loveless marriage of endurance seemed beyond her power to bear, especially now that she had been granted a glimpse of what happy marriage could be. Still, she would do it for Edward if she had to.

The real cruelty was to Julius, her brave, honorable, wonderful Julius, who had already suffered so much. It was inflicting this further pain that ate her up from inside. That she had sent him away broke her heart, because even if she found a means to defeat Dunnett and Timothy, Julius could never trust her again.

But at least pride would keep him away from her now. She knew that much. And Edward would be safe.

Tears tightened her throat, made her whole face ache. But she would not shed them. Instead, she rose early, and when Edward did too, she took him to the beach and they made a castle with a moat of seawater. For a few minutes at a time, she almost forgot the tragedies closing in on her life and swallowing Julius with them.

She had to change hastily to join Miss Talbot punctually for breakfast in her sitting room.

"We have a busy day today," Miss Talbot remarked mildly, although her eyes were sharp on Antonia. "Barely time to answer a letter or two and take my prescribed water before we go to Braithwaite Castle. I must admit I am eager to see more of the place, are you not?"

"Indeed I am," Antonia said with an effort at brightness.

"And Edward is included in the invitation," Miss Talbot reminded her. "I understand there will be many children of all ages, including the earl's own, and staff to care for them so their parents may indulge in other pursuits. Lord Tamar, the painting marquis, will be showing some new works. He is related by marriage to Lord Braithwaite, of course. And there will be poetry readings, music, dancing..."

"It does sound delightful," Antonia responded. Or it would have if she could only have enjoyed all those things with Julius. As it was, she hoped, miserably, that he would not be there. "And it will be lovely for Edward to be with other children."

Miss Talbot nodded and ate in silence for some time. At last, she said casually, "Does your betrothed accompany us?"

"I believe he would like to," Antonia managed. "But you are under no obligation."

"I care only for your wishes in the matter." *Not his.* The unspoken words hung between them, more uncomprehending than angry.

"I believe life will be simpler that way, if you can bear it."

"Oh, I can bear it. I am even prepared to be insufferably rude, if it will help."

Antonia's heart swelled at this sign of loyalty and friendship. Miss Talbot could not understand why she had chosen Dunnett over Julius, and it was not something that could be explained.

"Oh, no, it would make no difference," she replied.

Miss Talbot blinked. "Antonia, if you have changed your mind, if you have doubts at all, I am more than happy to give him his marching orders in words he will clearly understand. Or Linfield will do it if you think a male touch is required."

"Oh no," Antonia said urgently, "please don't do that."

"Very well, I won't. But remember, we are both your friends."

"That is something I will never forget," Antonia said, and cleared her throat to cover the sudden huskiness of her voice.

ALTHOUGH ANTONIA IMAGINED she was prepared for a trying day, she soon realized everything was about to get worse.

She and Miss Talbot arrived back at the hotel after taking the waters at the pump room, to discover Lord Linfield ensconced on one of the foyer sofas. He wore what Antonia thought of as his diplomatic face—an expression of deep interest coupled with a consideration that no one could mistake for agreement.

"Oh dear," his sister murmured with some amusement. "I wonder who they are?"

Antonia wondered too, casting her gaze over the couple opposite him. All she could see was the backs of their heads, and yet was there not something familiar about the shape of the gentleman's balding patch? And the style of the lady's still thick but graying hair?

Catching sight of them, Linfield did not betray relief, though he rose to his feet with some alacrity. "Ah, here she is," he said kindly to the couple, while his eyes met Antonia's as though trying to convey some kind of message. "Look, here is a surprise for you, Mrs. Macy."

The couple stood up, and she saw that it was indeed her parents. It felt like yet another blow, something else she had to deal with, someone else, no doubt, to fight, and that caused even more guilt to consume her. What daughter was so unnatural as to be displeased to meet her parents?

The daughter who had just discovered that they had lied to her ten years ago and every day since, destroying every possibility of her happiness.

And yet she had to smile and go to them, kissing their cheeks and exclaiming, "A surprise indeed! What brings you to Blackhaven? Are you too in need of the waters?"

"We came to see you, of course," her father said.

"Having quite given up on you visiting us in Hampshire," her mother added.

"My apologies," Miss Talbot said. "I keep her lamentably busy, do I not, Antonia? Won't you introduce me to your parents?"

She could do nothing else. She didn't know whether to be glad or sorry when Miss Talbot said, "You will join us for luncheon, of course?"

"We have to go out in the afternoon," Antonia said, to avoid any misunderstanding. "Miss Talbot has an engagement at the castle."

"Oh." Her mother's face fell. "I was hoping for a comfortable chat with you. Perhaps you could come up to our sitting room now?"

"Mama, I have duties—"

"I can manage without you until luncheon," Miss Talbot said.

THE CAPTAIN'S OLD LOVE

"And then you may show your parents the way to my sitting room. A pleasure to meet you, Mrs. Temple. Mr. Temple."

Linfield bowed and offered his sister his arm. There was nothing for Antonia to do but accompany her parents. By the time they reached their rooms, the sheer coincidence of their arrival had struck her.

As soon as her father closed the door behind them, she said, "Have you come to press me into *another* marriage of convenience?"

Her mother bristled. "Well, if you would do it for yourself, it would save us considerable trouble! But there you are, almost three years in his company, and you are not even engaged!"

Antonia's mouth fell open. She sank onto the nearest chair, staring at her mother. "You want me to marry *Lord Linfield*?"

"Of course we do!" her mother exclaimed. "What else have you been about in this mad start? Companion indeed! I admit I thought you a fool at the time, but having met him, I concede he is a quite charming man, extremely gentlemanly, and of course you would be a baroness, which is no small thing."

"Mama, I will never be Baroness Linfield," Antonia stated.

"Don't say never, my dear. You may think you have lost out on that suit, but it is most interesting that he is quite against this latest mésalliance you are attempting."

"M-mésalliance?" she repeated.

"With some friend of Timothy Macy's. I daresay Lord Linfield is mistaken, and certainly it does no harm to make him jealous, but you must take it no further. I believe Linfield can be brought up to scratch very quickly if you manage him properly."

"Mama!" Antonia said, aghast.

"You are quite right, Antonia," her father said, glaring at his wife. "That was all quite unnecessarily vulgar, but in the gist of it, your mother is quite right. Linfield seems an excellent fellow. It will be a very good match for you."

"I think he must be allowed some say in the matter," Antonia said. She didn't know whether to laugh or burst into tears. "And since I am no longer eighteen, so must I." She looked from one to the other, determined to understand them perfectly. "Then you did not follow me to Blackhaven to urge my marriage to Mr. Dunnett?"

They both stared at her.

"Why on earth would we do that?" her father demanded. "He is a nobody."

"He is Timothy's nobody." Her smile was frigid. "Like Francis."

Her parents exchanged glances, and her father had the grace to blush. "Not the same thing," he blustered. "Not the same thing at all. Francis Macy was a gentleman. Besides, we have cause to doubt Macy's opinion. And Dunnett's."

"Dunnett's?" She stared at them. "You know Dunnett?"

"You can do better than a mere solicitor, my dear."

"He isn't a solicitor!"

"Yes, he is," her father said irritably. "In fact, he was the solicitor recommended by Timothy to deal with your marriage contracts, which is why Timothy is now a rich man and you have nothing."

Antonia stared at him. She would not have believed him, except there was a certain symmetry to the whole picture. Dunnett had always been Timothy's creature.

"I would not say she has nothing, dear," her mother said. "She does have Lord Linfield."

It was like living in a madhouse. Had they always been like this? Had she just not noticed because life was so new and interesting when she was young? And then, of course, she had hardly seen them.

She drew in a deep breath. "I do not have Lord Linfield. Nor do I wish to have him, which is fortunate, because although he has been a good friend to me, he has no interest whatever in making me his baroness. Besides, I shall have to leave Miss Talbot's employ when I marry Mr. Dunnett, not because I want to but because this is where all your lies and machinations have led. Do you wish to see Edward before luncheon?"

"Edward?" They both looked at her, as if they had difficulty keeping up with her words.

"Your grandson," she said patiently. "Who is the only reason I forgive you for said lies and machinations."

JONATHAN DUNNETT WAS conscious of a sense of anticlimax. Although all his complicated plans were coming together—even if he had had to adapt and adjust them a little—he found considerably less satisfaction than he had expected in his gently born bride. He did not mind her anger. He had every belief in her eventual subservience. It was her *distaste* he found impossible to deal with, because he could not quite put his finger on what she was doing.

Before the Talbots and Macy, she spoke to him with perfect courtesy. She did not draw her person or even her skirts aside when he approached. Nor did she refuse to meet his eyes. But it was as if she did not see him, as though her mind was somewhere else entirely. She did not even trouble to introduce him to her employers as her betrothed. Well, he would make sure everyone knew at this damned garden party.

That he actually cared about such things made him uneasy.

Before going to the hotel to accompany his betrothed and the Talbots to the castle, he regarded himself in his bedchamber mirror with approval. He looked like the perfect gentleman, a suitable husband for any gently born companion. So what was that odd expression in his eyes?

With a twinge of unease, he thought it might have been vulnerability. And that was something nobody else should be allowed to see, ever, least of all *her*. He had waited ten years for her, ever since Macy had pointed her out as the wealthy woman he wanted for his brother and asked him to draw up contracts that would subtly make her money theirs. Timothy had been convinced the girl's father would never trouble to read them, providing he trusted his solicitor. Dunnett was very good at being trusted.

He had made a thoroughly good job of the business. He had been paid well, and both Macy brothers had spent the girl's money with abandon. He didn't mind that. He would undoubtedly have done the same himself. Everyone was happy, with the possible exceptions of the married couple themselves.

And yet Dunnett had never been able to quite forget Antonia Temple. Something about the turn of her neck, the shape of her mouth, her grace of movement... He had assured himself there were thousands of women just like her, and there were. But she was the one who had stuck in his head.

Even after ten years, when he had seen her name among the guests expected at the hotel—one of the clerks was very useful that way—a curious excitement had overtaken him. He meant to leave Blackhaven in style, and she would be the icing on his cake. It was clearly intended by fate. For she was an impoverished widow now, a dependent companion at someone else's beck and call.

And so he had formed a new plan, summoned Timothy Macy, and looked forward to a different kind of life.

Finally recognizing Julius Vale as the suitor Timothy had sent packing ten years ago had caused him a bad moment. So did the girl's unexpected backbone. But he would not give her up.

Throwing his shoulders back, he reminded himself that he was in charge, that he held all the cards and she was very much his creature now. It was possible he would have to bring all his plans forward, in which case, her obedience was essential. He must show her from the beginning who was master.

Nodding to himself, he turned from the glass and picked up his hat.

ANTONIA HAD THE insane desire to laugh all through luncheon, and yet she knew if she did, she would never stop weeping. Fortunately for harmony, Dunnett did not join them until her parents had departed on their own business, and she saw no reason to inform him of their presence. No doubt Timothy already had.

But now came the most difficult part of the day, the garden party at the castle, where it was perfectly possible she would encounter Julius and probably his entire family.

Edward, of course, was literally bouncing with excitement, which made the carriage appear to be even more crowded than it was on the short drive up to the castle. Dunnett, whose face had fallen ludicrously at the sight of the child, quickly recovered his beaming smile.

"Are you quite sure Lady Braithwaite is prepared for him?" he asked.

"Of course. She has children of her own. There will be many present from other families, too, I believe, of all ages." It gave her some satisfaction, because he had so clearly imagined it to be a much more sophisticated affair. Well, it probably would be, in parts.

On the other hand, she tried to keep Edward in his seat and stop him running from window to window of the carriage, bumping into knees and tripping over feet, for a new fear suddenly chilled her blood. If Dunnett became too annoyed with Edward, would he not persuade Timothy to send him away to school anyway? After the wedding, of course. She must extract guarantees, for without them, her whole sacrifice would be in vain.

"Sit still, my monkey!" she said, plonking him back on his seat. "You will spoil Miss Talbot's gown, grabbing at it like that."

"Sorry, Miss Talbot," Edward said. "I thought I was going to fall over."

"You would not, if you kept to your seat," Dunnett muttered.

As if she hadn't heard, Miss Talbot said, "Oh, there is no harm done. It is so exciting going up such a steep hill, is it not? And the castle looks so grand. Look, you can see it better from this window."

It crossed Antonia's mind that Miss Talbot was deliberately egging Edward on to misbehavior, perhaps imagining it would scare Dunnett off. She did not understand the danger, and Antonia could not tell her.

She was relieved when the carriage finally came to a halt and a liveried footman opened the door, let down the steps, and handed down the ladies.

Dunnett muttered, "Thank God. I will be glad to have the boy out of *her* influence."

Antonia said, "It is just high spirits with him. He will calm down."

Fortunately, there was time for no more. Lady Braithwaite, a young lady of unusual beauty, was there to welcome them and present a plethora of vivacious sisters-in-law, all but the youngest two of whom were married. Their husbands appeared to be playing with a gaggle of older children in the gardens, where a large marquee had been erected, with a covered walkway leading into the castle.

"We know it's going to rain," Lady Braithwaite said wryly. "It's just a question of when! The grass is rather wet for pall-mall, but as you see, the gentlemen are doing their best."

Among those gentlemen, Antonia recognized the earl himself. The others were all young, too—she guessed them to be his brothers-in-law and friends—and making a rather hilarious if messy game among the mud. It did not appear to disturb the countess, who smiled now at Edward. "Shall we go and find the other children? I believe they are playing bowls in the upper gallery in a no doubt vain attempt to keep them clean for the first hour."

Edward, who, since Vienna, was not remotely overawed by titles, happily took the countess's hand. The sisters and a brother-in-law swept them all inside, where they were able to abandon any outerwear they wished and admire the great hall of the castle.

Their party had been among the first to arrive, but by the time Antonia and Miss Talbot emerged from the cloakroom, the hall was filling up with local gentry she had never seen before, and some visitors to the town whom she had.

Mr. Dunnett appeared to claim her almost immediately, apparently eager to separate her from Miss Talbot and Lord Linfield.

"Sir, I still have duties to Miss Talbot," Antonia reminded him. "I cannot abandon her."

He sniffed. "She did not introduce me as your betrothed."

"A mere oversight, and hardly important if the news is going to be brayed from the pulpit on Sunday."

"*Brayed?*" he said, clearly inclined to offence.

"You are quite right. I daresay Mr. Grant has never brayed in his life. My unfortunate tendency to levity."

Dunnett recovered his smile. "I like a lady to have humor."

"Humor aside," she said, accepting his arm with reluctance, "why do you want to marry me so much that you let Timothy hold my son's wellbeing over my head to achieve it?"

The smile vanished again. "You misunderstand. Timothy is only concerned for the boy. Your unsatisfactory position in Lord Linfield's household—"

"Being so unsatisfactory," she interrupted, "I cannot understand why you made the offer."

He looked down at her with something very like irritation. Certainly, there was no admiration in his bland eyes, let alone love or even passing lust—she could recognize all of those.

"I am at your feet, madam," he said. "Ever since I first met you."

"Three days ago?" she said, with blatant disbelief. Another, quite startling, thought sprang into her mind, catching at her breath. She lowered her voice. "Mr. Dunnett, is Timothy somehow *compelling* you?" If so, surely they could ally to thwart Timothy and still somehow keep Edward safe?

But Dunnett actually laughed. Worse, there was genuine amuse-ment in his eyes. "Oh, no, you quite misunderstand, my dear. It will be my joy to make you my wife." And there at last was the flash of lust she had expected earlier. Even without his words, it would have made her blood run cold.

Dear God, can I really do this again? And it would be worse this time because she knew what to expect of marriage, and she had the knowledge of true love with Julius. That must be enough to see her through…

If she could not find a way to wriggle out of it.

A ship to Ireland, perhaps, where she could make a new life for herself… And how long would her savings last then? What would they live off if she could not find another position? There were not many Miss Talbots in the world.

She smiled and nodded to Lady Launceton across the room then looked around for Miss Talbot. Somehow, Dunnett had maneuvered them away from her employer after all, but she was sitting down with Miss Muir and the elegant lady who was the doctor's wife, a one-time princess by her previous marriage. Antonia tried to steer Dunnett toward them, but he remained unresponsive. Instead, he took them inexorably closer to Timothy, who appeared to have buttonholed Lord Braithwaite just inside the open front doors of the great hall.

Antonia saw that it had begun to rain. And then Julius's tall frame blocked her sight of it.

Chapter Fifteen

NVOLUNTARILY, ANTONIA JERKED in the other direction, tugging Dunnett's arm. But he kept going, merely patting her hand on his sleeve in an avuncular kind of gesture, totally belied by the steel of his hold.

"Ah, Vale! So glad you could join us," Braithwaite said, holding out his hand to Julius. There was a certain dignity about the earl, but he seemed to be both kind and perceptive. It was his duty to welcome his new guests, but Antonia could tell from Dunnett's stiffness that he had hoped to be spoken to first. Probably he even meant to distract his host altogether from Julius, who was now shaking Braithwaite's hand and introducing his companion.

"My sister, Miss Delilah Vale. Delilah, Lord Braithwaite."

Of course, it had to be Delilah. The woman's eyes barely flickered in Antonia's direction, just once and then away. Antonia wanted the ground to swallow her. The last thing in the world she wished for was to be standing here in front of him, awkward and obvious, as though flaunting Dunnett.

"How do you do?" Braithwaite said, bowing over Delilah's hand. "Are you acquainted with Mr. Macy?" For the first time, he appeared to see Dunnett hovering at his elbow, beaming, and Antonia, a faint, aching smile fixed to her lips as though with glue. "Of course, you know Mr. Dunnett and Mrs. Macy."

Dunnett opened his mouth and said it, smiling all the while directly into Julius's eyes. "My betrothed."

Julius didn't even look at him. But there was undisguised contempt in his eye, in the curl of his upper lip. He looked straight at Antonia, and her heart shriveled. "Mrs. Macy," he murmured.

"I hope we shall be seeing the rest of your family, too?" Braithwaite said easily. He must have sensed the charged atmosphere, but he was an experienced host.

Julius tore his gaze free of hers, and for some reason she felt as if he had struck her. She would have preferred it. His voice was perfectly steady as he replied, "Yes, I believe they will all appear, even the twins. But we are holding up your other guests."

He and Delilah moved on, regal and aloof. Neither so much as glanced at her. Delilah must have been speechless with triumph, feeding his hatred instead of helping him to understand and forget her...

Unfair. This is not Delilah's fault, nor Delilah's mess to deal with. It is mine. And Antonia wasn't dealing with it. She was walking on Dunnett's arm, helpless and afraid and...

"Ah, Mrs. Macy!" Unexpected rescue came in the shape of Kate Grant. "Delighted to find you here. And you, Mr. Dunnett. Have you seen the pictures on show yet? Some of them are quite stunning."

"No, I haven't yet," Antonia said, smiling brightly. "I would love to."

"I would rather listen to some poetry first," Dunnett said, and she understood that it was merely to exert his power. Perhaps he disliked being Timothy's creature. When could that have possibly begun, anyway? As much as ten years ago, he had been doing Timothy's bidding, pretending to be a solicitor to misadvise her father. How? Why?

Dunnett was gazing at her, his posture rigid, expecting her to move. Of course, he had expressed an interest in going to hear the poetry readings.

"Then why don't you?" she said, slipping her hand free of his arm. "I shall go with Mrs. Grant and find you at the poetry readings later."

"A little of Mr. Dunnett goes a long way, I find," Mrs. Grant said with a conspiratorial smile as they climbed the stairs to the gallery. "Though, of course, I should not say so. We would be lost at the hospital without him."

At least she didn't appear to know Antonia was engaged to him, which hopefully meant Dunnett had not yet spoken to Mr. Grant about the banns. Kate led her to a mezzanine gallery where many paintings were displayed, both amateur and professional, by the look of them. Stunning seascapes mingled with pictures of the castle in slightly bizarre perspective. Accomplished portraits, some of which seemed to see into the sitter's soul, hung beside the ordinary.

Without the oppression of Dunnett's presence, Antonia allowed herself to enjoy the paintings, and the company. She halted in front of one of the most alluring portraits—a raven-haired young woman with dramatic black eyebrows and an expression of utter mystery. She might have been laughing at the world, fighting it, or even pleading with it. Her mouth might have betrayed a hint of vulnerability, but her eyes were deeper than the oceans, thoughtful and yet utterly implacable.

"I know her," Antonia said suddenly.

"You do?"

Antonia dredged up the memory. "I met her at a reception in Vienna. In fact, everyone was admiring a painting hanging in her drawing room. It was by Lord Tamar, whom she called the finest artist of his generation."

A tall, dark man, who had been looking at the paintings opposite, turned toward them, nodding familiarly to Kate before he brought his steady gaze to bear on Antonia. A rueful smile played on his lips.

"Did she really say that?" he asked.

"This is Lord Tamar," Kate said dryly.

"Then yes, she did," Antonia said.

"She'd never say it to my face, you know," Tamar drawled. "But I'm touched. I believe you made a rare sighting of my sister Anna. Was she well?"

"She and the comte both were."

She didn't quite understand the cause of Tamar's laughter, though she was glad enough to entertain him. He seemed amiable and easygoing, and talked happily about his paintings. Engagingly, he also drew their attention to other works he particularly liked, enthusing about color, light, and style. Antonia almost forgot her own troubles until she turned and saw Delilah watching her from the other end of the gallery. At least Julius was not with her.

Antonia merely inclined her head while misery flooded back, and she remembered that she had promised to join Dunnett at the poetry reading. She excused herself to Mrs. Grant and the charming Lord Tamar and went back down to the great hall, dragging her heels a little and pausing to exchange greetings with whomever she recognized. There was no sign of Miss Talbot or Lord Linfield.

She found the poetry readings in a comfortable chamber with many sofas and upholstered chairs. Some people were seated to listen. Others chose to stand in little groups. Mr. Dunnett was among the latter, beside an army officer and the young lady who must have been his wife, judging by the intimate way she touched his arm. Antonia could not help the pang of loss for her own happy marriage, though she did her best to quash it. She had made her decision and must have the courage to stand by it.

Cornelius Vale lounged in one corner of the room, his shoulder against a tall cabinet while he glowered as though both discontented and attentive. The whole family must be here. She wondered if they all hated her or if Julius had told no one and only Delilah guessed. That would be like him…

One of the Earl of Braithwaite's youngest sisters was reading the newest poem by Simon Sacheverill. She read with unexpected grace and feeling, and in spite of herself, the words caught Antonia and swept her along. They were curiously haunting, lyrical, and beautiful.

Lady Helen's lovely voice did not falter, but she finished with suspiciously sparkling eyes, as though moved to unshed tears. But Antonia was not given a moment's peace to appreciate it properly, for Dunnett had seen her, and came to her at once.

"Do you care for poetry, Mrs. Macy?"

"A little. I cared for that poem a great deal."

"I suppose Sacheverill is fashionable for a reason, but Lady Helen read it magnificently. Let us mingle a little more."

Since he offered his arm, it would have caused comment to refuse. She left the room with him, feeling stiff and conspicuous, while he clearly wanted to show her off, looking for opportunities to announce their engagement. For some reason, this appalled her, and she felt desperate to prevent it, as though if it was not said aloud, it could not happen.

Foolish and pointless. She had agreed because she had to.

As they strolled across the hall, children's laughter drifted in from the front doors. "I think I will just go outside and see if Edward is there and contented."

"You must not pander to him, my dear," Dunnett objected.

"Caring is not pandering," she said tartly. "And since care of Edward is the reason for our agreement, I assumed you would know that." She moved at once toward the door, trying to withdraw her hand from his arm, but again he retained it, patting it soothingly. It made her flesh crawl, but at least he tried no further to dissuade her.

The rain had gone off, and a group of very small children were rushing around the lawn on wobbly legs, frequently falling over and howling with laughter. That was what Antonia had heard from the hall. Edward, being all of six and therefore at least double the age of the infants, was not among them. Instead, he was the youngest of several older children dancing in the marquee.

For the first time that day, Antonia smiled with genuine pleasure. A fiddler was playing a merry country dance, and one of the earl's sisters—Lady Tamar, Antonia thought—was guiding the children through the steps. Her partner was a tall, smiling boy of about fourteen. It was clearly more fun than a serious lesson, and the children's steps were more exuberant than accurate.

Edward, skipping happily down the line with a girl several inches taller than him, caught sight of Antonia and grinned. She smiled and waved, miming applause, and he grinned even more.

When the dance ended, Lady Tamar and the fiddler himself led the cheers and claps. Several of the children collapsed on the lawn, breathless with happy laughter. Edward ran enthusiastically across to Antonia, seizing her hand and spinning her around.

"Mama, Mama, I was dancing!"

"I know, I saw you!" Antonia said, laughing and digging in her heels before she got dizzy. "And very fine you were, too."

"A gentleman does not drag a lady about," Mr. Dunnett said, glaring at him.

Edward blinked at him with clear incomprehension. "I'm six," he said.

Laughter bubbled up inside Antonia.

"Michael's going to play football with us," Edward said, tugging at her hand. "Girls can play, too. Do you want to, Mama?"

"Don't be ridiculous, child," Dunnett snapped. "Your mother is not—"

"Perhaps Mr. Dunnett would like to play?" She looked him in the eye, challenging him from instinct and sudden, confusing knowledge. "I'm sure you'd like to know each other better."

For an instant, Dunnett's expression betrayed his answer. He most definitely would not. The distaste vanished almost immediately into a bland smile. But she had already seen. He had no interest in Edward at all. If anything, the boy irritated him. So why was he so keen to take him on? Just to please Timothy? Would they conspire to send Edward away, whatever she did?

Edward, always willing to give someone a second chance, grasped Dunnett's hand instead. "Come on, then!" he urged.

Dunnett tore himself free. "I am hardly dressed for it," he snapped, then, with effort, he smiled at Antonia. "On this occasion."

But Edward had forgotten him already. His whole face lit up. "Captain!" he yelled, and hurled himself across several yards to fling his arms around Julius's legs. "Do you want to play football with us?"

"That is unacceptable behavior," Dunnett pronounced.

Obviously Julius did not think so, for he bent to give Edward a brief hug in return, before extricating himself from the boy's grasp. For an instant, Antonia met Julius's gaze and the world seemed to stop.

Does anything else truly matter?

Then Julius smiled—at Edward rather than at her—and walked off with the lad in the wake of the bigger boy and a trail of smaller ones. Another gentleman, clearly the father of one of the children, strode along with them too.

Edward. Edward matters.

"Unacceptable," Dunnett repeated tightly. "Things will change."

"They will," Antonia agreed. What she could not yet see clearly was how. But at least she finally realized that bringing Edward under the same roof as Dunnett was just as bad as sending him away to school.

Abruptly, she dropped Dunnett's arm. "Excuse me," she said coldly, and ducked out from under the covered walkway, setting off across the damp lawn in pursuit of Edward. Until she saw Timothy walking from the side to intercept her.

Her heart jolted. She had to be cleverer than this. She must not let Timothy see her rebellion until she had a means of fighting him. All she would achieve with this show of temper against Dunnett was having Edward sent away immediately. Timothy had to think she was submissive to Dunnett. She didn't yet understand why, but it was all that would give her the time to find out.

She halted, as though she had forgotten something, then turned and hurried back toward the house. She could just make out Dunnett's back as he walked along the covered path in the same direction. She would catch up with him at the door, suggest listening to the music she could hear beginning in the great hall.

"What can I do?" said a quiet voice beside her.

She glanced in surprise and saw Delilah Vale. "Do?" she repeated, confused because she expected attack, not offers of help.

"I am not blind," Delilah said, "though perhaps I have been. Someone is coercing you." Antonia could not admit it, but Delilah must have seen the answer in her eyes, for she said, "He will help. Tell him the truth. And tell me what I can do."

Delilah's eyes were not trusting. They were wary, challenging, even angry, but somehow not unkind—or not yet.

Antonia drew in her breath. "Help him," she said. "Whatever happens, I know it is over, but I would spare him whatever pain..." She had to break off to swallow down the rising sob in her throat. She sped up to escape the other woman, murmuring, "Excuse me," as she fled back to Dunnett.

For now.

THE MUSIC WAS beautiful, played by a mixture of professional and amateur musicians, including the earl's sister Lady Alice, who was not merely accomplished but extraordinarily talented.

Antonia remained by Dunnett's side throughout, even when tea was served. The children hurtled through the hall at that point, though they were quickly herded upstairs to the nursery by several maids and a young man in spectacles. Edward waved to Antonia from the staircase, and she waved back.

She forced herself to be patient while they drank tea and ate dainty sandwiches and pastries, and then, while an orchestra began to set up in the gallery on the opposite side to the paintings, she strolled again with Dunnett, allowing him to decide the direction and the people they paused to speak to.

After this, she would consider her duty done for the day. Although she might have to dance with him once. And then, perhaps, Miss Talbot would be ready to leave this torture, and Antonia could plan…

Dunnett halted to bow to Mrs. Winslow, the squire's wife. Beside her, her husband seemed to be in serious conversation with a stout, elderly gentleman and Colonel Doverton from the local regiment.

"Are you acquainted with Mrs. Macy?" Dunnett said proudly, as though preparing an announcement.

Antonia tensed, but Mrs. Winslow retained her gracious, almost condescending manner as she answered, "Of course. We met at the last assembly ball, I believe. How do you find Blackhaven, Mrs. Macy? Is it still to your liking?"

Beside her, Mr. Winslow was saying, "…bizarre discovery of guns!"

"Very much," Antonia answered Mrs. Winslow. "It is a charming town, and everyone has been so welcoming."

"Guns?" repeated a startled Colonel Doverton. "A couple of pistols abandoned by smugglers, perhaps?"

"Oh, no. Crates full of weapons," Winslow replied. "Rifles, pistols, ammunition for both."

Dunnett was still smiling, although his gaze shifted rather rapidly to the gentlemen.

"Well, I hope you will stay a while longer," Mrs. Winslow said. "Are you acquainted with my daughter, Lady Sylvester Gaunt? She missed the last assembly ball."

"Just sitting there, in a cave?" said the older gentleman.

"Yes, on the beach by Black Hill. Sir Julius found it, along with a boat."

Guns! Was that what the horse thieves had bought with their ill-gotten gains? That made the whole matter suddenly much uglier.

Keeping her anxious thoughts to herself, Antonia tried to keep her attention on the Winslow ladies. But while she exchanged polite greetings with Lady Sylvester, a gentle young woman with smiling eyes, she was suddenly very aware of Dunnett at her side, stiff and silent, and when she cast a quick glance up at him, his attention had clearly wandered to the men's conversation. And he didn't like it. He didn't like it at all.

"...to do with the horses being driven over his land last week," Mr. Winslow was explaining. "They were clearly landed from the ship skulking up and down the coast, and their sale probably paid for at least some of the arms in the cave."

Dunnett knows! The thought almost stunned her. *Somehow, he is involved in this!* In which case, it was vital he heard no more, just in case Mr. Winslow was about to reveal their plans to catch the thieves and Dunnett was able to warn them.

"Oh, I think the dancing is about to begin," she said excitedly to Lady Sylvester. "I must just speak to Miss Talbot before... Your escort, Mr. Dunnett?"

With a quick, apologetic smile, she seized Dunnett by the arm and all but dragged him away. And there was nothing he could do except comply, or else make an obvious scene that would hardly reflect well on him.

There, how do you like it? Antonia thought with malicious satisfaction.

"I fail to see why you are in such a rush to speak to a woman you see every day," he said coldly.

"She still employs me, sir, and as such has more call on me than you do." Now that they were far enough away from the dangerous conversation, she felt it was safe to release him, so she did. "So do not let me detain you on what is clearly an unpleasant errand for you."

She sailed on without him, though rather to her annoyance, by the time she reached Miss Talbot, he had caught up with her.

"As long as I don't miss our first dance," he said mildly.

Inwardly, she gritted her teeth, for she needed him out of the way so that she could get a message to Julius about him. If she could just speak to Lucy or even Delilah…

Outwardly, she smiled, and gave her hand to him for the waltz, wondering that he could not feel the revulsion of her flesh. Then she thought he probably could and simply did not care.

Which brought her back to the other mystery. Why did he want to marry her? She had no money, no property of her own. If her parents were correct, Dunnett himself had seen to that ten years ago while pretending to be a solicitor. Was he again obliging Timothy, who wanted her remarried so that she would have no claim to Masterton Hall?

Or…did he actually *like* her in some perverse way that took no account of her own feelings? He certainly did not like Edward, and that rang the loudest warning bell of all.

The urge to discuss it all with Julius overwhelmed her like a physical pain. Even now, he would help her. She knew that, even without hearing Delilah's words. But he needed a clean break from her. She would not inflict her problems on him. This was something she had to manage on her own. Somehow.

Timothy was the one who had control over Edward. If she could drive a wedge between Timothy and Dunnett, so that she could reject the latter without any disadvantage to Edward… She would have to do so quickly, but it was definitely worth thinking about.

Would Timothy not be appalled if Dunnett truly were involved with the horse thieves and hidden guns? Could that be the wedge she needed?

While her mind spun with plans to bring him down, her body waltzed and her mouth made trivial conversation about the age of the castle, the quality of the orchestra, and the charm of today's event.

As the music ended, the more urgent problem of how to shake Dunnett off came to the forefront of her mind. He seemed determined to keep her at his side. Perhaps an excuse to speak to Timothy would make him drop his guard, because at the moment he seemed to be treating her like a dog with a bone.

"Ah, Mrs. Macy." Lord Linfield appeared, apparently out of nowhere. "Would you care to dance?"

Dunnett, in the act of drawing her hand to his arm, pinched her skin hard through her glove, though he had to know that to refuse a gentleman in public, where several people had overheard, would be offensive and cause just the kind of talk he appeared to dislike. Perhaps the pinch was merely a warning. She certainly took it as one, though not in the way he intended.

"Thank you, my lord," she said, sliding her hand free to bestow it upon Linfield instead. There was nothing for Dunnett to do except bow and walk away, leaving Antonia with a sense of massive relief that she was at last in the company of a friend.

"You seemed in need of rescuing," Linfield murmured, moving toward one of the country dance sets forming up.

"Was it so obvious?" she asked.

He bent his head toward hers. "I speak as a friend, Mrs. Macy. You and Edward will always have a home with us. There is no need to marry a man you do not like."

She cast him a glance of genuine affection. "Thank you. And you are quite right."

"If either of us can help, we will."

"I might yet ask you to—when I can work out what it is."

"Then let us simply enjoy the dance."

THE CAPTAIN'S OLD LOVE

As befitted a man who had been active at the Congress of Vienna, Lord Linfield enjoyed his dancing, and he was good at it. A charming, graceful partner, the exhilarating exercise of the dance, and the sheer fun of the set did much to restore her spirits and her optimism.

"Where shall I escort you?" he asked lightly when the dance ended at last. "In search of Edward? My sister?"

Only a few feet in front of her, she caught sight of Lucy Vale. "To Miss Vale first, I think," she replied, still breathless from the dance.

To her surprise, he swung her around in the opposite direction, where she came face to face with Delilah. And Julius, who had just halted at his sister's side.

Chapter Sixteen

JULIUS HAD COME to the castle solely because he was sure Antonia would be there with Miss Talbot. Otherwise, he would not have left the watching of the guns and the ship to others. His concern for Antonia went way beyond that. Just as last night, he knew from her stiffness, her fixed smile, the curiously desperate veiling of her expression, that she was not only unhappy but frightened. And just for a moment, when they had come face to face at the front door to the great hall, he had seen her grief and her loss.

He might be furious, hurt, offended even, that she would not confide in him, but such useless feelings could not compete with his need to help her. He did not distress her further by haunting her footsteps. Mostly, he watched her surreptitiously, and when Edward ran to him, his heart felt curiously full. He was happy to go off with him and play football with the children. In fact, it turned out to be a hilarious game, thoroughly enjoyed by all.

But Antonia's expression still haunted him—that flash of new, appalled understanding. Perhaps she finally realized she had made the wrong decision by allying herself with Dunnett. Certainly, it was something to do with Edward.

When he put his coat back on after the game and strolled back up to the castle, Delilah caught him.

His heart sank. He did not want another quarrel with her. Nor did he want her making Antonia's life even harder.

"She's being coerced," Delilah said low.

He blinked at her in surprise. "I know." His lips twisted into a smile at her almost equal astonishment. "I know her very well."

"How is he forcing her? What are we going to do?"

His heart warmed at the *we*. It was always more comfortable to have the formidable Delilah on one's side. "The *how* is through Edward. The *what to do* is more difficult. She needs to confide in someone."

His mind knew it should be any friend. His heart wanted it to be him.

He glanced curiously at Delilah, who was frowning direly. "What changed your mind about her?"

"She smiles too much, and it doesn't touch her eyes. She hates Dunnett to be near her—that appalls me. And then... I spoke to her."

His eye narrowed involuntarily. "Tell me you did not scold her."

"I asked her what I could do," Delilah replied without offense. She met his gaze. "Do you know what she said?"

"How could I?"

"She said I should look after you."

His heart turned over. He could not speak.

Delilah said, "You have to talk to her. After tea, there will be dancing. That is your best opportunity, when she cannot refuse."

He regarded her almost with amusement. "One would think you had been organizing assignations for years."

"This is my first," Delilah replied with mock modesty.

It was agony trying not to watch Antonia dance with Dunnett. Although her smile flashed frequently, her shoulders were so tense that he was afraid she would shatter. He wanted to pound Dunnett into the ground for doing this to her. Instead, he strolled around the floor, exchanging pleasantries with a few acquaintances, one of whom—Colonel Fredericks, once commanding officer of the local regiment, now something more nebulous to do with intelligence—appeared to know about the hidden guns in the cave.

Mostly, he kept his eye on Macy and shadowed Antonia around the dance floor, ready to intervene.

Lord Linfield was too quick for him, which was only mildly annoying. He liked Linfield, however unreasonably jealous he might be of the man's friendship with Antonia, and was glad that at least she was safe for the length of the dance. He amused himself by noting his siblings' often surprising interactions on and off the dance floor. One or two were probably heading for heartache. But at least they were alive, with something to fight for.

As he was.

This time, as if positioning a ship for battle, he was ready and in perfect position.

When he stepped up beside Delilah, facing Antonia and Lord Linfield, she looked stunned, and he took shameful advantage.

He held out his hand. "My dance, I believe, Mrs. Macy."

For an instant, she looked so hunted that he was actually afraid she would run, despite the scene it would cause. She even cast quick, pleading glances at both Delilah and Linfield. But they had turned to each other.

She swallowed and raised her hand to his. It was trembling as he laid it on his arm and led her toward the center of the dance floor, where other couples were already gathering. Even in England, even in Blackhaven, Society loved to waltz.

Her touch, the feel of her so close, definitely distracted him. But he held on to his plan for her sake, kept his attention moving, making sure he knew where Dunnett and Macy were at all times. Dunnett plunged onto the dance floor, but other couples got in his way, and by the time the orchestra struck up the introduction, he was already looking a trifle foolish. He did not quite glare at Julius, but his eyes definitely held malevolence.

Julius smiled and ignored him to take Antonia in his arms. She felt frail, like a bird whose bones could be crushed by a moment of carelessness.

"Antonia," he said softly as they began to dance, but she interrupted at once, unexpectedly brisk and down to earth.

"I'm glad of this opportunity. You need to know that Dunnett is somehow involved in the business of the horses and the guns."

Whatever he had expected from her, it was not that. "What makes you think so?"

"He was with me when Mr. Winslow was talking about it. The words definitely affected him, and I don't know what he means to do about it. I'm afraid he is more—or rather less—than a charitable hospital administrator. I think he is a flim-flam man and, God alone knows how, is involved with guns. You have to be careful."

"So do you," he said grimly. "You must not marry him, not on any account."

Her eyes fell before the ferocity in his. "I know," she said, so low that he barely heard her. And yet the conviction in those quiet syllables flooded him with relief. "I need to drive a wedge between him and Timothy so that Edward will be safe."

There were so many questions fighting to be asked, but he stuck with the most important. "How do they threaten Edward?"

"Timothy will send him away to school if I don't marry Dunnett."

He had to keep control of his fury as well as his pity. "Dunnett will send him away anyway."

"I know that now. Even if he doesn't, it will be just as bad. I will not give my son into the power of such a man."

"Good girl." He drew in a breath. "Do you think Macy is also involved with the guns? How well do he and Dunnett know each other?"

"He knew Dunnett before he came here. A long time before. I don't know how they met, but according to my father, Timothy recommended him as the best solicitor to negotiate my marriage settlements ten years ago. He must have been doing Timothy's bidding then, though I doubt he is a real solicitor. Timothy told me they have some kind of business together, but I cannot believe it is horse stealing and gun smuggling. He has always been so respectable—"

"So *outwardly* respectable," Julius interrupted. "They are the worst of people. I have the feeling it was he who persuaded your parents of my family's lack of respectability. You are worried about me."

As he had intended, the change of subject took her by surprise. For an instant, the sheer loss and misery in her eyes caught at his breath. His arms ached with the need to hold her close and comfort her.

"Of course I am." Her voice sounded hollow, though she held his gaze, still dancing as if her body moved without the control of her mind. "I never intended this. But Edward has only me."

"No," Julius said intensely. "He also has me."

Her stricken eyes met his. "Oh, Julius, don't," she whispered.

"Don't you trust me?"

"You know I do. And I am grateful. If you can give me anything to use, to prevent Timothy supporting Dunnett in this—"

"We will do it together. But what is Dunnett's motive? Does he love you?"

She frowned, appearing to think about it. "No. If he loved me, he could not do this to me or to Edward. I thought he must at least desire me, and he might, but it does not seem to be in any *personal* way. I used to believe Timothy was doing him a favor in promoting this marriage between us. But now I think he just wants me married to be rid of my claim to Masterton Hall."

"If that was the case, he might have as easily let you marry me. Either way, you lose Masterton Hall."

"I know, but he has no means of controlling *you*."

His eye widened. "And you think he has a means of controlling

Dunnett? To what end?"

"I don't know that. But it could be something to do with whatever their business is together. Or with the guns."

"And the hospital," Julius said.

"The hospital? Everyone agrees Dunnett is a wonder there, even those who don't like him."

"Exactly, and so everyone has stopped supervising him. He has just moved most of the hospital's funds into an entirely different account belonging to a supposed broker in London. My belief is that the account belongs to Dunnett himself, under a different name."

She stumbled, and he held her closer in order to preserve her balance. She didn't seem to notice. Or perhaps she secretly didn't mind. "Seriously? How do you know?"

"I went with Dr. Lampton this morning to look at the hospital's supposedly healthy bank account. Now the bank is tracing the money to try to get it back."

"Then he will be arrested?" Antonia asked eagerly.

"Not yet. The hospital board want to trace the money first and get it back before it vanishes altogether. They don't want Dunnett accusing one of them of extracting the money instead."

"Unlikely!" she exclaimed.

"Extremely. My worry is that he will use the time to abscond. With you."

Her lip curled with contempt. "He won't."

His heart lifted at the certainty in her voice. "You need to be careful," he urged. "Make sure you are always accompanied by someone other than him or Timothy. In fact, if you marry me now, it might spike his guns, as it were."

"That is no reason to marry." The pain was back in her eyes.

"I thought we had a reason," he said softly.

The music was coming to an end. He had to dance her toward the far end of the floor, to avoid both Timothy and Dunnett. She didn't seem to notice.

"Don't," she said, her voice hoarse. "I have done this for the second time. I might trust *you*, but you will never trust me. I know it is over for us." She leaned closer, and just for an instant he felt her breath on his lips and inhaled the light rose scent of her skin. "I will always love you."

She had timed it perfectly, so that he had to release her as soon as the words were spoken. Antonia slipped from his hold, straight into the waiting company of Miss Talbot.

Savagely, he wanted to create a scene anyway, to force her hand, force her to marry him, whatever the scandal or gossip. She had given him that right with her final words. Knowing, as they both did, that he would not take it.

Or, at least, not yet.

Inhaling a deep breath, he turned away and saw Macy approaching him with some determination. Julius rather wanted a fight with someone, so he was happy to let them meet.

"Macy," he murmured, choosing to stop in front of him.

Macy opened his mouth and then, belatedly, realized there were far too many people around for his purpose. "Give me the favor of your company," he said between his teeth.

With an exaggerated gesture, Julius invited Macy to go ahead of him, and the older man stalked off. Julius was conscious of a childish desire to go in the opposite direction just to see how angry Macy got, but in the end, he reminded himself he might learn something, and strolled after the man's vanishing back.

He caught up with him outside, just to the left of the front doors.

"Sir," Macy said haughtily, "did I not explain to you that you were to have nothing further to do with my sister? And yet I find you dancing with her the very next day."

"Ah, yes. That must be because, as I know *I* explained to *you*, you have absolutely no authority over either of us."

"If you imagine that, you are an even bigger fool than I took you for," Macy snapped.

"What, because you are vile enough to hold a threat to your own nephew over your sister-in-law's head? You really are a commoner, Macy." And Julius walked off, leaving the man opening and closing his mouth silently like a landed fish.

There was little satisfaction in it, though. For it had struck him that despite Macy's plausibility, he really wasn't terribly clever. He might convince a gullible couple not to wed their only daughter to a man with an ex-mistress in Lisbon and an unconventional family that contained an old rake of a parent and three illegitimate children. He might even have contrived to introduce Dunnett to the Temples in order to influence Antonia's marriage contract with Francis Macy. But could Timothy really *control* a man like Dunnett, who appeared to be successfully embezzling an eye-watering sum from the hospital that lauded him, while he also organized a secret transaction of stolen horses for arms?

What if it was the other way around? What if Macy did what *Dunnett* said?

Then why did Dunnett really want Antonia, with or without Edward?

Julius needed to know, but what bothered him more than anything was what she had said to him just before declaring eternal love.

You will never trust me. I know it is over for us.

The words ate at him so much, he knew he was glowering. And anyone who observed him closely would have seen that he did so mostly in Antonia's direction while he prowled the hall and the galleries, always at a distance from her, yet always keeping her in sight.

While she still loved him, it would never be over. And she had declared that she always would. That lit a fire in his heart—and, if he was honest, in his loins. He wanted to marry her now, take her to his bed, and give her all the joys of love of which he was capable. And convince her she was wrong about the trust.

But it was not in his nature to ignore problems. If he trusted her at all, he had to consider her words.

Did he trust her? Despite his undeniable love, during their life together, would he be constantly on edge, waiting for the next betrayal? Betrayals made no doubt for his own good or Edward's, as she saw things, the decision made without consulting him. Such independence was part of her character. She was not afraid to make decisions, to defend those she loved, even at her own expense. He loved her for that.

Ten years ago, she had been too open, too trusting, to have done this without at least talking to him. Their parting then had been possible only because they had not been allowed to see each other. If they had, the lies would have been apparent. Yet now, when she could have talked to him, she had acted alone, dismissing him against her own heart, her own wishes, when together they could find a solution.

The misery of those ten years had taught her that—the unhappy marriage she had not fought until it was too late, the threats of her brother-in-law since, the need to keep her son safe. And now Julius, too.

He understood she had been trying to look after all of them. But it was she who did not trust.

Not entirely true. She had not believed a word of the lies concocted by Macy and Dunnett, so she did believe in Julius's love. Just not in the strength of it. And that, surely, would come with time.

His greater understanding did not ease his mind, although the niggle of anger faded. While he spoke to Winslow and Colonel Fredericks about the guns, he watched her dancing with Aubrey. Her smile, her whole posture, seemed curiously tragic, almost as though she had always expected unhappiness, as though she deserved nothing else.

Well, he would not have that.

He excused himself and made his way through the throng. Aubrey had released her to one of Lord Braithwaite's brothers-in-law—Hanson, the member of Parliament who had played football with the boys. They were talking. He passed her a glass of wine from the table.

"Sir Julius, how delightful to see you here." Miss Muir stood in front of him, and he could hardly bat her aside. "Your whole family, in fact. I have just had the most agreeable talk with your sister, Mrs. Maitland—such a charming lady…"

While she talked and he listened and watched Antonia, part of his mind wondered what Miss Muir's life had been like during all the years he had been gone. If she had loved his old roué of a father. Had Sir George broken her heart? Or had Miss Muir broken his? Was it possible this eccentric spinster was the reason for his father's serial misbehavior?

The possibilities calmed his impatience. She was a lady worth knowing. This town was full of such people.

More than that, an upsurge of grief hit him.

He had not seen much of Sir George in his adult life. When they did meet, they tended to quarrel. And yet his father had been the constant background of his life, unquestioningly loyal, knowledgeable, humorous, fun, even upright in his own unique way.

Julius's throat tightened. He missed his father. And he liked Miss Muir, whatever their story had been.

By the time he left her with her Spanish sister-in-law—another tale he had yet to hear—Antonia was walking outside through the front doors. A quick glance showed him that Dunnett was dancing, and Macy was deep in sententious conversation with a tolerant Mrs. Doverton.

Julius followed Antonia. At first, he could not see her. Then a glimpse of lavender caught his attention, and he saw her beyond the marquee, hurrying toward the lawn where the children had played football. He set off after her, limping quite badly. Tension seemed to have stiffened his leg.

A couple of ladies were wandering the grounds, too, and Julius instinctively stepped behind a large oak to avoid them. He would not trap Antonia with scandal, tempting as it might be. This was too important.

From the tree, he saw her hurry onto the lawn and pick up a small blue coat from the ground. Edward's. Julius hadn't even noticed the boy had forgotten it. She began to walk back. The other ladies had paused to admire the scenery, pointing things out to each other. They would be bound to see him if he stepped out to confront Antonia now. They might even join them, engage them in conversation there was no time for.

Antonia was keeping to the path by his tree. For an instant, he thought she had seen him and was coming that way deliberately, but her eyes were on the distance, her mind clearly lost in unhappy thoughts.

He flicked a glance at the ladies, who had their backs to him at that moment, and took his chance.

Reaching out, he grasped Antonia's wrist and hauled her behind the tree. He took her by complete surprise, and her mouth was already open to cry out. He had even warned her not to walk alone. Which made him want to laugh, only there was no time before her scream would ring out.

He covered her mouth was his, and she fell back against the tree. He pinned her there, driven wild by her softness in his arms, the thundering of her heart against his, the feel of her lips suddenly recognizing his and yielding. Then she pressed back with her mouth, her whole body, not merely surrendering but kissing him with wild, desperate passion.

She flung her arms up around his neck, tangling her fingers in his hair. He swept his hand down her back from nape to buttocks, glorying in her delight, in her every sweet, sensual response.

This was not what he had intended. He had come to talk to her. And yet this said more than words... He gave them another moment, and then another, as if he would make the kiss last forever, as if he would ravish her, take her here and now...

Gasping, he wrenched his mouth free.

"Never tell me whom I trust or don't," he raged.

That wasn't what he had meant to say either, so he wasn't entirely surprised that she blinked at him in bewilderment. Her beautiful, usually clear eyes were clouded still with desire.

Gently, he took her face between his hands. "We act together in this," he whispered. "In everything. We will *talk*, Antonia."

She stared up at him, emotions crowding in her eyes. Her fingers clenched in his hair, dislodging the strap that held his eye patch in place.

Only the other night, he had made love to her with tenderness and abandon, and managed to keep the patch in place the whole time. Yet now, in full daylight, it slid off. He made an instinctive grab for it, but it was too late. Her gaze was riveted to his empty eye socket.

His vulnerability swamped him, almost like shame. He could not bear it. Whirling away from her, so she did not have to see it, he strode off through the trees, clumsily tying the eye patch back in place as he went.

Chapter Seventeen

A NTONIA STARTED AFTER him, wondering what on earth had just happened in the last five minutes. Bombarded by a whirlpool of emotions, she had been flung from calm thoughtfulness to fear, to sudden, blinding hope that she had been wrong—and then, like a bucket of cold water, came the realization that she had been right all along.

He did *not* trust her.

Oh, perhaps he knew she would not make any further promises of marriage to other men, but that suddenly seemed trivial beside this much more intimate doubt. That she was shallow enough to be repelled by his empty eye socket.

Catching up her skirts, she charged after him through the trees, glad for the first time of his lameness holding back his speed. Wrestling with his eye patch slowed him down too. Apparently, he did not even hear her at first, because quite suddenly he halted and spun around to face her. His wide-eyed surprise was almost ludicrous.

She stalked up to him and seized him by the hand to prevent him rushing off again.

"How dare you?" she said furiously. "How dare you tell me I have to trust you when you show such singular lack of trust in the depth of *my* feelings? Even my humanity? How *dare* you lecture me about talking to each other when you run away at the first hint of your own pain?"

He stared at her, his face whitening beneath its weathered bronze. The truth of it must have hit him like a blow, and just for an instant she was glad of it. Until she saw his shame.

"I'm sorry," he said hoarsely. "You should not have to see... I never wanted you to see...the disfigurement."

She swallowed, her heart beating hard. So much depended on this moment.

Instinctively, she carried his hand to her cheek. She even managed a watery, rueful smile. "What did you think? That we could somehow live in intimacy for the rest of our lives, share a house, a bed, waking in the night for children and illness and other emergencies and never see all of each other? I do not want such a marriage as I had with my first husband."

"I know." His fingers moved against her cheek as if they couldn't help it. "It...took me by surprise."

A frown twitched her brow. "You think it repels me. You are afraid of...*disgust?*"

"I am afraid of pity!" he burst out. Then, as if ashamed, he dragged her face to his shoulder. "*Your* pity," he whispered.

Her arms crept around him, gently, as though feeling their way, as her mind was. "I pity your pain," she said into his coat. "As though I could suffer it with you. I pity every injury I see, and God knows there are plenty of those, especially from the war. If I feel more for yours, it is because I love you. And you have no business loving me if you believe an empty eye socket makes you less desirable to me."

She raised her head and then, slowly, her hand. His breath caught. He made a faint movement as though to halt her, and then held still and rigid, letting her take off the eye patch again. Deliberately, she drew down his head and softly kissed the puckered flesh.

"Part of you," she said. "A tiny part, and as beloved as the rest, sacrificed in duty and bravery." Then she covered it again and fastened the patch in place, while he gazed at her with startled wonderment.

Slowly, he relaxed. His arms came around her. For a long moment, they held each other, his faintly stubbly cheek to hers. It was a moment of peace that made her want to weep with gratitude.

"We are finding our way, you and I," she whispered, her throat aching. "Hindered as well as helped by the past. But we know the love is there. I won't hide from you if you don't hide from me. Do you plan to marry me, Julius? Or not?"

"I've been planning to for ten years," he said before pressing a quick, hard kiss to her lips. "I consider us still engaged. If you do."

"Then let us decide how best to flummox Timothy and Dunnett and keep Edward safe."

He released her reluctantly and began to walk back toward the castle, although he still retained her hand. "I think we need longer than we have. We must not let them think they are opposed just yet. We should go in separately. But Antonia? Take care."

He paused and drew her closer for another long, tender kiss, which she returned with gladness. Then he released her, and his lips twitched into his beloved, crooked smile. She caught a lock of escaped hair from an equally loose pin, and repaired the damage as best she could. Then she shook out Edward's coat again and walked away from him out of the trees and past the marquee.

The sky had darkened. It would rain again soon. But despite the danger still hanging over them, her heart felt light and sunny, confident and brave.

IT WAS DUSK by the time Julius returned to Black Hill. He barely heard the excited chatter of his siblings in the carriage, or in the house. Conscious of a new, deeper happiness trying to burst out of him, he wanted to pace the deck at speed, feel it roll beneath his feet, while the sight and smell of it filled his senses. As she did.

Since he could not settle, he decided to ride to the cliff edge and see if anything was happening. He saddled his own horse, since the stable staff had all been sent to bed, tied a lantern to the side of the saddle, and rode carefully toward the sea.

When he estimated he was about a hundred yards from where he had found Halford that morning, he dismounted and tied Admiral's reins around a scrubby tree.

Extracting the glass from his pocket, he put it to his eye and pointed it toward the sea. His heart gave a thump, because there, surely, was the ship they were waiting for. He detached the lantern and walked warily on until a sudden click made him freeze.

A man loomed out of the darkness, pointing a pistol directly at him.

"Captain," Halford said with relief, and lowered the weapon. "Come and see this. Something's happening. Best put out the lantern in case they see it. There's plenty of light on the beach."

"Is there, by God?" Julius said, dousing the lantern flame before dropping down beside Halford.

He was right. There was a little glow of light on the beach below, from three lanterns and a small fire. Four men sat around the blaze. There was no sign of the boat. And the ship seemed to be at anchor, coming no closer in to shore.

"How long have they been there?" Julius murmured.

"Maybe an hour. Ate and drank a bit."

"Did they come from the ship?"

"No, over the rocks from the north, and they met with the evil-looking ruffian who was already here. They seemed to know each other. But they don't seem in any hurry."

"They don't," Julius agreed. "They must be waiting for more long-boats from the ship. Have you seen anything that looks like signaling?"

"No, not unless the fire itself is a sign. None of them seem to be paying much attention to the ship."

But the timing was right. It must be tonight. According to Antonia, Dunnett knew the guns were discovered. And since he had cleared out the hospital's account, he must be planning to leave. Perhaps the storm damage to the ship had delayed his departure.

In any case, as soon as they began to load the guns, Julius would gallop to Blackhaven harbor, board his borrowed ship, and signal Captain Alban and the revenue cutter... He doubted it would be much of a battle, but still his nerves tingled and his blood heated. He was ready for action.

The men below trampled out the fire, as if they had no further need of it, and retreated into the cave. Their voices, low and desultory, faded into silence.

Julius and Halford waited. And waited. No one came out of the cave again. The ship remained at anchor and in darkness.

"Looks like it's going to be tomorrow night," Halford said, with a sigh. He lay down under the canvas shelter. After another quarter of an hour, so did Julius, though every sense remained far too alert to allow him to sleep. Although he did doze eventually, knowing from experience that any noise or light would wake him.

It was dawn that woke him in the end, and the light patter of rain on the canvas overhead.

He sat up and reached for his spyglass. The ship had gone. He crawled over and peered down to the beach. The tide was in, leaving little space between the cave entrance and the sea. During high spring tides, especially when there were storms, he recalled, the cave could get flooded—another reason his father had objected to their playing there.

Nothing would happen for the next couple of hours. He left Halford still dozing and walked stiffly back in search of Admiral.

After breakfast, he returned, with some bread and ham for Halford's relief, Johnston.

"Anything?" Julius asked hopefully.

"Not a peep," Johnston growled. "Wouldn't know there was anyone in there. Maybe Halford dreamed it."

"Only if he and I were sharing the same dream."

Half an hour later, when there was still no movement, Julius crept down the "secret" path to the beach, while Johnston kept his pistol trained on the cave mouth. Every so often, Julius paused and strained his ears, but he heard nothing, not a snore or a murmur or a footfall below.

When he dislodged a stone and it bounced down to land on the rocks below, he flattened himself against the cliff so that he couldn't be seen from the cave entrance, and silently cursed himself.

Nothing happened.

Even more uneasily, he continued his descent in silence. On sudden impulse, he picked up the stone that he'd kicked loose, carried it toward the cave, and hurled it at the foliage covering the entrance. Then he ducked behind a rock and peered out.

Still, nothing happened.

He exchanged looks with Johnston at the top of the cliff, then pointed toward the cave. Johnston shook his head violently, but Julius paid no attention. Something was very wrong here.

Although he entered the cave warily, he already knew there was no one there.

The longboat was, though the bedroll he'd found before had gone. Worse, when he jumped down to the ground and moved around the boat, there were no crates of guns or anything else. Those, like the men from the beach, had vanished.

LORD LINFIELD JOINED them for breakfast in Miss Talbot's sitting room the following morning. He seemed thoughtful and distracted, which was not unusual, until he said abruptly, "Mrs. Macy, you're not really going to marry that fellow Dunnett, are you?"

Antonia blinked. And decided on honesty. "No. I thought I might have to, but I won't do it."

"Good. If you have to leave us, Vale's the better man by far. Apply to me for anything you might need." With that, he got up from the table, nodded, and went out.

"Well, there you have it," Miss Talbot said, half amused, half irritated. "He is trying not to pry while assuring you of our support."

"I know. I am grateful. And touched." She drew in a breath. "Dunnett is a bad man. I believe measures are afoot to arrest him, but in the meantime, he must not suspect I am anything but submissive. I shall have to see him if he calls, but I would not be sorry if my duties to you kept me very busy."

Miss Talbot's gaze was shrewd. "My health is not good. I believe I am having a relapse."

"Oh dear," Antonia said with the beginnings of a smile.

"Precisely. You must take me to the pump room, and then I shall need you for all sorts of errands."

"It is my pleasure as well as my duty."

Miss Talbot snorted in a most unladylike fashion. "Then be so good as to fetch my bonnet and reticule, and the pelisse that matches this gown. Do you think Edward should come with us? In case we go to the beach—the sea air might do me good."

"I am certain it would," Antonia replied gravely. "Let me fetch him."

It was as the three of them strolled up the high street—at least, Antonia strolled; Miss Talbot tended more toward a totter while grasping Antonia's arm, and Edward bounced two paces ahead—that she saw Mr. Dunnett.

She merely glanced down a narrow side street from habit, to avoid any emerging traffic, and recognized Dunnett's back. He was easily recognizable to her now from any angle, something to do with the way he held himself—just a little too straight, a little too haughty, and yet his head held very slightly forward and to the side, as though bent in a contradictory obsequiousness.

Her stomach gave an unpleasant twist, and that was before she took in the man talking to him. She remembered him only too well—the "pirate" who had threatened them on the beach near Black Hill.

"Mama, can we buy a bucket from the market?" Edward piped up. "Then we can make proper towers for the castle and collect water for the moat!"

At once, Antonia bent her head to Edward. If his voice attracted their attention, she hoped they would not guess that she had seen them.

"What a good idea," she said, walking on calmly while her mind raced.

Though she'd hoped to see Aubrey at the pump room, so that she could pass a message to Julius telling him what she had seen, the place was unusually quiet. Apart from themselves, there was only one elderly gentleman, who had much to say about gout.

They did not linger for longer than it took Miss Talbot to drink a glass of water, after which they repaired to the beach. Antonia spread a blanket on a useful rock of the correct height for Miss Talbot to sit, while she and Edward built sandcastles around her feet.

Antonia kept looking up, hopeful against all reason that Julius would stroll along the sand from one direction or the other. Miss Talbot watched her but said little.

Once, she asked, "Have your parents come to prevent your marrying Dunnett? Or to encourage it?"

"Prevent it. They feel I could do better."

"Sir Julius?"

"Lord, no." Antonia met the older woman's gaze. "In fact, I doubt they know he is in Blackhaven. Please don't tell his lordship, for it will mortify him—it certainly mortifies me—but they seem to have decided I should marry him."

Miss Talbot blinked. *"Denzil?"* she exclaimed with all a sister's contempt.

"Your brother is perfectly safe from my wiles," Antonia said hastily. She managed a rueful smile. "Though not necessarily from my parents'."

"Oh, I wouldn't worry about *him*," Miss Talbot said.

Eventually, Edward's hunger drove them back to the hotel, where he was invited to join them for luncheon in Miss Talbot's sitting room. While the older lady fussed over his sandy hands and face, Antonia took their outer clothing along to her own chamber.

She had only just inserted her key to the lock when Timothy materialized beside her.

Was he also involved with the stash of guns in the cave? Was he physically more dangerous than she had previously imagined? If Dunnett was under his thumb, she must assume so.

Unless… Could this be the wedge she had been hoping to drive between them? Would he not be shocked by this additional trade of Dunnett's? She could imagine Timothy turning a blind eye, even benefiting from, embezzlement. But the dangerous business of gun smuggling was surely too alarming for him to contemplate.

"Timothy," she said as graciously as she could. "Is there something urgent? Miss Talbot is expecting me directly."

"No doubt. I have been waiting for you for some time."

Which at least meant he had not been able to bully the hotel staff to let him into her bedchamber again.

She turned the key and opened the door, then stepped inside and threw the garments toward the nearest chair. Sand flew off them in all directions. She turned at once to leave again, but Timothy had already followed her into the room.

"If it is so urgent, the coffee room is convenient," she said. "But you will give me leave to ask Miss Talbot's permission."

He closed the door with a snap. "What I have to say will not take long. It does not require discussion. Despite assurances, you have not yet given your notice to Miss Talbot. You will do so as soon as you return to her rooms. If necessary, you will sacrifice salary to leave her employ tomorrow. You will also make time to accompany Dunnett to the vicarage this afternoon, to arrange the calling of banns. Unless Dunnett has had the time to acquire the common license he mentioned."

He smiled thinly. "How fortunate that your parents have arrived in time to see you safely married once more. Finally, I was appalled to see you dancing yesterday with Julius Vale. You will not see him again."

With effort, she held on to her anger. She had to appear submissive and yet still in character. She let her shoulder slump.

"I will speak to Miss Talbot this afternoon, and I have already said I will marry Mr. Dunnett. However, in a town this size, it is impossible to avoid anyone. Refusing to dance with Sir Julius would have been rude and unacceptable in polite society. I know you are too conscious of family pride to wish me to appear so."

His eyes narrowed. "Mind your insolence, Antonia."

"You are mistaken," she said dully. "Allow me to pass if you wish your instructions followed."

He opened the door and went out ahead of her without a word.

Her breath caught. *I am losing an opportunity here...* "Timothy," she said. "A moment longer, if you please."

DUNNETT WAS HALF annoyed, half pleased with himself as he swaggered down the high street toward the bank. He didn't like that he had to change his plans, particularly not because of Julius Vale, whom he had begun to hate with a loathing, but he rather liked to imagine the captain's face when he saw his great discovery had vanished. No doubt he would lose face and credibility among the local gentry, who would assume the arms cache had never existed, and that gave Dunnett considerable malicious pleasure also.

He strolled into the bank, civilly waited his turn, and then presented the latest banker's draft to the clerk.

"Good morning! This is payable to the hospital account. I shall draw fifty pounds now for expenses, and the rest should be transferred to the investment account."

The clerk took the draft and put it in a drawer before raising his eyes to Dunnett's. A rare chill passed through Dunnett's veins.

"I beg your pardon, sir, but that will not be possible today. The board of trustees has insisted all transactions be carried out by one of them, so perhaps if you return later with one of those gentlemen…"

Dunnett tried for joviality and a winning smile. "Don't be silly, man—they didn't mean me."

"Nevertheless, sir, I must follow my instructions."

Dunnett's quick eye had already spied the manager hovering by his office door. He knew this game had ended.

"Well, you are wasting my day," he said, a little testily, as might have been expected. "And that of whatever trustee has to give up his time for so trivial a matter. Good morning!" Dunnett spun on his heel and stalked out. The hairs on the back of his neck stood up, just as if he expected the heavy hand of the law on his shoulder. Again.

But he made it to the street unmolested.

It was time to go. The guns could not be loaded on board safely until dark, but no one, surely, had connected him with the ship. The excisemen had already searched it and found nothing. He grinned wolfishly and crossed the street toward the hotel. He and his bride would be safe there.

"MAKE UP YOUR mind, Antonia," Timothy said irritably. "What do you want of me?"

"To warn you," she said, her heart bumping so fast it should have made her voice shake. She opened the door wider, and after a moment's hesitation, he walked back inside. This time, she closed the door, although she made sure she stood nearer it than he did. She still had the room key clutched in her hand.

She took a deep breath. "I appreciate you are trying to do your best for the family, for Edward...but are you quite sure tying our fortunes to Mr. Dunnett's is the best way forward?"

He stared at her, not quite hiding his astonishment. "Yes. Very clever man, Dunnett. We have had business dealings together before."

"And now *I* am such a business?" She had to fight to keep the indignation from her voice. "Again? Why, Timothy? How? Are you really in such desperate need of his services?"

A hint of confusion passed over Timothy's face. "I don't know what you mean."

"Timothy," she chided. "He tries very hard, but he is hardly of our class, is he?" She thought that quite a clever move, playing on his snobbery. "He is not a gentleman."

"No, but he's damned good at making money," he said. "You'll have everything you want. And so will I."

"With respect, Timothy, I'm not sure that is true. In fact, to have any standing at all in Society, we both need to cut our ties to him immediately."

He gazed down at her, supercilious disbelief quite clear in his face. She gazed back until a flicker of doubt entered his eyes. "What are you talking about?"

"I think you know he is not a mere administrator of a charity hospital," she said quietly. "Or even a solicitor, though it is what you told my parents. You know he is a flim-flam man. But I am sure you cannot also know that he is embezzling from the hospital funds and is about to be arrested. He is also deeply involved in a scheme of horse stealing and smuggling arms, probably to rebels in Ireland. You need to drop him, Timothy, and at least pretend to be as shocked as I am."

Timothy's mouth gaped, but his surprise seemed to be less at Dunnett's criminality than the fact that she knew about it.

"He is an unsatisfactory servant who has let you down," she said. "You had better tell me everything so that we can plan our story together and avoid the scandal about to break over Dunnett's head."

He didn't seem to grasp what she was saying. She actually seized his sleeve and shook it. "Timothy, *he will go to prison!* He might even be transported or hanged! Do you want to go with him? How deeply involved *are* you?"

Abruptly, the door slammed into her back, and she staggered forward.

"Up to his neck, my dear," Dunnett said, walking into the room and closing the door with a terrifying snap. "It seems we are all in the mire."

Chapter Eighteen

"**T**HAT'S RIDICULOUS," WINSLOW said, staring at Julius with incomprehension. "Five crates of arms cannot vanish! One of you must have fallen asleep."

They stood with Johnston on the beach, just outside the cave.

"I didn't," Johnston said indignantly. "At least, not so heavily that I would have missed the crates being loaded into boats and rowed out to a waiting ship! And I trust Halford."

"Then how do you explain it?" Winslow demanded.

Johnston sighed and dragged his rigid fingers through his already untidy hair. Bits of grass remained threaded through it. "I can't."

But memory was stirring in Julius, tugging him back into the cave.

"What? You think the guns and the smugglers might have magically reappeared again?" Winslow said.

"No," Julius said, edging around the longboat to get to the far right-hand corner of the cave. "The arms were here and now they have gone. The longboat, which would have carried at least some of the crates, is still here. It has not sailed, with or without arms. Accept for a moment that we did not fall heavily asleep and miss all those men and arms sailing away. They must have gone somewhere. Somehow. And it was not by boat."

"Through the rock, perhaps?" Winslow said sarcastically.

Julius, feeling along the wall by the light of the lanterns they had lit, turned and looked at him over his shoulder.

Winslow's jaw dropped. "Seriously?"

"I used to play here as a boy," Julius said. "There are tunnels, built by smugglers last century, or probably the one before that—during the civil war, even. They're all over these cliffs, even under Blackhaven itself, according to rumor. My father forbade us to go near the tunnels after I almost got caught when one collapsed. I don't know how long these men have been coming here, but long enough, I suspect, to shore up the roof. Ah, here's where my father had it blocked off."

The stone, once cemented in place, came away easily in his hand. He dropped it at his feet and lifted the next before turning to Winslow. "They couldn't take the boat, but they could—and did—take the arms."

Winslow strode toward him. "Where to, man? Where does the tunnel go?"

"To the Black Cove, just outside Blackhaven. It's been used by smugglers for years. No one will bat an eyelid, except the excisemen, if there is movement there of a dark night."

"But it's miles from here to Black Cove!"

"By road. Not so far directly under the ground."

"Then you think they'll move the arms aboard from there tonight?" Winslow asked, tugging at his lip.

"I do."

"Then we can't take the chance of letting them load the crates. I'll speak to Colonel Doverton about lending us some men tonight. And you and Alban can take care of the ship."

"First," Julius said, "I have a few errands in Blackhaven." Chief among them was the desire, the need, to see Antonia, to assure himself of her safety, and to assure her of his love.

He should, of course, go home to change so that he did not call upon her trailing sand and smelling of horse. But some urgency drove him to turn Admiral's head immediately in the direction of the town.

"Exactly where does this tunnel come out?" Winslow shouted after him.

"I'll meet you at the cove and show you," Julius called back, and gave Admiral his head.

Half an hour later, he clattered into town at a gallop, and almost ran down the vicar.

This was entirely Mr. Grant's fault for hurling himself in front of Admiral's hooves, and Julius was understandably furious as he wrestled the horse under control without harm to the vicar.

"What the devil's the matter with you?" he demanded, appalled by the possibilities so narrowly averted.

"Dunnett has been in to the bank," Grant said. Like the rest of the hospital trustees, he was appalled by Dunnett's betrayal and eager to get the money back. "He knows we're onto him."

WITH THE PRECIPITATE arrival of Dunnett in her chamber, Antonia realized many things. First, that she had misunderstood his relationship with Timothy. Dunnett was not subservient. Timothy was. Second, that Dunnett already knew he was, in vulgar parlance, rumbled, and that he had a plan. And third, if she wanted to know that plan, she might have to go along with it, at least partially.

Her advantage had gone. Dunnett now stood between her and the door. And behind her was Timothy. Threat closed in on her from all sides.

We are all in the mire, he had said.

"Then how," she said with surprising calm, "do you propose to get us out again?"

"Move on, of course," Dunnett said. "To Dublin's fair city, with a new name, a new wife, new wealth, and new opportunities to earn more. You won't need a bag. You can buy more suitable gowns in

Dublin."

Her breath caught. "You want to go now?"

"No point in waiting for old Winslow to come at me with his clod-hopping constables and the town watch. They'll have turned out the regiment by tonight."

"I...I will need time to collect Edward's things," she said, playing for time.

"You misunderstand, my love," Dunnett said. His eyes, once almost obsequious, were like flint, and with a jolt she realized he meant to compel her. "Edward will not accompany us. He will stay here with Macy."

"That was not the deal!" Antonia exclaimed, although she had no intention of ever letting Dunnett anywhere near Edward.

Timothy paled. Dunnett ignored him. "You're not going to make a fuss, are you?" he said, his voice tight and chillingly soft. He flexed his fingers and curled them into a fist, as though to be sure Antonia understood he could and would *insist*. One blow could knock her into unconsciousness, and then she would have no control at all.

She swallowed. "Of course not, but I—"

"Then pick up your bonnet and let us go."

"Is Timothy not...?"

"Oh, Timothy will stay here and play the gulled gentleman. I really don't feel like carrying him any further."

"That isn't what you said when you needed Masterton Hall for your damned flim-flam!" Timothy said bitterly.

Antonia turned to him, her eyes wide. "Is that why you wanted me away from Masterton Hall?"

"It was a useful address, not connected to either of us," Dunnett said. "A lot of letters and parcels containing money were sent there, to a large variety of names. We could not have you becoming suspicious, or—er...collecting evidence."

"And now you don't care?"

Dunnett smiled. "Exactly. As my wife, you could not testify against me anyway. But we shall vanish across the sea and reappear as a different couple."

"Is that what you do?" she asked, fascinated in spite of herself. "Change your name and circumstances, always just one step ahead of the law?"

"One step is enough." He stretched out his hand and lifted her bonnet from the chair. "Usually. Goodbye, Macy. You should still be able to salvage something. Come, my dear."

Antonia hesitated. She needed to get out of this room, where the weight of physical threat from both men seemed to crush her. On the other hand, she had no intention of going anywhere with Dunnett that was not very public. And she did not want him to think she was giving up Edward too easily, considering what a fuss she had made about him before.

Surely, in the hotel, or in the street, they would meet someone she knew, or someone who would help her? At least to pass a message, if she was subtle enough. If she could just get him to tell her about the guns first, then she could bolt.

"You will be kind to Edward?" she said in a rush to Timothy. He looked outraged, betrayed, and she tried to will him with her eyes to do something about it, to tell Julius, the Linfields, Mr. Winslow— anyone. But before he could answer, she swung back to Dunnett. "And we shall send for Edward from Dublin? Won't we?"

"Perhaps," he said with impatience. "Let us go."

Her fear did not ease much as they left the room.

"Where are we going?" she asked loudly, setting off toward the main staircase, which would take her past Miss Talbot's room, and Lord Linfield's.

But Dunnett seized her arm and jerked her in the opposite direction. "This way."

He took her down the staff stairs, which were at least busy with people who, hopefully, would remember seeing her. Why did Dunnett not care? Because he had the means to get clean away?

She had an even nastier moment when they emerged from a back door beside the kitchens and she saw a carriage harnessed to a pair of horses waiting in the stable yard beyond.

How stupid to imagine she could keep control of this situation! She took a deep breath and opened her mouth to scream, just as Dunnett tugged her away from the carriage and into the lane that led to the high street. He even laid her hand decorously on his arm, although he took the precaution of holding it there. He did not trust her.

Which reminded her of another mystery.

"You don't need anything from Timothy, do you?" she said, frowning. "So why do you want to marry me?"

To her amazement, he actually blushed—the color seeped under his skin so quickly, it looked painful. "You are beautiful and intelligent," he said with an effort at carelessness. "We shall do well together."

Seriously? So there was something personal after all? It was astonishing enough that he actually seemed to like her, but did he really imagine that his crimes, separating her from her son, and compelling her into marriage were helping his cause? Or was he just one of those men who was not concerned with a woman's feelings because his own were enough for him?

That caused a fresh burst of alarm within her. So she concentrated on what she had to know.

"Do you really have to leave so quickly?" she asked. "From what I hear, they have not yet traced the missing money to any account of yours."

"And hopefully they won't, but I don't feel like taking the chance. Besides, other matters are afoot."

"The guns. Did you know they found them?"

"I know Julius bloody Vale did," he said viciously. "But don't worry. He's lost them again."

Her heart thudded. "Has he? How?"

His gaze, scanning the street ahead, came back to her. "You'll see," he said confidently.

"Are they really destined for Irish rebels? People will die, you know."

"People die all the time. I don't see why I shouldn't be the one to make a little money out of it."

"I suppose it's quite clever," she mused, darting her gaze around in search of people she knew. "Steal lots of horses in Ireland, sell them over here at fairs where no one's likely to recognize the animals, and buy much more lucrative arms with the proceeds. Or are they stolen, too?"

"Most of them," Dunnett said, and again she felt a chill in her blood. He was telling her because he didn't believe she would be able to tell anyone else. *Why not?*

"Where are they now? On board your ship?"

"No."

"Where are we going? To see Mr. Grant?" Another panic seized her. "Do…do you have a special license?"

"No, though in retrospect, that would have been best. Sadly, we have no time to call upon Mr. Grant. Our wedding will have to wait."

"Oh." She glanced at him, trying to read his intentions without giving away her own fear. "What is it you intend?"

He smiled and patted her hand. "A pleasant stroll on the beach with my betrothed. Is that not romantic?"

They turned into the market square crowded with stalls and customers. For Antonia, it provided a few moments of safety, though he had still told her nothing about the guns, and she was reluctant to bolt and play hide-and-seek among the stalls.

Someone jostled her from behind, and she spun around, praying it was not Timothy or, worse, the evil "pirate" from the beach. But she found herself blinking into the smiling face of Leona Vale. Beside her, inevitably, was her twin brother.

"Mrs. Macy!" Leona exclaimed. "I'm so sorry. I hope I didn't hurt you?"

"Of course not. The market is so crowded, is it not?" Antonia felt she was babbling, and was afraid that at any moment Dunnett would pull her away, before she had the chance to convey any message at all. She could not even find the words. Hiding her desperation, she smiled brightly. "What is it you are looking for?"

"Oh, we're just following our noses," Lawrence said cheerfully.

Did she imagine the very slight emphasis on the word following? Were the twins actually following her? For Julius?

"Well, carry on with that," she prattled, as Dunnett began to pull her on. "Good luck! Oh, and tell your family I am asking for them!"

The twins waved, already turning to the nearest stall, and she wondered if she had misunderstood everything. The twins could easily have been making mere meaningless conversation.

"Who are they?" Dunnett demanded with distaste.

Thank God he never paid attention to children, or he could easily have remembered them from Braithwaite Castle.

"To be honest, I cannot remember," she lied. "But I have definitely met them somewhere."

She dared not look back over her shoulder as he drew her past the rest of the market and around the corner to the harbor. She barely looked at the ships and fishing boats tied up there. Dunnett appeared to, though, as he strolled along, an unctuous smile on his lips while his arm and his hand over hers made it impossible for her to pull free without a major scene. At least there were people around, and it seemed he really did mean to walk on the sand. And he chose the town beach, usually the busiest and most easily seen. Although she remembered only too well Julius kissing her behind the rocks…

"Are we waiting for something?" she asked at last, trying to keep the anxiety from her voice. If she screamed here, would anyone come to her aid? "Have you hidden the guns near here, and we are going to take them with us?"

He actually laughed at that. "I am not so stupid. And no, there is no need to wait."

Drawing her with him, he walked toward a small blue rowing boat that was tied to a hook driven into a large rock.

Panic surged. More questions tried to spill from her lips, but instead she let out a hoarse cry of alarm as a man loomed up from the bottom of the boat where he had been lying.

It was the "evil pirate" she remembered only too well. It was impossible to know if he recognized her, or if he cared. He only grinned ferociously at her alarm, while Dunnett patted her hand and smiled.

The pirate untied the boat and began to tug it down to the water. Antonia's blood seemed to freeze in her veins. In the boat, away from the shore, from people, she had no prospect of help. She had gone far enough. It was time to leave, and if that involved screaming her head off, so be it.

Dunnett, keeping hold of her, strolled after the boat. Antonia glanced wildly around the beach, seeing only a few children with parents or nurses, and a middle-aged couple with a small dog. At the edge of the harbor were some fishermen mending their nets—they might help her.

And then, on the steps, she glimpsed Lawrence Vale, for once without his sister. He lifted his hand, an oddly calm, friendly gesture. And abruptly, reasonlessly, she knew everything would be fine. Lawrence knew where she was going. He would see where Dunnett took her, while Leona, presumably, had gone for help. They had understood her perfectly.

She suspected Dunnett meant to row around to Black Cove or even Braithwaite Cove, both of which were infamous locally for smuggling. Lawrence could follow easily over the cliffs, keeping them in sight.

Sooner or later, Dunnett and the guns would be in the same place, and she would be the witness who would see him convicted. Edward would be safe from him. And with this knowledge, she could keep Timothy at bay also.

So she made no fuss when Dunnett helped her into the boat and climbed in after her. She did not even object when the pirate pushed the boat into the water and jumped in himself, splashing seawater from his boots over her skirts.

"I had hoped for more time with you in Blackhaven, my dear," Dunnett said with apparent regret. "But never mind; we shall be married in Ireland as soon as the opportunity offers. And if it doesn't— well, no one will know. A wife opens up so many possibilities. Something tells me you will enjoy a life of adventure and riches."

There was something vaguely taunting about his tone that caught at her nerves.

She tilted her chin, meeting his gaze. "You sound as if you are prepared to dishonor me. What if I do not choose to be dishonored? What if I do not choose this life of riches and adventure you promise?"

Dunnett smiled mockingly. "I rather think you should have thought of that before."

With a jolt, Antonia realized they were not hugging the coast around to the next cove, but pulling out into the sea.

"Besides, what choice will you have? Alone with a man who enjoys all the privileges of a husband? Our fates are tied, Mrs. Macy. Or rather, Mrs. Dunnett."

She ignored him. There were several ships in the distance, but Dunnett's pirate was rowing directly and speedily toward one that looked suddenly familiar. Of course, the ship that had brought the horses and had lurked off the coast near Black Hill.

Her stomach twisted in knots. Dunnett knew, damn him, that

alone on a ship full of men like the one rowing them now, she would be glad of his "husbandly" protection.

But it won't be for long, will it? I can demand to see everything and learn everything until the guns are brought aboard, and then Julius will attack and we shall all be safe.

Only somehow, even repeating the words silently in her head, they sounded naïve and even silly. She should have taken her chance and fled with the twins in the market.

Dunnett was watching her like a cat with a mouse, as though he saw her thoughts quite plainly on her face.

"Why?" she said. "Why me? Why force me with lies when you could easily woo some other woman more suited to your purpose?"

"She would not be more suited," Dunnett argued. "She would not have your grace, your quality. It is something that cannot be learned, you know, not properly, the manners of a true lady. Or gentleman, although I imagine I shall come close now that we are together."

She smiled. "Do you imagine I am too much the lady to stick a knife between your ribs?"

For an instant, she could have sworn surprise flashed in his eyes, but then he was smiling again. "Actually, that is exactly what I think. A lady would not even strike a gentleman, let alone stab him. Imagine all that blood, and all those lies to tell, before you are hanged anyway for murder. Besides, I don't believe I am immodest to foretell that you will grow to like me very well. I knew that dry old stick you married last time."

"Francis?" she said. "Then my father is right. You did pretend to be a solicitor and made sure the Macys could spend my dowry with impunity."

"It put both brothers in my debt," he said with a shrug. "And therefore under my instruction. Timothy was quite useful for a while, but I always knew you were worth ten of them both."

"And how, pray, did you know that?"

"I saw you once, ten years ago," he said almost dreamily, "when

Timothy and I first discussed the plan. You walked past with me with Vale, so close that your skirts brushed against me. Such beauty and spirit and the grace of a true lady... I could not understand why the Macys wanted you. Except for that tidy little dowry. It seemed a shame, a waste, if you like, but I did what they asked."

His lips quirked. On anyone else, it might have been attractive. Antonia's blood chilled, even as she wondered if she could use it against him.

"Only I never quite forgot you," he said. "And now my patience, my loyalty, has been rewarded. Will you be able to climb the ladder, or will Horry here carry you?"

With fresh alarm she saw that they were almost alongside the ship. But in this moment, she was free. She could probably jump over the side before they could stop her. Though of course she could not swim, and they were likely to catch her and haul her back before anyone else could save her. She would gain nothing. She might even die.

Or she could climb the ladder and wait for the guns to be brought on board, and then for Julius's attack. When that happened, she would fight with everything she could find to help.

"I can climb," she said coldly.

She had done so before, onto Julius's borrowed ship. What a beautiful, perfect day that had been. Followed by an even more beautiful night...

Horry's rough hands shoving her after Dunnett onto the ladder dragged her out of her memory and back to quite desperate reality. Why had this seemed such a good idea back in the safety of the hotel?

The wind whipped at her hat, blowing it to the back of her neck. Cold pierced straight through her clothes to her skin, and large, heavy spots of rain landed on her upturned face as she climbed. Horry was too close behind her. She had to resist the urge to kick him hard and see if he fell off into the sea.

Dunnett was helped on board, and hands reached for her.

Someone stepped in front of him, clapping a hand on Dunnett's shoulder, while a seaman threaded a rope over his hands.

"You are under arrest, Mr. Dunnett," said a voice she could not allow herself to believe in.

Landing on the deck, she stared at the man in front of them.

"Julius!" she cried with joy, and hurled herself into his arms.

Chapter Nineteen

FOR A MOMENT, the sheer joy of discovering him here outweighed everything else. The safety of his arms, the fierce pressure of his kiss, and overwhelming gladness swept her away.

Only gradually did she become aware of the cheering of the sailors and the ribald comments being bandied about.

Julius lifted his head. "Well. At least you are pleased to see me."

"At least?" she repeated. "What else did you want?"

"Your *not* turning up with the villain of the piece!"

As his arms fell away, she straightened her hat and tried to recover her dignity. "I was trying to discover where the guns are. But Julius, how on earth did you get here so quickly?"

"Grant and Lampton waylaid me with the news that Dunnett had been to the bank and knew he was rumbled. We thought he would bolt, so we decided to take the ship immediately. It was a simple matter."

Dunnett, his hands tied, arms held by two burly sailors Antonia recognized from Captain Alban's ship, glared from Julius to the crew. "None of them are mine!"

It seemed to be said more to himself than anyone else, but Julius chose to answer him. "No, yours are under arrest, too. They didn't put up much of a fight."

"Did they tell you where the guns are?" Antonia asked eagerly.

"I didn't ask them. I know they're in the tunnel that comes out at the Black Cove. By now, Colonel Doverton should have them and the rest of Dunnett's sailors in custody."

Dunnett swore furiously. "How the *hell* did you know where we'd moved them to?"

"Common sense and local knowledge. It was my escapade as a lad that saw the tunnel sealed up, but I remembered its existence—after the vanishing crates gave me a bit of a fright. There was nowhere else they could have gone."

Antonia found herself glaring at Julius. "Then I came with him for nothing?"

"I won't say nothing," Julius said with feeling. "It certainly shook me up to see you in the boat with them." Barking orders at the crew, who started back on their duties, including hauling away Dunnett and his piratical henchman, Julius dragged her further along the rail. "Seriously, Antonia, have you no sense of danger?"

She would have retaliated, except that she saw he was not really angry with her. He was afraid. "I took a calculated risk," she said. "Because the twins saw me, and I knew I would be safe. I wanted to help."

He seized her in another embrace, muttering something against her cheek. "He was compelling you," he said. "I saw that much."

"I chose to let him. No one will ever compel me again."

He drew back. "Not even me?"

She felt her whole being melting into her smile. "You have never compelled me. I might make an exception... Oh! Do you suppose we could go back ashore? Miss Talbot and Edward are expecting me for luncheon, and oh, Julius, did I tell you my parents are here? They want me to marry Lord Linfield, poor man, and I don't think they even know you are in Blackhaven."

Julius began to laugh. The sound was so infectious that soon not only Antonia but all the crew she could see were smiling.

LEONA AND LAWRENCE had done Antonia's bidding only too well. Not only were most of the Vales waiting on the beach to cheer their return, but Lord Linfield, the Grants, the Lamptons, Bernard Muir, old Colonel Fredericks, and Colonel Doverton too. Antonia felt herself blushing wildly while she laughed and apologized and thanked them all. With Julius by her side, his arm lightly but quite openly at her waist, she had never felt so happy or so proud in her life.

Colonel Doverton reported that the arms cache and the rest of Dunnett's sailors were safe in custody. After which Julius surprised her by inviting everyone to the hotel for tea.

"Antonia missed luncheon," he explained, grinning, and everyone laughed, especially Lord Linfield.

Accordingly, they all processed from the harbor down the high street, Antonia on Julius's arm at the front. Several townspeople and shopkeepers stopped to smile at them, as though their sense of fun was infectious. Euphoric, Antonia realized what a lovely place to live this would be. Even without Julius, it could have become home. With him… She was speechless with happiness.

The twins materialized on her other side.

"Thank you for watching over me," Antonia said warmly. "Did Julius put you up to it?"

"Delilah," Leona said. "She said she knew better than anyone that neither Dunnett nor Macy could be trusted."

Beyond them, Delilah met her gaze with a faint, rueful shrug. Antonia mouthed, *Thank you,* and rather to her surprise, Delilah flushed. But she didn't look displeased. On the contrary—Antonia thought she saw the first glimmerings of friendship.

"We didn't know whether we should rescue you in the market or just keep following you," Lawrence said. "Then when you spoke to us, we took it to mean we should get help. So Leona went to tell everyone while I kept watch on you."

THE CAPTAIN'S OLD LOVE

"You are very quick and very useful people to know," Antonia said, which seemed to please them enormously.

The sheer numbers seemed to take the hotel doorman by surprise, but since he recognized nearly everyone, he greeted them all politely and held the door for them to pass into the foyer, where Julius requested a large table for tea.

"And champagne," Aubrey added.

Julius scowled at him, clearly about to countermand the order, and then he shrugged and relaxed. "Why not? We are celebrating, are we not?"

Antonia knew what he meant. "Will you speak to Mr. Grant?"

His smile took her breath away. "I will."

A large table was quickly prepared in the center of the tea room. While they waited, Lord Linfield went off to fetch his sister and Edward.

"You said your parents were here," Julius murmured. "Should we not invite them to join us?"

Antonia had decidedly mixed feelings about that. "They might spoil the party," she said ruefully. "Besides, can you be civil to them? Understanding that they are very unlikely to be civil to you!"

"Today, I can be civil to anyone." Accordingly, he sent a maid scurrying to invite Mr. and Mrs. Temple to join them.

As they made their way into the tea room, Edward ploughed his way through to Antonia and Julius, dragging her employers by the hand. "You didn't come back for luncheon and there was apple pie! Goodness, is this a party?"

"Yes, it is," Julius said.

"So, best manners, young man," Antonia said, ruffling his hair. "And please don't drag Miss Talbot about like a toy. Sorry, ma'am," she added to her employer.

"Don't tell him," Miss Talbot said, "but I actually quite like it. And it's good for Denzil! Now, let us hear about your adventures."

Everyone sat down and contributed what they knew. It all made a very exciting tale, and Antonia wasn't entirely surprised to see Edward bouncing up and down on his seat, or people at other tables clearly listening in.

Mr. Winslow appeared while tea was being served, along with his rather rakish son-in-law, Lord Sylvester. Naturally, they joined the party while Mr. Winslow reported that Timothy had been stopped by the constables on the outskirts of town.

"Doing a bunk," Mr. Winslow said severely, "in vulgar parlance. He is implicated in all Dunnett's crimes, so I presume someone will press charges against him."

Antonia's satisfaction faded into unease. "I want him to face justice," she said to Julius. "Only his name is Edward's name, and I would hate that to be besmirched."

"Actually," Julius said into a sudden silence she was at a loss to account for, "I was hoping he would change his name to Vale. If you and he would like that."

Her smile was slow but felt as though it split her entire face.

"Yes!" Edward shouted, and a storm of congratulations ensued.

Champagne glasses were raised. Mr. Grant rose to his feet, smiling. "I presume you want me to call the banns on Sunday?"

"If you please," Julius replied.

"Then to your health and happiness!" Mr. Grant said, and everyone stood and repeated the toast.

Which was when Antonia noticed her parents standing in the doorway, rigid with disapproval. Julius's hand grasped hers, and she realized she had stopped breathing. She exhaled in a rush, and they both rose to their feet as everyone else sat down.

Antonia went to her parents as if nothing untoward had occurred. "I'm so glad you are able to join us. Let me introduce our friends."

But their attention had moved beyond her to Julius, who stood a pace or two behind. Her mother looked outraged.

Her father threw his head back like a rearing horse. "There is no need to introduce *him*! We remember him perfectly. I am astonished that you dare show your face, sir."

Antonia lowered her voice so no one but the four of them would hear, but she made sure her anger came clearly through every word.

"Why is that? Because you lied to him and to me, making each of us break our word and leading to ten years of misery? To say nothing of the loss of my dowry, which should have been my security. You should be delighted to know that both Dunnett and Macy are in custody and will stand trial, thanks to Captain Vale.

"You will be further delighted," she added between her teeth as her mother tried to speak, "to know that we are celebrating the resumption of our betrothal and will be married within the month. Edward will take Sir Julius's name, as shall I."

Her father's mouth opened and closed, but no sound came out.

Antonia nodded with satisfaction.

"*Sir* Julius?" her mother repeated, hope struggling with doubt in her voice.

A breath of laughter escaped Julius, and suddenly Antonia saw the humor in the whole situation. It bubbled up inside her while Julius bowed to her mother and shook her father's apparently numb hand.

It was Julius who swept them across to the table, where everyone shifted good-naturedly to make room.

"Oh, rats!" Miss Talbot said suddenly. "Now I really *do* need a new companion!"

As though it released the sudden tension introduced by the Temples, everyone began to laugh. Antonia sat back down beside Julius, and below the table wrapped her fingers around his. He squeezed back, and she knew that now, all would be well. She sat back and gazed around the table with utter gladness.

At last, she would be with Julius, the only man she had ever loved, and Edward would have a lively, secure home. All these people had become her friends. Most of them would be her family.

Whatever happened next, she was ready to embrace it with all her heart.

Epilogue

A LITTLE OVER two years later, on their second wedding anniversary, Julius and Antonia stood on the deck of Julius's ship, gazing out to sea.

The ship was crewed by their own servants, who doubled as extra gardeners, grooms, foresters, and gamekeepers at Black Hill. Some of them were too infirm to be considered fit for service in the Royal Navy, or even as merchant seamen, but with each other's help, they worked to their strengths, and Julius was satisfied that his ship was safely sailed. Otherwise, he would not have brought his wife and unborn child—or the baby currently in her specially constructed cradle in the cabin below, watched over by her protective older brother Edward.

"It has been a lovely trip," Antonia said, resting her head on her husband's shoulder. "Was it enough for you?"

They had sailed around the southern Hebrides, stopping to explore a few of the beautiful islands, and now they were heading back to Blackhaven.

His arm crept around her waist. "More than enough. The longer I am with you, the less I crave the sea. Besides, it is...better with you." Somehow, she saw what he did in the vastness of the sky and the ocean, sharing his thoughts so completely that the experience was at once more intense and less necessary to his serenity. It was no longer lonely. His restless spirit had found peace. "Are you ready to go home?"

She placed her hand protectively over her stomach. The baby would not be born for another four or five months, but he was sure she was already nesting like a bird, eager to make everything perfect to greet this newest member of the family. "Quite ready. I miss the twins and everyone else."

She turned her face up to his, and his breath caught all over again at the profound happiness he read there. "I was thinking, maybe next year or the one after, we could take a longer trip with everyone, perhaps to the Mediterranean? There are so many places I want to see. And Edward and the twins would love it."

His arm tightened. "So would I." In fact, the possibilities of their life together were endless, and each was delightful. He lowered his head and kissed her, and that was best of all.

About the Author

Mary Lancaster lives in Scotland with her husband, three mostly grown-up kids and a small, crazy dog.

Her first literary love was historical fiction, a genre which she relishes mixing up with romance and adventure in her own writing. Her most recent books are light, fun Regency romances written for Dragonblade Publishing: *The Imperial Season* series set at the Congress of Vienna; and the popular *Blackhaven Brides* series, which is set in a fashionable English spa town frequented by the great and the bad of Regency society.

Connect with Mary on-line – she loves to hear from readers:

Email Mary: Mary@MaryLancaster.com

Website: www.MaryLancaster.com

Newsletter sign-up: http://eepurl.com/b4Xoif

Facebook: facebook.com/mary.lancaster.1656

Facebook Author Page: facebook.com/MaryLancasterNovelist

Twitter: @MaryLancNovels

Amazon Author Page: amazon.com/Mary-Lancaster/e/B00DJ5IACI

Bookbub: bookbub.com/profile/mary-lancaster

Printed in Great Britain
by Amazon

34945449R00145